DEAD AIR

Also by Joe Lee

ON THE RECORD

DEAD AIR

BY JOE LEE

DOGWOOD
PRESS

Library of Congress Control Number
2004093761

Printed in the United States of America

Jacket design by Bill Wilson
Cover photo of Emily Myers by Bill Wilson
Author photo of Joe Lee by Leslie Lee

DOGWOOD
PRESS

DOGWOOD PRESS
P.O. Box 5958 • Brandon, MS 39047
601-919-3656
www.dogwoodpress.com

For Leslie

ACKNOWLEDGMENTS

My thanks to Don Bartlett, who spent hours patiently answering procedural questions about police work. Dr. Steven Zackow answered every last medical question I threw at him, as did retired pathologist Dr. James A. Pitcock. Wayne Carter, a former Jackson television colleague and now a reporter at WVEC-13 in Norfolk, Virginia, was my television consultant. Sherita Sekul furnished important information about the investigation of cyber sex crimes. My wife, Special Assistant Attorney General Leslie Lee, served as a sounding board from the beginning and offered crucial legal expertise.

My editor, Allison Mays, deserves loads of credit for her patience, humor, creativity and insights. Thanks as well to Special Assistant Attorney General Glenda Haynes, Andy Smith, Joseph and Marilyn Lee and Charles and Vicky Staehle for reading early drafts and offering their thoughts. Thanks to Bill Wilson for his excellent design work and photography, and to Barney and Gwen McKee and Cyndi Clark at Quail Ridge Press for technical support.

This book was written in 2003 while Leslie was on active military duty. Thank you for your service to our great country, and thanks to all who have served in our armed forces in the past or are doing so at present. Your sacrifices will never be forgotten.

SATURDAY NIGHT

"**S**orry to bother you, Jerome. A body has been found. Need you and McDaniel to have a look."

Homicide detective Jerome Washington sagged at the news from the desk sergeant. He was accustomed to being awakened at all hours, and his wife of twenty-five years and their teenaged children understood his responsibilities and were proud of the work he did to keep the community safe. But the killings just never seemed to stop, and there were days he wondered if the constant danger and time away from his family was worth what he tried to give back. This was one of those days, a warm, late-spring evening with a light breeze which blew grill smoke across his south Jackson backyard.

Washington was a fixture in the neighborhood, a tall, well-built black man whose legendary athletic past and years of law enforcement experience made him a natural leader. His wife and kids had the same qualities, and families of both races gravitated toward them. It wasn't surprising to find him at the grill, expertly cooking hot dogs and hamburgers while wisecracking with a dozen lounging adults and a flock of kids who were enjoying his trampoline and above-ground pool. Nor was it a shock that he was called away in the middle of a neighborhood get-together he'd organized. The festivities would continue without him, but the evening wouldn't quite be the same.

"Where we headed, Sarge?"

"A vacant lot on Gallatin near the interstate."

"All right," Washington said, panning the yard. His wife heard the cell phone and already had her supportive look in place when he met her eyes. She would insist that the fun continue and that the radio remain on the soft-soul station Washington favored when he was around. "I'll rustle up Mac and we'll buzz you back once we're headed that way."

* * *

Late that evening in northeast Jackson, Shawn Forrest struggled to her feet in the shimmering vanilla candlelight. She swayed, her head lolling back and forth. Her long, brown hair fell across her flushed face and brushed her cheekbones. The dark-haired man caught her before she pitched forward and smashed her face on the glass coffee table. One of the three wine glasses fell to the white Berber carpet below, scattering a series of red drops. Shawn's plaid sundress hiked up and revealed a pair of shapely legs.

"Have you driven a Ford lately?" she said in a slurred, singsong voice. She burst into drunken laughter, which gave way to ominous rumblings in her throat.

The dark-haired man smirked. "Shawn, if Jack and Leigh could see their little princess now."

"Just do it, will you?"

"Relax," he said, turning to the blond. A look of urgency was on her face. She glanced over her shoulder, then turned back to him. "Everything's under control, kid."

Shawn met the man's eyes and tried to slap him, but her wild swing barely grazed his cheek. She collapsed into his arms and made retching noises, then went limp.

"Oh, God, she's getting sick! Do something!"

"This will actually work to our advantage," the man said, grabbing a cushion from the beige leather sofa. "Grab her ankles."

DEAD AIR

Carolyn Davis smiled to herself. The evening had been spent at an Italian restaurant in Ridgeland with a reputation for tremendous food. It was her first time there, and she savored the soft candlelight and the intimacy of the small tables nearly as much as the mouth-watering lasagna, caesar salads and white wine. Eric Redding was intelligent but down to earth, serious yet playful, and liked television without living and breathing it. He was a decade older and divorced, also without his mother after losing her to a terminal illness. So much in common, yet so many headaches at the thought of dating this man, which seemed very possible after tonight. Not only was Eric a colleague, he was white. It was a first date in a lot of ways.

Normally disinclined to share herself with anyone she didn't know well, she found it easy to open up to him about her desires and shortcomings. He displayed a surprising capacity to listen, something she'd seldom seen in the self-centered men from her past. Gossiping about newsroom colleagues made for easy conversation, but he was comfortable with race relations, religion and politics. They had much more in common than she would have imagined.

The kiss nearly knocked her off her feet. They'd been at her Clinton home for an hour, talking easily on her worn sofa with David Sanborn on the stereo. He flashed his warm smile, but she didn't know what was coming until he took her into his arms. The embrace, which was rock solid and lasted a full minute after the kiss, was even better.

Now she was curled up in his arms, her hands in his. He kissed the top of her head, commenting again on how nice she smelled. She remarked that she couldn't take her eyes off the alternating black and white fingers in her lap. She waited him out, straining to hear as the music ended and the air conditioning kicked off simultaneously.

He was snoring.

"Eric? Wake up, honey."

He moaned, which became a soft laugh. "I apologize. It's not the company."

"You're a morning weather anchor and get up at three o'clock each day," she said, a twinkle in her eye. "That's your story and you're sticking to it, right?"

"A true story. So where were we?"

"Looking at my hand in yours and thinking about Shawn Forrest's series on race last year. Remember that crap?" She adopted a mock announcer tone. 'Have we reached a brighter day in Mississippi? Shawn Forrest of Channel Five News digs deep to find out if relations between the races have improved.' Before you began snoring," she said, throwing a soft elbow into his ribs, "I was going to say that a tight shot of a mixed couple's hands would have been great for a promo."

"A mention of Shawn Forrest is a great way to cool off a hot evening."

Carolyn giggled. "Isn't that the truth. You and Claire Bailey gripe about getting up in the middle of the night to do morning show, but you miss Shawn altogether. Count your blessings."

"Claire says the same thing." He got to his feet. "Way past my bedtime. Maybe we can do this again."

"Definitely," she said, taking his hands. "Off to Philadelphia for the Cronin trial on Monday, so there goes my week. But how about next weekend, assuming I can break away between newscasts? Believe it or not, I'm quite the cook. Make you a plate of down-home food that will have you on your knees."

He kissed her again, a lengthy moment during which she imagined him staying the night. She started to ask if he wanted to meet for breakfast but opted against it. Best not to push. A final hug and he was gone.

* * *

12

Tracey Walton moped into her kitchen and gazed at the pint of ice cream in the freezer. Hurt that Parker had bailed on her, she'd spent the evening in front of the television. Supper was a huge hunk of cheesecake and a box of Pop Tarts. Her old friends Ben and Jerry were beckoning, although she watched her figure these days and kept them at a distance. Tall, redheaded and shapely after years of being heavy and dateless, Tracey had been introduced to Parker Ford two months ago and fallen hard. It was love at first sight and ended her pledge of virginity until marriage. He taught her to drink and experiment with drugs, which she embraced after a strict religious upbringing. The hard living was taking its toll on her nursing skills, but she loved him and would do anything he wanted.

Tears welled in her eyes. It was nearly midnight and he hadn't called. Was he really in Grenada with his rock band or in someone else's arms? She wanted him inside her, preferably after he'd given her a stimulant and electrified her central nervous system. Already wired from a sugar high, she reached for the New York Super Fudge Chunk and gazed out the window overlooking the pool. It was from this same window that she'd spotted Shawn Forrest several months ago.

Shawn was the pretty television anchor on Channel Five, and she emerged from a black Lexus which Tracey had seen periodically in the parking lot. Tracey watched as she unloaded groceries, making a series of trips to a second-floor apartment in a neighboring building. Tracey found the courage to trot downstairs and identify herself as a regular viewer, and Shawn was polite and shared Tracey's gripe that the new speed bumps in the parking lot were too tall. As luck would have it, Tracey ran into her the next night in the midst of a large group at Hal & Mal's, and this time Shawn refused to speak. Hurt, Tracey wrote her off as a snob and hadn't seen her since.

A dark-haired man and a blond now emerged from Shawn's apartment and started down the stairs. The blond looked back over her shoulder. Tracey watched, shoveling ice cream into her mouth. Must be nice to have a perfect body like Shawn. Must be nice to drive a Lexus and have so many friends you could blow off folks who were just trying to be nice. Must be nice to have it all. But Shawn didn't have Parker.

The phone rang. Tracey dropped the ice cream in her hurry to reach it and didn't bother checking the Caller I.D. unit. She scowled when a female apologized for getting the wrong number. Fuming, she sidled back to the window in time to see a car exiting the parking lot. The Lexus was still there. Tracey had played tennis a few times, and she wondered what Shawn would do if she knocked on her door sometime with racquet in hand. She cast the thought aside and planted herself on the sofa, armed with her ice cream and the cordless phone. Parker would call soon.

MONDAY AFTERNOON

Channel Five assistant news director Rod Faber rubbed his temples. He was on hold, waiting for the Jackson Police Department spokesman to update him on a five-year-old who was injured in a drive-by shooting several hours ago. The delay wasn't the problem. He wanted to know why Shawn Forrest was running so late.

Faber was notified that the boy was out of surgery. He made his way across the raucous newsroom to news director Jim Yarbrough's office. Yarbrough was on the phone but waved him in, gesturing at one of the padded, straight-backed chairs across his desk. Faber nudged the door shut.

"Promotions," Yarbrough whispered, covering the mouthpiece and rolling his eyes. Faber smiled back. Yarbrough, a handsome, dark-haired guy in his late-thirties originally from St. Louis, was out of patience with the new tease writer. The youngster didn't know a thing about news promotion, and Yarbrough, who got his start in the business writing teases fifteen years earlier, made the mistake of offering his help on days he struggled with the creative juices. Now the kid was asking each day, unable to write even a few seconds of compelling copy about the top stories on the upcoming newscasts.

Yarbrough hung up and groaned. "Not only does he not have promos produced for Shawn's medical series, he's suggesting he and I sit down and do some brainstorming."

15

"Like there's not enough to do back here," Faber said in his New Orleans brogue. He was a stocky, bespectacled redhead, a television whiz kid in his late twenties who was going places. They had worked together in New Orleans, Faber in an assignment role and Yarbrough as assistant news director. When he was hired in Jackson, Yarbrough brought Faber in before even thinking about the anchor team.

"So what's up? Kid in the drive-by gonna live?"

"Hopefully. The next twenty-four hours are the big test. Carolyn says there's movement in the Cronin trial, and Gayle said there was practically a fistfight at the City Council meeting this morning."

"I think we can do an entire show on the council, Rod. Show the viewers that we once had a group which actually cared about working together, instead of the grandstanding we get now," Yarbrough said, gazing at the Peabody citation adorning the wall to his left. Videocassette tapes and news writing tomes filled two bookcases; a third housed television monitors which allowed him to view the three competing newscasts from his desk. "Interviews with past and present council members, other city officials. Be thinking about a thirty-minute documentary, something we can run in prime-time in November."

Faber glanced at the clock above the bookcases. "Has Shawn called in?"

"She's at U.M.C., remember? Doing the shoot for the series our young promotions flunky hasn't gotten with her about."

"The shoot was at two. She didn't show."

Yarbrough raised an eyebrow.

"I've paged and tried her place. The series doesn't start for a week, and she'll get it done, just like she gets everything done at the last minute. But I don't like her rolling in this late. Gets everybody's attention." He pitched his voice down. "The word is out about her contract."

"Where's the freakin' leak?" Yarbrough said, glaring as he

gazed out at the newsroom. It was divided into gray cubicles, and reporters were at computer terminals working on stories. The sports director was on the phone. The executive producer was leaning over the shoulder of the five o'clock producer, pointing at something on her screen. The chief meteorologist was wisecracking with a photographer as they readied for a live shot at a community fund-raiser. Business as usual.

"I think she is. Nobody in management would say anything, so nobody's gonna know unless it's her. And eighty thousand a year sounds pretty outrageous to people making one-third or one-fourth as much, especially when she sashays in at three-thirty or four every day."

Yarbrough sighed. "I'll speak to her. She gives me any lip, I'll talk to Rick. I don't care if her daddy's a bigwig at corporate. I can't have the newsroom bitching about Shawn new's contract when they're supposed to be focused on May ratings."

* * *

An hour later Yarbrough approached Gayle Kennedy. A short, slender blond in her mid-twenties who anchored the noon news, she was killing the remaining minutes of her day on the phone. She curbed her conversation when she saw Yarbrough.

"Go freshen up. You're doing the five and six."

"Where's Shawn?"

"Good question. Wouldn't hurt to be on standby for the ten."

"Five and six are no problem. But my college roommate is in town, and we had dinner plans."

"Gayle, I don't have a lot of options, and you're always asking for opportunities."

A shrug. "Okay. Can you see where we are on scripts?"

"They'll be on the set when you get there."

"And maybe a drop-dead time that I know I'm working the late show? Hate to cancel dinner, then have Shawn walk in at the last minute."

"No problem." Yarbrough paused, forcing a smile at the tease writer as he walked through. "She was pretty upset at her husband, wasn't she?"

"You don't think she went to Hattiesburg to make up and blew us off, do you?"

"I'm wondering. And there will be hell to pay if she did."

*   *   *

The Spring Center building was on Pearl Street in downtown Jackson, several blocks from the Hinds County courthouse. The homicide detectives were in a musty, dimly-lit room on the second floor. The desks of the two-man teams were butted against each other, so Washington was often face-to-face with his best friend and partner of twenty years, Tim McDaniel. McDaniel was a tall, lanky white man with close-cropped black hair and a dry sense of humor, which had meshed perfectly with Washington's gregarious tendencies over the years. They had grown up together in south Jackson and followed in the footsteps of fathers who served the department in a racially-torn era a generation ago.

McDaniel was a better typist than Washington, and he composed the case summaries on his computer while Washington offered input over his shoulder. The objective was to provide the District Attorney's Office with as much information about each player and event as possible. Some cases took minutes to recap; others took hours and required updates when new information was found. There were detectives in the department who threw the summaries together, eager to move on to the next case and get the District Attorney off their backs. Washington and McDaniel didn't rest until they had transcribed every last notation in their copious notes, and they had a reputation with D.A. Blair Bennett for superior police work.

"Sam!" Washington said, his deep voice carrying the room. The jackets were off and the ties were loosened at this point in the day, and only a couple of detectives were still at work. "We're done. Your copy is printing."

Lieutenant Sam Cowan emerged with a steaming cup of coffee. He was a red-faced, heavyset man who was closing in on retirement after a generation with the department. He was an all-business sort who rarely smiled on the job, but he had tremendous respect for the loyalty and dedication shown by Washington and McDaniel over the years and backed them to the hilt.

"Just talked to U.M.C.," McDaniel said, looking up from his screen. "The little guy is out of surgery."

They were summarizing a drive-by shooting in a west Jackson neighborhood which left a man dead and his five-year-old boy in critical condition. The case was a slam dunk—there were half a dozen eyewitnesses to the shooting who were willing to talk, and a young man was already in custody. It now went to the D.A.'s office.

Cowan shook his head. "My grandson just turned five. What's the prognosis?"

"Fifty-fifty. Next twenty-four hours are crucial," McDaniel said. He printed the two-page summary. "I'm e-mailing this to Bennett as we speak."

Cowan retrieved the sheets from the printer and glanced over them. "Nice work," he said, addressing both men. "Jerome, you still got time to make your little girl's softball game?"

"Headed that way," Washington said, reaching for his keys.

Cowan turned to McDaniel. "How's your mother-in-law?"

"No change. No news is good news at this point." McDaniel's mother-in-law was dying of a terminal form of leukemia and had moved in with them after being told she had little time left. "A family from church is meeting us at the house to watch her and the kids. Insisted that I take the wife out for a nice meal and get away for a couple of hours."

"We're thinking about you, Tim," Cowan said, gripping

McDaniel's shoulder. He slapped Washington on the back as he walked past. "Thanks, fellas. See you tomorrow."

*   *   *

Yarbrough was still in his office at nine. Gayle had handled herself well with co-anchor Jeff Walker at five and six, both shows highlighted by strong live shots from Philadelphia, Mississippi. Carolyn Davis was covering the trial of a white neurosurgeon who interrupted a robbery at his northeast Jackson home last summer and shot two unarmed black teens who were trying to escape. One had died; the other lived and told police that the doctor screamed racial epithets as he chased them through his yard and fired. The doctor vehemently denied the accusations and seemed certain to be acquitted until Carolyn interviewed his wife just before trial. Asking questions gently but firmly, she extracted a tearful admission confirming the teen's statement. A plea was reached, avoiding a trial and creating a win-win situation; Carolyn had broken the story and added a big feather to the station's cap, and the company wouldn't have to pay motel fare and expenses for a trial which Carolyn thought might last two weeks.

Yarbrough called general manager Rick Sewell at home. They had already talked twice.

"Not a word from Shawn. I told Gayle to plan on the ten."

"When did you try her last?"

"Half an hour ago. Look, I didn't say anything earlier because I thought she'd show, but we ate with Shawn and her husband Saturday night. You've met him, haven't you?"

"Yeah, he's a meteorologist in Hattiesburg." Sewell paused. "You had dinner with them? What was the occasion?"

"Six of us: Samantha and me, Shawn and Darren, and Gayle and a friend of hers. No occasion, really—sort of a peace offering after the flap over Fifth Street Elementary. I had some promotion ideas, thought I'd run them by her. A way for us to have some good food and a couple of drinks and see if we could check our egos at the door."

A snort. "Noble to be sure, but I don't know how realistic. And Gayle and Shawn at the same table? Like to have seen that."

Yarbrough glanced out at the newsroom. Reporters and producers were hustling to finalize their stories for the late news, but heads popped up every few minutes. Everyone was mumbling about Shawn, and the fact that the news director was still in his office indicated that it wasn't being treated lightly.

"They were civil. The problem was Shawn and the husband—a scene in the parking lot."

"Great. Could she have gone to see him and opted not to join us?"

Yarbrough took his time. "I know this is a sensitive subject with her daddy at corporate, but she's the one member of the team who knows she could get away with it, even in a rating period. Honestly, Rick, I expect her to bebop in tomorrow all smiles as if nothing happened."

"That pisses me off. She got every dime she asked for and went out of her way to screw Gayle out of the five o'clock show. I can't believe she'd turn right around and blow us off in a power play." He paused. "How well do you know the husband?"

"First time I'd met him. Not very sociable, although he may be charming under better circumstances."

"Touch base with me first thing tomorrow. If Shawn walks in, send her home and tell her to check with me if she has any questions."

*　*　*

Carolyn kept time as a B.B. King recording drifted from the living room. She was seated at the kitchen table in James Norris's rural Madison County home and watched as he studied the chess board. He had crafted much of his furniture by hand and made money on the side with his carpentry skills. His refinished wood floor and built-in bookcases in the living room were especially attractive, and the place always smelled of varnish. Tonight it smelled of peppery fried chicken, okra, cornbread and tomatoes.

"Checkmate," he said with a grin, drawing out the word. Norris was a short, stocky black man in his late thirties, a radio veteran with a love of woodworking and photography. He was divorced and shared custody of his twelve-year-old son with his wife, who lived in Greenwood. Originally from Jackson, Norris had dated Carolyn's oldest sister two decades ago. He'd been at Channel Five almost ten years, starting as a part-time news photographer after being left without a job when the radio station he worked for was sold. Now he was the chief photographer and managed a group of ten employees. "Chess, Scrabble and Monopoly. Anything else I can kick your butt in?"

"Go on, shoot your mouth off," Carolyn said in mock indignation. "You got some nerve. I drive all the way out here and cook my butt off for you, and you can't win any more gracefully than that?"

Norris laughed and consulted the satellite guide. He was a diehard baseball fan and idolized Barry Bonds so much he'd named his son after him.

"Giants hosting the Dodgers. Want to catch a couple of innings and see Barry hit?"

"Better get home," she said, reaching for her purse. She gave him a quick hug. "I enjoyed this, Norris, even though you wouldn't let me win anything. Sorry about complaining so much. I'm just lonely."

"The right man is out there, Davis. Trust me."

"I just hope I meet him before I retire. I'm beginning to think my short-lived marriage was the only chance I'll get." A wistful sigh. "What about you? Ever want to get married again?"

"Sure. But like I've said, the ex and I both want to wait until

Barry's out of the house before either of us forces a step-parent on him."

She smiled. "You're a good man. And a good friend."

"So are you, kid. And you're a hell of a cook. Drive safe, and watch out for deer. Saw one right in front of the house the other night."

She lingered at the door, wanting to tell him about the date with Eric Redding. He was the one person she would share it with, but she wanted to see if Eric showed any more interest before spilling her guts.

"One of these days, Norris, I'm going to pull a Shawn Forrest and just not come to work. Must be nice, huh? The ten o'clock producer said she's been keeping track of Shawn's hours the last couple of weeks, and she's been in the building a grand total of forty hours. She's making eighty thousand dollars to work twenty hours a week? Please."

"There's no way in hell she's making that much money. Just keep up the good work you're doing. Did great in Philadelphia today, kid."

Carolyn smiled. "Couldn't do it without my best friend pointing the camera. Good night."

TUESDAY

Yarbrough sipped coffee at his desk and gazed at the discrepancy report from last night. Minimal mistakes on the three evening shows, although incorrect video aired twice at ten. He would speak to the girl who ran tapes during the newscasts—that crap simply wouldn't be tolerated during rating periods. There was another e-mail from Claire Bailey, the morning show anchor. The friction between her and a member of the studio crew was increasing, and she was demanding a meeting. Yarbrough was rubbing his temples when Sewell summoned him.

A pair of leather couches flanked the oak desk in Sewell's spacious office, and family pictures and citations from the city adorned the walls. An enlarged photograph of him reporting from a fire in Pensacola twenty years ago was a reminder of his news background. He was a dignified, polite man in his mid-fifties with carefully-styled, graying hair and almost always in a suit.

"Morning, Jim. Close the door." He nodded at the flat-screen television, which was muted. Claire Bailey was reading news during a local segment in the network morning show. "Her contract is about up, right?"

"That's correct."

"Sweet kid and tries hard, but we were so cash-strapped then. Even though Eric's a good meteorologist and liked out in the community, we'll never put a competitive morning show on the air as long as she's front and center."

"You're preaching to the choir. She's a good step below the competition, and I can listen to my wife if I want non-stop whining. Now there's a camera operator she can't get along with."

Sewell lowered his voice. "And she's gotten fat—there's no other way to say it. The consultant even said something. What the hell are we supposed to do? One of our sports guys in Pensacola got heavy, and there was a meeting. Everybody was professional, and the guy lost forty pounds. But if we men say something to a female about her weight, we're liable to get sued."

"Tell the consultant to handle it herself."

"I will, if we offer her another contract. We'll decide that soon. So where do we stand with Shawn?"

"Just tried her place. Not answering her pager or cell, either. You tell me."

"Let's try the husband." Sewell asked the receptionist to hold his calls, then clicked the speaker. The phone in Shawn's apartment rang five times before the voice mail picked up. He left a message, then dialed the station in Hattiesburg. The receptionist sent him to the morning show producer, who gave him Darren Clarke's home number. A man answered on the fifth ring, sleep in his voice.

"Darren Clarke?"

"Yeah. Who's this?"

"Rick Sewell in Jackson, general manager at Channel Five."

"Yeah, Shawn has mentioned your name," Clarke said with a yawn. "What can I do for you, sir?"

"Sorry to bother you this early—I know you work late each night. Our news director Jim Yarbrough is here, and you're on speaker." A brief pause. "We're looking for Shawn."

"What do you mean? She's in Jackson, isn't she?"

"She didn't show up yesterday. Missed a promotions shoot at a local hospital and didn't come in for any of the newscasts. We didn't get an answer at home or on her cell last night, and nothing this morning. Thought we'd see if she was with you before we called her parents."

"No, she's not here," Clarke said, clearing his throat. Sewell imagined him sitting up, trying to get his bearings. "She just didn't show up for work yesterday? Damn."

Sewell glanced at Yarbrough. "I understand you and Shawn had dinner in Jackson Saturday night. I'm not trying to nose into your business, but Jim said there was some discomfort at the end of the evening. Did you see Shawn yesterday or Sunday?"

"No, I didn't. We parted at the restaurant Saturday night. I'd driven up for dinner, then turned around and came home." A sigh. "This television marriage stuff isn't always the best of both worlds. But I can't believe she just wouldn't come to work, especially in ratings. Try her mother—she goes over there a lot. I'm sure you know they're in Atlanta."

They exchanged cell numbers and hung up. Sewell gazed at Yarbrough.

"I'm in his shoes and someone said my wife hadn't shown for work and nobody could find her, I'd be on my way here. And that comment about his marriage was odd."

"It was more than discomfort, Rick. It was downright ugly in the parking lot."

"I realize people fight, and maybe she ran to her mother. But we're in ratings for God's sake! We can't go from one show to the next not knowing if she'll be here." He shook his head. "Let me call her father. If they haven't talked to her, I suppose the next step is the cops. Gosh, I hope something hasn't happened to her."

* * *

26

Norris was on his way to the station when Yarbrough paged. He asked him to stop at Shawn's apartment before coming to work. Norris accepted the assignment without question and called back ten minutes later.

"She didn't answer the door, and I got her voice mail when I tried her cell."

"Is her car there?"

"I'm standing next to it. Suitcase in the backseat."

Yarbrough groaned. Faber heard it and looked up from the assignment desk. "Don't come in just yet, James. Run an errand or ride around the block and I'll call you right back."

*   *   *

"Hey, kid. Just wanted to make sure you were up."

"Norris, Yarbrough said we didn't have to be in until ten, remember?" Carolyn said, sleep in her voice.

"It's almost nine, so get your butt out of bed. By the way, I'm standing next to Shawn's car in front of her apartment. Yarbrough asked me to check on her before coming in. Nobody can find her, so I'm waiting on the cops."

Carolyn grunted. "This sounds serious."

"Keep your cell on. I'll call you back."

Norris didn't like Shawn, never had. Beneath the phony team spirit was a veiled threat that if you looked at her the wrong way, you were screwed because her father was vice-president of news at the company's corporate office in Atlanta. Norris had never forgotten their confrontation when she questioned his photography skills during a live shot. He replied that he would take her criticism seriously the day she anchored at a station her father had nothing to do with, and when they were alone Shawn hissed that there would be hell to pay. Norris, who made a personal oath long ago to never flaunt his race in a job setting, intoned that hell would freeze before she or anyone else of her pigment threatened his job security. An unspoken truce was reached, but they weren't friends, and he wouldn't shed tears if something had happened to her.

A youthful officer with the Jackson Police Department arrived. Norris introduced himself and explained why he was there. The officer called for backup and hunted down the landlady, a nervous sort who puffed on a cigarette. She watched Shawn on television each night and described her as a good tenant who had lived at the complex six months and had few guests. An older patrolman arrived then. The young cop made the introductions, then looked over the grounds—brown brick buildings in good condition with carefully-tended landscaping and a pool with crystal clear water. An elderly woman lugged a basket of clothes toward the laundry room, but no one else was in sight.

"We can get a warrant, or we can waive it with the exception that you, as manager of the premises, are willing to let us in," the older cop said calmly. "We'll just need your signature."

"Let's go in there. I want to make sure she's okay. She's such a sweet, young thing."

The four of them climbed the wrought iron staircase. Norris's heart was beating faster. He glanced over his shoulder and was grateful for the quiet. He had shot video many times of police kicking doors open with onlookers jockeying for position, and he knew there would be a crowd if the public was aware that the cops were opening Shawn Forrest's door.

The landlady fumbled the keys and dropped them. The older cop placed a gentle hand on her shoulder and said to relax. A moment later the key was inserted. The landlady hesitated, then pushed the door open. She screamed and reeled backward. Norris caught and steadied her, his vision momentarily blocked. Then his eyes began to water.

* * *

Washington and McDaniel arrived together. They watched as two technicians in white coats from the Mississippi Crime Lab tossed fingerprint powder and bagged and tagged items near the body. The stench of vomit and decay made it difficult to breathe, and the techs were wearing thin masks similar to what the detectives wore while cutting their lawns.

"Hi, fellas," the older tech said. He was a short, squat man named Bernie with a bad comb over, but easily the best of the bunch in this sometimes sloppy outfit. "There's broken glass on the carpet near the body. We just removed a shattered picture frame from one of the hands of the deceased. Looks like it had been slammed against the corner of the coffee table, based on the abrasion here," he said, pointing to a scratch on the edge of the table closest to Shawn's head.

"You're saying she was holding it when you got here?" Washington said.

A snort from the young male tech a few feet away. "We assume," he said, heavy on sarcasm, "that someone who thinks he's pretty clever broke the picture, then placed it where it would look like she was holding it. That might make sense if this woman drank herself to death. But look at this," he said, gesturing at a cushion from the sofa. It now had a white tag affixed to it with a stick pin. The numeral one, in red magic marker, was visible on the tag. "Pretty sure this was used to suffocate her, so it's hard to believe she died while breaking the frame."

"You guys don't know who this is, do you?" Bernie said. His partner and the detectives turned to him, and he pointed at the destroyed frame. Shawn and a dark-haired man were in formal wear and holding wine glasses aloft. "That's Shawn Forrest from Channel Five. That's the first thing I saw, and I thought, 'whoever this is must know Shawn Forrest.' And I just now realized it's her. She's so messed up I hadn't made the connection."

"It is, Jerome," McDaniel said, stepping forward and looking closely at the body. "My wife watched her every night."

"You're right, Mac. Damn."

"Don't move, Tim. Something's at your feet," Bernie said.

He told his partner to close the door and dim the lights, then aimed a pen flashlight near McDaniel's shoes. Nothing appeared at first, but Bernie gently patted down the carpet with gloved hands. A moment later an earring fragment was bagged and tagged. "We'll let you know if we find the rest of it."

"Make sure you get the computer," Washington said from the bedroom.

"We're still taking prints, Jerome. We haven't even looked in there yet."

"No, man—I mean bag and tag it. We don't get it now, we'll need a warrant later. And I'm told that's her Lexus out there. Black, with a Georgia tag."

"Keys?"

"That's probably her purse on the kitchen table," McDaniel said, striding that way. He grabbed a paper towel from a rack near the sink and signaled Bernie over. He tilted the designer bag, careful not to leave prints. Among the items which tumbled out was a set of keys. An athletic club membership card was visible, as well as several grocery store cards. A large black car key with an emblazoned Lexus logo stood out.

"Excellent. We're on top of it, fellas. We'll get her prints while we're here."

The detectives stepped outside, both gasping for breath and squinting as the bright sunlight greeted them. Nothing like May humidity after a few minutes with a decaying body. Washington took a statement from the landlady, who was shaken and wiped smeared makeup from her face. McDaniel approached Norris and introduced himself, spotting the Channel Five golf shirt. Norris had stumbled down the stairs and lost his breakfast in a nearby hedge, then gathered himself and phoned Yarbrough. The news would spread like wildfire. That was the nature of the broadcast business—everyone talked, even to friends at competing stations. He would place calls on his cell once he had the opportunity and had just alerted Carolyn.

"Did you know her well, Mr. Norris?"

"We weren't close. Her daddy Jack Forrest is with corporate—Colonial Broadcasting in Atlanta. Vice-president of news."

"Never hurts to know people in high places. Married? Kids?"

"Her husband is a meteorologist in Hattiesburg, and they have a house there. No kids. She worked with us during the week and went home every weekend—made no secret about getting the hell out of Dodge as soon as Friday's late news was over." He glanced at the Lexus. "Packed bag in plain view."

McDaniel took notes on a small pad. "What about an emergency, all hands on deck?"

A sardonic grin. "Not Shawn."

"I'm sure management knows how to get in touch with her parents and husband."

"That's management now." A silver Audi roared into the parking lot. Sewell and Yarbrough jumped out, grave looks on their faces. "Younger guy is the news director, Jim Yarbrough. Older guy is the general manager, Rick Sewell."

"I may get back to you," McDaniel said, handing him a business card.

"I'm easy to find."

*   *   *

An hour later McDaniel merged his dark blue, city-owned Ford Taurus into traffic on Old Canton Road and headed toward the interstate. The crime lab techs were still at the apartment and had been joined by the medical examiner.

"We better solve this right quick, my man," Washington said, smirking at his partner. "Sewell didn't quite say it, but that's what we better do. And you can imagine what our big dogs are going to say."

"He's right about the local media doing anything for an angle."

"His station, too, Mac. They're the worst—I'm sick of that first-on-the-scene crap. We'll see if they boast about being first when one of their own is found dead. The sense I get is that the station wants this solved in record time—and they also want to own the story."

"Could be. Yarbrough is a little smooth for my taste—may know more than he's telling. But let's walk through it. Three couples had dinner at Que Será Será Saturday night: Yarbrough and his wife, Gayle Kennedy and her date, and the late Shawn Forrest and her husband."

Washington consulted his notes. "That would be Darren Clarke. Let's see him now."

"He's in Hattiesburg. We're liable to pass him on the highway, Jerome."

"Let's start in that direction. We'll call his station before we get past Richland and make sure someone has talked to him. He works the evening newscasts, and Sewell said he probably gets to work about two each afternoon. He could be asleep or at the grocery at this hour. If they haven't caught him before we do, Mac, we may spring the news. Much as I hate that, it wouldn't be the first time."

Washington radioed the station house and spoke with the desk sergeant, who approved the two-hour drive down Highway 49. Washington estimated that they would be back in Jackson mid-afternoon. He waited fifteen minutes, then tried the Hattiesburg television station. He was put through to the general manager, who had unsuccessfully tried to catch Clarke at home. He gave Washington the street address and promised to call if he spoke with Clarke.

"Yarbrough said Clarke booked after the spat in the parking lot and wasn't seen again," McDaniel said from memory. "Yarbrough and his wife had everyone to their place for drinks after dinner, so it was five of them without Clarke. Shawn had too much to drink and couldn't drive. Yarbrough and Gayle Kennedy were the designated drivers. Gayle dropped off her date, who was also drunk, and Yarbrough drove Shawn home in the Lexus and parked it where it is now. Yarbrough and Gayle got Shawn upstairs and left her on the couch. She was passed out but breathing when they left, and Gayle took Yarbrough home."

Washington nodded at his pad. "That's exactly what I have. We'll talk to Gayle when we get back and get the name of her date. We need to talk to Yarbrough's wife, too. That's the cast at Que Será Será. Maybe a waitress or someone saw something." He paused as McDaniel veered around an old pickup entering the highway from a county road in the Star community. "So why does Yarbrough know more than he's telling?"

"He seemed reluctant to admit they'd all been out drinking."

"Television folks have lives, too."

"Of course. Just something about him. We'll see what forensics comes up with, but you ask me, Bernie's right: Somebody turned her lights out."

* * *

Thirty minutes later an impromptu department head meeting took place in the Channel Five conference room. The managers, several of whom were in tears, then paged their troops for an emergency staff meeting. It was Sewell's goal to address the entire group before the noon newscast, since Shawn's death was the obvious lead story across the city once it was common knowledge. Yarbrough contacted the competing news directors and passed the information along, asking that they not release Shawn's name until the five o'clock show out of professional courtesy.

By eleven-thirty most of the seventy station employees were in the building. Sewell summoned them to the cavernous studio which housed the news set. An engineer flipped on overhead fluorescent lights, leaving the harsh on-camera lights off.

"I'll make this quick," Sewell said hoarsely, his eyes circling the room. "Most of you are aware that Shawn Forrest wasn't at work yesterday." He paused, gathering himself. "In the last

33

hour, we've gotten official word that Shawn was found dead in her apartment this morning."

A collective gasp. Although many knew by now, the fact that Sewell was presenting it to them drove the shock home.

"Jim and I have already given statements to the police. Foul play has not been ruled out, and an autopsy will be performed. Jack Forrest and his wife, as well as our news consultant from corporate, are on their way from Atlanta and will be here mid-afternoon. Funeral arrangements are incomplete."

Sewell heaved a sigh, clearly fighting to keep his emotions in check. His reaction was believable and had many dabbing at their own eyes.

"The unfortunate thing about this business is that it doesn't stop when there's a tragedy. In fact, we have a newscast in twenty-five minutes. We will withhold Shawn's name until the evening shows—we'll report that a body was found, and that the name is being withheld pending notification of family. We've asked the other stations to do the same, and I'm sure they'll cooperate. Shawn's death will be the lead story everywhere tonight, and I'll be on the set with Gayle and Jeff at five, six and ten. We'll have some background pieces, and James—James Norris, are you back yet?"

Norris raised his hand from a pocket of photographers near the rear of the studio.

"James represented the station this morning when Shawn's door was opened by police, and he shot site video for us," Sewell said, his voice cracking. "I know that was as tough a task as anything that's come across your plate. We're very proud of you, sir, and we thank you for your professionalism."

Norris nodded and acknowledged the supportive looks of his teammates. Sewell gathered himself.

"Let me say one more thing, folks: Shawn was adored in the community, and because she was one of our most visible anchors, the competing stations and media of all kinds will be putting a microscope to every conceivable angle out there. This means that all of you will be getting questions from friends and family as well as folks you don't know. I ask you not to share any information with anyone at this time. We will get you the latest on the investigation as soon as we have it—you have my word. In the meantime, I ask all of you to step lightly today and over the coming days and weeks, and muster as much consideration for your co-workers as possible. It won't be easy getting through this."

*　*　*

Hattiesburg was a college town of approximately 40,000, an attractive place with a sprawling, centrally-located campus. Still on Highway 49, the detectives passed M. M. Roberts Stadium, then turned west on Hardy Street. The university was to their right, and fast food outlets and small shops popped up as the school faded from view. McDaniel, consulting his notepad, turned left on 34th Street and passed a pair of stop signs. He turned again and entered an upper middle class subdivision awash in shady redbuds and pines.

"There it is, Mac. Corner lot. What I'd give for some of those trees in my neighborhood."

"I hate not knowing if his station reached him."

"But if he had something to do with it, sure gives us a leg up to spring it."

McDaniel parked along the curb and smiled at the chorus of crickets as he emerged. The house was perhaps twenty years old, a single story brick dwelling with a wood privacy fence around the back yard. The two-car garage was closed. Washington checked his watch as he rang the doorbell. It was just before noon. A full minute passed, and the detectives were contemplating a visit to the back. Washington knocked sharply. Fifteen seconds passed. Then they heard footsteps. The door was opened by a dark-haired man of medium height in his mid-thirties. He was in gym shorts and pool slippers. No shirt, a nice tan and a healthy application of cologne.

"Darren Clarke?" McDaniel said, displaying his badge.

"Yeah, that's right." Clarke looked from Washington to McDaniel. "Jackson police? I assume this is about Shawn. So where was she?"

A long moment passed. "Our deepest sympathies, sir," Washington said softly.

Clarke frowned, then turned pale. "No. No way. Oh, my God."

"May we come in, sir?" McDaniel said.

An odd flash in Clarke's eyes. He let them inside the foyer. There was a formal dining room with upscale furniture and a stocked bar to their right. A more casual living area was in view, but this was apparently as far as he wanted them. He took a seat on a wingback chair in the dining room. The detectives remained on their feet.

"No one from your station has contacted you?" Washington said.

"No," Clarke said softly, eyes on the floor. "Shawn's station called, so I knew she was missing."

"Her body was discovered about two and a half hours ago."

Clarke rubbed his temples and started to speak, then whirled when the sliding glass door opened. A youthful female voice boomed through the house.

"Baby, there's a wasp out there that's going to be the death of me!"

McDaniel and Washington darted into the foyer. A short, well-built blond of perhaps twenty stood there, her eyes the size of saucers. She was dripping wet and wore a lime green two-piece swimsuit. It was clear that the girl was on familiar terms with the host.

"Look under the sink, Patti," Clarke said from the dining room in resignation. "Then go back outside."

The girl rummaged through a cabinet, then beat a hasty retreat to the pool. The detectives watched, then returned to Clarke.

"We talked to your general manager on the way down," Washington said. "He said he came over here."

"I ran some errands," Clarke said distractedly. "But I always have my pager on, and it never went off." His eyes were filled with tears when he looked up. "What happened?"

"There will be an autopsy, but she appears to have asphyxiated on her own vomit. Suffocation would be my guess. Toxicology tests will be ready in a few days, maybe a week." Washington paused, sitting on a mahogany sofa covered in velvet. McDaniel joined him and pulled out his notepad.

"We need to ask some questions," Washington said. "We understand you were in Jackson Saturday night."

"Shawn and I had dinner with people from her station."

"And you were in separate cars. We know there was a fight after dinner. If there hadn't been a fight, would she have followed you back here for the weekend?"

Clarke's eyes were on the floor. "No. Patti rode with me and back."

Washington frowned. "Was Patti at dinner?"

"Of course not. I dropped her at the mall in Ridgeland, then met Shawn at Que Será Será. Patti met a friend and caught a movie. I picked her up when it was over."

"Why bring your girlfriend on a trip to see your wife?"

"I came because I'd heard things about Shawn and somebody else."

"So you came to confront her? You were going to do that at dinner in front of everyone?"

"Lay off the sarcasm, Detective. I was going to speak to her in the parking lot, but someone had tipped her off about Patti, apparently. She hit me with it the instant I walked up and didn't speak the rest of the meal. The blowup was in the parking lot when I was leaving."

"We're told she went to Jim and Samantha Yarbrough's house for drinks after you left."

Clarke shrugged. "I didn't see her again. I walked around the mall until Patti called. Bought a shirt and a book. I can show you the receipts."

"So Shawn pretty much stole your thunder. What then? You and Patti head back to Hattiesburg?"

"We went to Shawn's apartment. I have a key—I've spent the night before, when things were better." He rubbed his eyes. "We wanted different things. I like it here and signed a long-term deal. She was from Atlanta and wanted to climb the ladder and get to network."

"How long were you married?"

"Five years next month."

"How long has Patti been around?"

"Since last fall. Being alone five days a week had gotten old. And Shawn had gotten in the habit of driving to see her mother every couple of weeks, and there were times I didn't find out until she was already in Atlanta." He paused. "Look, I loved Shawn once. We weren't on good terms the last year or two, but the last thing I'd do . . ."

"Let's talk about the apartment. Find what you were looking for?"

"No."

"Take anything?"

"No."

"How long were you there?"

"About half an hour."

"So you just poked around her things and split?"

Clarke sighed. "Patti and I made love, then had a glass of wine."

"Where did you make love?"

"In bed, Detective."

"You had wine there, too?"

"Wine was in the living room. Left the glasses there."

"There was a third glass, Mr. Clarke. Someone else with you?"

"No. Just the two of us."

"So how would that third glass have gotten there?"

Clarke shrugged. "No idea."

"Is Patti local?"

"She's from Jackson, just goes to school here."

"She knew you were seeing Shawn Saturday night?"

"Yes."

"Were you with her at midnight?"

"Yes."

"Where?"

"Here, in this house. At midnight we were probably in the pool."

"Mac, why don't you go speak to Patti."

McDaniel nodded. Clarke started to get up, but Washington motioned him down.

"Stay put, sir. He won't take long with her. And I'm almost done with you."

* * *

Patti sat in a pool chair and stared straight ahead. A canned Mountain Dew in a foam hugger was at her feet. He took the chair next to her, wrinkling his nose at the smell of chlorine.

"Patti St. John, I understand. I'm Detective McDaniel. How old, young lady?"

She removed her sunglasses and looked away. "I knew you guys were cops. Nineteen next month."

McDaniel's eyes widened behind his own shades. "Can I see some identification?"

Patti rose without a word and strode into the house. She returned a moment later with a valid Mississippi driver's license. Shame and fear were in her blue eyes. She looked mighty young, and the childlike voice didn't help.

"Tell me about Darren."

"He's the best thing that ever happened to me. He loves me. And I love him."

"Do you know why we're here?"

She lowered her head. "Some people have nothing better to do than sit around and talk about everyone else—someone at the sorority house found out I'm sleeping with a married man and made sure my parents were told, right? You just don't know how vicious those girls are."

A frown. "Miss St. John, this isn't about you and Darren. Darren's wife is dead. We're homicide investigators."

Patti looked at the water, then back at McDaniel. Terror was in her eyes now.

"We know Darren was in Jackson Saturday night. Were you with him?"

"No, sir. I was at the sorority house. I stay over here with Darren during the week, but not on weekends because—you know . . ."

"Can someone verify you were there that night?"

"Yes, sir."

"All night?"

Patti faltered. She took a swig of Mountain Dew and set down the can shakily.

"Miss St. John, please tell me exactly what happened. I can't help you if you don't."

"Am I a suspect?"

"Not at this time."

She stared straight ahead and told a story which matched what Darren gave. McDaniel wrote little.

"Did he suspect Shawn of having an affair?"

"None of my business. I didn't ask."

"Is it possible that he took things out of the bedroom or closet, things you didn't see because you were in the living room?

Documents, perhaps, or a roll of film—something he could put in a pocket?"

"I suppose. I didn't ask. I felt funny about being there."

"What time did you leave?"

"Nine-thirty. I remember the clock in his car as we pulled out."

"And you spent the night with him, here at this house?"

"Yes, sir. He dropped me at the sorority house on the way. I got some clothes, freshened up and drove here in my car. Parked next to him in the garage. He said it was a special occasion since it was the first time my car spent the night, too," she said, attempting a smile.

"Did he say anything else about Shawn?"

"Not until the next morning. He doesn't like to talk about her around me—doesn't want to hurt my feelings. But he said she was a hideously selfish person. Those were his exact words."

"If your car was in the garage, he assumed she wasn't coming home?"

"He told me about their fight. He didn't expect her home."

McDaniel flipped back a page. "If your parents live in Jackson, I assume you're at the sorority house during the school year. Roommate?"

A nod.

"I'll need her name and how to get in touch with her. Ditto for your parents."

Patti groaned. "Jamie knows, but please don't tell Mom and Dad. They'll kill me."

McDaniel gestured at the pad. Patti wrote and handed it over. Then he removed a print ink pad from his jacket.

"What are you doing?"

"Like to get your fingerprints. We're getting a set from everyone we're talking to about the case."

"Is Darren going to give his?"

McDaniel stifled a laugh. "I assume so. No reason not to if you have nothing to hide."

She sighed, then offered her small hands. McDaniel took the prints and got to his feet.

"Thank you, Miss St. John. We'll be in touch if we need anything else."

* * *

The arrival of the detectives raised eyebrows at the sorority house, a modern, three-story brick building which bore little resemblance to the Victorian-era homes on fraternity row. Patti's roommate Jamie Fontenot was between classes and summoned to the lobby. She was a tall, tanned brunette, clad in a clingy t-shirt with sorority letters and tight blue jean cut-offs. She led the detectives to a quiet corner of a large recreation room on the first floor. She was aware of Patti and Darren, but her eyes popped when the detectives revealed that Darren's wife was dead.

"I was in Jackson Friday night for a wedding rehearsal," she said, her voice naturally husky. "Patti called Saturday, said she was coming up and wanted to hang out." Her face darkened. "What happened?"

"That's what we're trying to find out," McDaniel said. "So you guys went to a movie in Jackson. Then what? You and Patti rode back down here together?"

"No, she was with him. I was in my car. Got here about ten-thirty and went right to bed."

"Did you see Patti after you left Jackson?"

"Just for a minute. She woke me up when she came in, but I went right back to sleep." Jamie glanced around. "You know how girls are, Detectives. When you put forty or fifty together, everybody knows who slinks out at night and tiptoes back the next morning. Patti tries to get in and out without a lot of fanfare."

"She say anything about the evening?"

"I haven't talked to her. Figured she was with him."

"Would you mind giving us a fingerprint sample?"

"No, sir."

McDaniel removed the ink pad and took prints. "Thank you, Miss Fontenot. We'll be in touch if we need anything."

* * *

Eric Redding signaled Carolyn into the weather office after the noon news and pondered quietly if Shawn was dead at the very moment they'd joked about her Saturday night. It wasn't the time to ask him over for dinner, but Carolyn took it as a good sign that they were comfortable with each other. She would know when to ask. And if he asked first, that would be even better.

She passed Gayle Kennedy in the hall and patted her shoulder as she walked by. Gayle gave a beleaguered smile in return. With Shawn gone, Gayle was filling in and no doubt felt the eyes of the world—it was probably akin to auditioning for a job at network.

Carolyn plopped down at her desk, Gayle's scent lingering. Gayle had the cubicle next to her and wore enough fragrance to sink a battleship. Carolyn wrinkled her nose and leaned back, fanning herself. A tiny flash caught her eye. She glanced around, her eyes stopping at a piece of metal on the worn carpet under Gayle's desk. Upon closer inspection it was part of an earring, probably the one Gayle was moaning about yesterday. She started to leave it in her desk and send an e-mail, but someone was approaching. Last thing she needed was for word to get around that she was snooping in a colleague's desk. She waited until the coast was clear, then dropped it into the pocket of her slacks.

* * *

Channel Five was in an elevated area of south Jackson, not far from Forest Hill High School. McDaniel followed a narrow, winding road past several small businesses and an industrial park before rounding a final curve. The road abruptly dead-ended into the vast station parking lot, and he nosed into a visitor's space near the front door. Acres of tall pines surrounded them on three sides, and a large, colorful facade with the familiar logo adorned the top of the single-story brick structure. Colorful flower beds and neatly-trimmed hedges ran the length of the building. A man in overalls and a cap was manicuring the grounds with a weed eater and waved as they walked past.

The front lobby had black and white tile flooring and was dominated by a huge, muted television set. Photographs of the anchor team, broadcasting awards and community citations were arranged to catch the eyes of visitors, and the station logo was emblazoned on the wall behind the receptionist's desk. The group shot of the anchor team included a beaming Shawn Forrest. The receptionist blanched when she saw McDaniel looking at it. She rang Yarbrough's office and announced his guests, then lowered her voice and said something they couldn't hear. It likely had to do with Shawn's presence in the picture.

Yarbrough appeared seconds later. "Gentlemen. Anything new?"

Washington stepped forward. "We need to speak with you, then we'll need Gayle Kennedy. Somewhere we can talk?"

Yarbrough led them to a carpeted room with padded chairs around a long, brown conference table. An enlarged photograph of the Channel Five staff was on one of the paneled walls. An easel and a videocassette player were at the far end of the room. McDaniel took in the surroundings, easily able to visualize Rick Sewell telling his managers of Shawn's death in this room. The air-conditioner came on then, hitting them with a welcome blast of chilly air.

"We'll need to speak with your wife," Washington said. "Where can we find her?"

Yarbrough clearly had a broadcasting background based on

his near-perfect diction. He explained that she ran a printing company in Clinton and gave directions. McDaniel nodded, familiar with the neighborhood.

"She's an old producer. We met in a newsroom fifteen years ago, so she knows what the troops are going through. By the way, Rick Sewell is on his way to meet Shawn's parents and get them to a hotel. Don't envy that."

Washington frowned. "I realize there's a lot going on, but the ball got dropped somewhere, Mr. Yarbrough. Darren Clarke didn't know she was dead. We had to tell him."

Yarbrough winced. "I know Rick talked to their general manager. Folks were probably flying in so many directions they didn't do the most obvious thing and find him before someone else did."

"Anyway, tell Mr. Sewell we'll need to talk to Shawn's parents. Fact, call his cell phone before he gets to the airport. Have him page us when they're at the hotel, and we'll go right over."

"I'll do that as soon as we're through."

"Tell us about Shawn. You were her supervisor. What was she like to work with?"

He tented his fingers. "Very good on the air; network quality in the not-too-distant future. On the high-maintenance side, though. Hard to motivate, carried herself a certain way. Knew she was going places and looked down on Jackson."

"Did that bother you?"

"Confidence is a very important thing. But there's a way to temper it with a dash of humility. We didn't see a lot of humility in Shawn." A smirk. "You know who her father is. That was waved at us from time to time."

"Anyone on staff have a beef with her?"

"Not enough to cause trouble. Word had spread around the newsroom about her new contract, though."

"And what was the significance of that?"

"She went from sixty to eighty thousand a year."

Washington raised his eyebrows and smiled. "Nice raise. Think she was worth it?"

"Not for me to say. I don't handle contract negotiations. Are there a lot of people in my newsroom who work just as hard and get paid a lot less? Absolutely. But Shawn tested very well in our market analysis. We're not first in the ratings, but we're a lot better off during the evening shows than before she got here."

"How would word spread about the contract? Management wouldn't discuss it, would they?"

A bemused smile. "No, we wouldn't. Not Sewell, not me, and not Rod Faber, the assistant news director. Fact, Rod and I were discussing why the troops were in the loop. We think she may have been telling people herself."

"Why?"

"Gamesmanship, perhaps. Folks knew her contract was up, and some were probably brazen enough to ask. It's a double-edged sword, Detectives. Quality anchors are a critical piece of the puzzle in a news-gathering operation, but they aren't the only important people on staff. They are the newscasts as far as viewers are concerned, though, so resentment builds fast if they act more important than everyone else. Shawn had a big advantage in this company because of her father, and there was some posturing. But she wouldn't have been headed to network if she couldn't deliver on the air."

"Who's taking her place?"

"Gayle Kennedy, temporarily."

"Would Gayle have a shot at taking over permanently?"

"I doubt it. It's my opinion that Shawn would have already been at network with Gayle's work habits. But Shawn was very natural on camera, easy with the viewers. She had something you can't teach—something I've tried like hell to teach Gayle and something she's tried like hell to get. But that doesn't mean

Gayle isn't a good anchor in her own right, and a strong reporter. Besides, the right consultant might see things a lot differently than ours."

"The consultant?"

"Works with the talent at all the Colonial stations and advises Jack Forrest."

"Who knew Shawn well at the station?"

Yarbrough couldn't hide a smile. "Shawn was only here when necessary. She didn't socialize with anyone in the newsroom to my knowledge."

"So what was the occasion for dinner Saturday night?"

"Call me the eternal optimist."

"It was your idea?"

A nod. "Dinner was my idea, and Samantha suggested that everybody come out to the house for drinks. Fifth Street Elementary is our adopted school, and the kids and teachers really liked Shawn. But Shawn didn't want to fool with it, and we had an argument a couple of weeks ago."

"Why? She thought it was beneath her?"

"To a degree. I wanted to kick around some marketing ideas at dinner—stuff that would have made Shawn look like a hero to the school and our viewers. And like I told Samantha, I wanted to coax Shawn into hanging with the troops a little. Truthfully, I wanted her around Gayle more. Gayle wouldn't admit it to you, but she was intimidated by Shawn, and you can't convince me it wouldn't have done Shawn some good to have at least one friend in this place."

"Was Shawn that hard to work with, or just a snob?"

Yarbrough couldn't hide a smile. "Little of both. Everybody was all for wearing jeans and drinking beer at Chili's or Copeland's, but she let it be known she wasn't coming unless we ate at Que Será Será. She knew the owner, and he made a big deal out of putting us at a certain table she wanted. It was a little silly, but that's what it took to deal with her."

"So is there anybody around here who knew her very well?"

"Talk to Jeff Walker. He's our prime-time male anchor. She seemed to respect him and may have gotten to know him a bit. But I don't know that for sure. Jeff, while an excellent anchor and a very nice man, isn't exactly the definition of an open book. The only other person Shawn seemed glad to see was Rick Sewell."

"We'd like to get a set of fingerprints."

"Tell me where to sign."

McDaniel took the prints. Washington gestured at the door. "Thank you, Mr. Yarbrough. We'll be in touch. Go see if you can catch Mr. Sewell, and send Miss Kennedy in here."

"She's doing one of the background pieces on Shawn for tonight, and it's about done. I'll tell her to step on it."

McDaniel had taken notes and not said a word. He'd watched Yarbrough carefully, and he opined that resentment of Shawn glowed on his face like a neon sign. Washington was about to respond when Gayle Kennedy edged into the room. She was made up and wore a tailored navy suit.

"I hope this won't take long," she said, forcing a smile. "I'm anchoring four newscasts right now, and you can only imagine how busy we are with all this extra coverage about Shawn."

Washington smiled. "It shouldn't. We just have a few questions. I'm Detective Washington, and this is Detective McDaniel. Tell us about Saturday night."

Her story matched Yarbrough's perfectly.

"What's the name of the guy you were with?" Washington said.

"Parker Ford."

"Boyfriend?"

"No. Don't know him well. Bartender on the reservoir. A neighbor, actually."

"Where can we find him?"

She gave the addresses of Ford's apartment and his club.

"Tell us about Shawn Forrest. Did you like her?"

"We weren't that close, but she showed me the ropes when I was new. I don't think what happened has really hit me yet."

"Guess with her gone, they'll need someone to anchor prime-time. That something you'd want? Might be the break you've been waiting for."

Gayle frowned. "Yes, Detective, my goal is to anchor prime-time, either here or somewhere else, but not at the expense of one of my co-workers."

"I see. What was your take on Darren Clarke?"

"First time I was around him. Didn't talk at all, didn't seem like he wanted to be there."

"Yarbrough is your boss, right?"

"Rick Sewell is the general manager, but Jim is the news director. I report to him."

"And you went to his house for drinks. You guys socialize often?"

A shrug. "He wanted several of us together to discuss a station promotion, then Samantha told us to come by for drinks. The whole evening was sort of a thank-you for our hard work. Damn generous, if you ask me. They've done that before—they don't have kids, and once or twice a year they have the reporters and anchors to their house. I think they just enjoy hanging with other television folks."

"So you socialize with Jim and Samantha occasionally. What about Shawn Forrest? How often did you see her away from the station?"

"Rarely. The last time was at a charity event. She didn't do stuff like that unless she had to."

"You said she showed you the ropes when you were new. She take you out for a beer, talk shop?"

"No, sir."

"What about Yarbrough? Have he and his wife done things socially with Shawn and Darren?"

"You'd have to ask them."

"What would be your guess, Miss Kennedy?"

Gayle glanced at her watch. McDaniel noticed a bead of sweat roll down her forehead and made a note of it.

"Probably not, Detective."

"Do you know James Norris?"

A frown. "He's our chief photographer."

"He said Shawn pretty much got the hell out of Dodge each Friday night and wasn't back until Monday. Doesn't sound like she was interested in putting roots down."

Gayle didn't try to hide her exasperation. "No, Detective, Shawn didn't hang around with the people in the newsroom, and no, I don't think she spent any time with Jim and Samantha away from the station unless she had to. No disrespect, sir, but what are you getting at?"

Washington leaned closer. "Here's what I'm getting at, Miss Kennedy: It strikes me a little odd that the six of you would have dinner. You and Jim—and I assume Samantha—were meeting Clarke for the first time. You were with a guy named Parker Ford whom you barely knew. Shawn was never here on weekends, yet she and her husband—whom she only saw on weekends—managed to have dinner with a co-worker and a boss in the city of Jackson. Was Clarke also coming to Jim and Samantha's place for drinks?"

"That's what I understood."

"When was dinner discussed the first time?"

"Jim mentioned it Wednesday or Thursday, I think."

"Do you know when he talked to Shawn about it? Did Shawn mention it to you?"

"It wasn't completely firmed up until Saturday. We weren't sure if Shawn and Darren would come. So, no, I don't know when he talked to her, and she never mentioned it to me." A pause. She addressed both men. "I'm not trying to be rude, Detectives, but I really wish you'd ask Jim these questions."

"We have," Washington said. "Was anyone else invited?"

"Not as far as I know."

"So tell me about being at Yarbrough's house. This was you and your date, Yarbrough and his wife, and Shawn, who was upset. Five of you. What'd you guys do?"

"Samantha tried to cheer Shawn up, and it worked to a degree. Jim brought out blooper tapes, and Samantha made daiquiris."

"Was it an enjoyable evening?"

"Parts of it. Everybody liked the blooper tapes. Shawn got pretty drunk, and after a while she was laughing and carrying on with Samantha. Parker got a little forward, but it wasn't anything I couldn't handle. He couldn't drive by the end. I drove him home, and Jim drove Shawn back to her place in her car."

"What about Samantha?"

"I don't know how much she usually drinks, but she was polluted. Went right to bed."

"What time did you leave Jim's house?"

"Around eleven. I dropped off Parker and pulled into Shawn's parking lot right behind Jim. Shawn couldn't speak coherently or walk straight, so we got her inside the apartment."

"Describe it."

A shrug. "Upscale furniture. Wine glasses on the coffee table. Other than that, not a hair out of place."

"How many wine glasses?"

"Three, I think. We weren't there two minutes. Shawn was a little hard to handle coming up the stairs, but didn't put up a fight when we laid her on the couch. We made sure she was breathing and left. We were in my car, and I drove Jim back to his house, dropped him off and drove home. Got in before one."

"And Shawn was okay when you guys left?"

"No danger that I could see. I thought we did the right thing by making sure she didn't get behind the wheel."

"You didn't call to check on her Sunday, make sure she was up and running?"

Gayle frowned. "We weren't close, Detective. Look, I fully assumed I'd see her Monday and that we'd chat a minute. But it never crossed my mind to call the next day. Believe me, I'm in shock about this. One day you're working with someone, the next day she's gone."

McDaniel looked up. "What did you do with her car keys?"

"Put them in her purse."

"Where was the purse when you left?"

"Kitchen table."

"Can we get a set of fingerprints?"

Gayle gave them without a word. Both men stood.

"Thanks, Miss Kennedy. We'll contact you if we need anything," Washington said. He waited until she was gone and turned to McDaniel, rubbing his hands together. "You can damn near hang meat in here."

A coy smile from McDaniel. "Didn't keep her from sweating like a pig."

"I noticed that, too."

* * *

Samantha Yarbrough was a chunky redhead in her late thirties, dressed in a white apron over a button-down shirt and jeans. She managed a locally-owned print shop which offered the same services as the major chains but catered to Mississippi College and the downtown Clinton merchants. She seated them in her cramped office, then excused herself to settle a dispute with a customer.

"I apologize, Detectives," she said, returning ten minutes later. She drained a can of diet soda, cracked her knuckles and sat behind a desk awash in paper. Nothing was on the gray walls, although a bookcase behind her held an eight by ten wedding photo. Samantha was thinner; Yarbrough was younger but looked virtually the same. "A big client is being unreasonable and all the charm in the world is getting me nowhere."

"We understand," Washington said. "Tell us about dinner at Que Será Será Saturday night."

Samantha's story was a replica of what Yarbrough and Gayle had given them.

"I'm really sorry about Shawn. A nice girl with a great future. But I was embarrassed for her. Didn't hold her alcohol well."

"How much did she have to drink?"

"We all had a beer at dinner. I made daiquiris at the house, and she had a second one. Had it to do all over again, Jim and I probably wouldn't have given her anything. She ate very little."

"Understand you didn't help drive anyone home."

A blush. "Nor did I need to. The bed was the best place for me."

"What time did your husband arrive home?"

"He said around one, but I don't remember him coming in. Slept like a rock."

Both detectives wrote. McDaniel looked up. "Gayle Kennedy told us that you spent most of the evening trying to cheer Shawn up."

"She'd found out that very day her husband was having an affair. Said there was no way he would have the nerve to show, but he walked up like business as usual. She said Darren was an insecure person who needed constant reassurance, and that wanting to stay in Hattiesburg long term was out of fear nobody in a bigger market would touch him. That was before she got so drunk I couldn't understand a word she said. She had the giggles at the end—played ping-pong with Gayle's date and had a big old time."

"Did she say where she was going at the end of the evening? Atlanta, perhaps?"

"Not to me, and I'm still kicking myself for not insisting she spend the night in our guest room." She shook her head. "Long distance marriages aren't worth it. Jim and I know from experience. Met him in Tulsa fifteen years ago. When he took this job, the station was looking for an executive producer, someone who would oversee the team of producers. Exactly what I wanted, since I was a producer for years. Problem is, that person answers to the news director."

"Your husband."

"That's where it broke down. Corporate nixed it right away. We were in New Orleans then, and I got miserable driving back and forth to see him. Finally moved here with no job, which was as good as suicide with the economy the way it was. I stumbled into the printing business through a temp service, and now I manage the place and practically live here. I help the station in a pinch. I produced a week of morning shows last month."

Washington frowned. "Your husband didn't tell us you worked at the station."

"This is where I am ninety-nine percent of the time."

"What was your take on Shawn's husband?"

Samantha frowned. "All I got was Shawn's side, so I shouldn't make a value judgment. Glanced at his watch all night. Evening couldn't end soon enough."

"Gayle said it was your husband's idea to get everyone together."

"He and Shawn had their ups and downs, and I think it was Jim's way of trying to meet her in the middle and start over. He tried hard to get her interested in working with the station's adopted school—they're going to be crushed that she's gone. I invited everyone to the house; I admit I love television and meeting anchor types, even if most of them are a little full of themselves."

Washington smiled. "You sound like a very supportive spouse."

"Jim's worth supporting. Good husband and a good leader in the newsroom."

McDaniel consulted his notes. "Gayle's date was Parker Ford. What was he like?"

"Long-haired guy with an attitude. She said he tends bar on the other side of town, plays in a band. Jim and I didn't think much of him. Little surprised Gayle would associate with him, to be honest. And he sure looked out of place at Que Será Será."

"What's your take on Gayle?"

"She's no Shawn Forrest, although she's come a long way. Jim hired her from Meridian, tried to polish her skills the best he could. She's cocky, like you have to be to make it in this business."

"Understand she'll work the prime-time shows with Shawn out. Any chance they're hers for good?"

"None. Not nearly enough experience. I'm sure Jim would say the same thing."

"Last thing: Fingerprints. We're getting them from everyone."

"I'll be happy to add mine, then."

* * *

"Faber!"

"Yo! Hey, James."

Norris held a digital videocassette aloft. "Come here, man."

Faber followed Norris and Carolyn into an edit bay in the newsroom and closed the door. The room was twenty square feet and featured digital editing equipment and soundproofed walls. Norris described the sound bites they'd gotten at Fifth Street Elementary, the Junior League of Jackson and the Metro Jackson Chamber of Commerce. Everyone they spoke with on camera was shocked and saddened at Shawn's death and expressed admiration for her efforts in the community. Carolyn had temporarily assumed Shawn's medical assignments, so they swung by University Medical Center on the way back to the station.

"We were wrapping up at U.M.C. when this woman in administration came up and asked if she could follow us outside," Norris said. "You'll find this interesting."

He depressed the play button and was heard assuring the

woman that her comments would not be put on the air. A woman of perhaps fifty in a pants suit came into focus. Carolyn told her to tell the story the same way she told it a moment ago.

"This was not long before last Thanksgiving, and Shawn was here filming something for your station on Alzheimer's patients. She spoke to three women who had a mother or father with the disease, and on camera she was sweet as she could be. But the second the cameraman turned off his lights, her warmth disappeared like the air was let out of a balloon. And here's this nice woman about my age whose mother is wheelchair-bound and in the advanced stages of the disease, and the woman asked Shawn if she would pose with her and her mother. Wouldn't have taken ten seconds—she had a digital camera with her, and a nurse was already volunteering to take the picture."

The woman shook her head. *"'I'm sorry, but I have things to do. Another time.' The woman tried to explain that her mother didn't have a lot of time left, and Shawn got right in her face. 'No! Now leave me alone!' She grabbed the cameraman's arm and told him to get moving, and we could hear her loud and clear as she marched off down the hall. 'I'm sick of this crap! You don't know what I'd give not to have to deal with these people!' It was the saddest thing I've ever seen. The poor woman in the wheelchair didn't know what was going on, but her daughter was in tears. We came very close to calling the station and telling you all that Shawn wasn't welcome at our hospital any more."*

Carolyn spoke off-screen. *"Why didn't you? Why not at least report it? Management needed to know that kind of thing."*

"In retrospect, we should have. But I decided not to say anything then. We decided to give her one more chance, which would have been the other day. I was going to sit her down and discuss the situation and get her to assure me it

would never happen again. If she apologized and said she'd had a bad day, all would have been forgiven, because we'd worked with her many times and never had a problem. But she didn't show up."

Norris stopped the tape. He and Carolyn glanced up at Faber, who was shaking his head.

"Interesting. Make Rick a copy of that, James."

"Safe to say you don't want that finding its way into a package," Carolyn said dryly.

Faber grinned. "I think not."

* * *

McDaniel merged onto the interstate after leaving the print shop. He glanced at his partner. "You look deep in thought."

"That's one lonely woman. She'd have invited us to supper if we'd hung around longer. She's stuck in this quiet little printing company when she'd rather be hyper in a newsroom."

"Jerome, I'm sure she's a nice person, but it raises a big red flag when she says she went to bed and let her husband drive around with Gayle Kennedy. I don't care if they were taking home drunk party guests. For all we know Yarbrough is in her pants. And why the hell didn't he tell us his wife works at the station? I don't care if she works there once a year—she knows the staff. I told you he wasn't telling us everything, man. I want to put some heat on him."

"I'm sure you'll get your chance. Where to now? The bartender?"

It was after three when they reached the apartment community inhabited by Gayle Kennedy and Parker Ford. It was on Old Canton Road and modest compared to Shawn's quarters. Gayle's building faced the busy street. Ford lived in back. A brunette in a tight mini-skirt emerged from Ford's door as the detectives approached. She marched past, climbed into a convertible and roared away. The men watched, then knocked. A tall, thin, long-haired man with a pony-tail opened up. He looked to be in his late twenties and was shirtless. He frowned as he took in the detectives.

"Can I help you?"

Washington introduced them, brandishing his badge. Ford stared, then motioned them inside. The small living room was messy, with stacks of compact discs and piles of magazines on the floor. A framed poster of the Allman Brothers with an inscription from Gregg Allman was on the wall. Expensive stereo components were visible. Cigarette butts were in a tin ashtray on the coffee table, and four empty Heineken bottles were nearby. The unmistakable scent of sex was in the air. Washington stepped forward, pen poised. He talked over the rock music issuing from the speakers.

"We passed a woman who was just leaving here."

Ford grinned. "That's not what this is about, is it?"

"You went out with Gayle Kennedy Saturday night, right? And turn the tunes down."

He silenced the music with a remote. "What about it?"

"You met Shawn Forrest?"

A snort. "What a bitch. And what a lush."

"She's dead. Did you know that?"

Ford deflated almost comically. "Oh, wow, man. What happened?"

"That's what we're trying to find out. Why don't you tell us about the evening."

The story more or less matched what the others had given. Ford made it clear that he attended because he thought the payoff would be a night in the sack with Gayle. It hadn't turned out that way.

"Did Shawn and Gayle interact much during the evening?" McDaniel said.

"Like I said, I was focused on Gayle's pants. I didn't pay

attention. Shawn and Gayle's boss's wife did the girl talk thing, I remember that. And Shawn got roaring drunk. Stuck-up bitch wouldn't look at me half the night, and at the end she's three sheets to the wind and we're playing ping-pong. Go figure."

"Reason we ask, Gayle and Yarbrough took Shawn home. They were the last people to see Shawn alive. You're telling us you weren't with them?"

"No, man," Ford said, frowning. "We were in Gayle's car, and she dropped me off here. She didn't say anything about where she was headed. I didn't ask once it was clear she wasn't coming inside." A pause. "You think she had something to do with it?"

"We'd like a set of fingerprints," McDaniel said, ignoring the query.

"Not a problem, dude," Ford said, holding out his hands. "Saw you looking at Gregg Allman over there. My band opened for them once. He liked our stuff and thought he might be able to get us a contract with his label."

"That so?"

"Yeah, man. I'll tell you, some nights we sound more like the Allmans than they do."

"We'll keep that in mind," McDaniel said with a straight face. Washington was looking at the floor, trying to keep from laughing. "We'll be in touch if we need anything."

* * *

Dr. Ben Pyle, fondly nicknamed Gomer because of his good nature, huge grin and profound southern accent, was the favored medical examiner of the Jackson Police Department. A tall, angular man in his mid-forties, Pyle played along with the teasing but was a highly-qualified professional who practiced at Rankin Medical Center. He had a large staff but looked at all potential murder cases himself.

"Watched her on the tube every night," Pyle said, gesturing for McDaniel and Washington to sit. His office was small and cramped, with plaques, citations and family pictures on the cinder-block walls. Medical tomes were in bookshelves, piles of paperwork in boxes along the floor. An orderly mess, but not a pig sty. The hospital had been remodeled in recent years, and the woodsy surroundings were a far cry from the downtown environment of the major Jackson hospitals.

"Foul play?"

"I assume so, Jerome," he said, tracing his page of notes with a ball point pen he removed from a white lab coat. "The vomit on the cushion is hers, and the indentations in the fabric indicate that it was placed over her mouth. What I'm not seeing is the popped blood vessels in her eyelids and skin particles underneath her fingernails, which would point to a struggle. There's minor bruising along her calves, heavier bruising on her shoulders. All the bruising appears to have happened about the same time."

"Like she was held down and someone else held the cushion over her mouth. A two-person job, or could a third person have been in on it? I ask because three wine glasses were found."

Pyle nodded. "The bruises match up to two sets of hands, but a third could have helped. Also a bruise on her right forearm, another on her left calf. But she wasn't beaten. No blows to the head or body, nothing like that. She had sex that night, although no bruising which would lead to an assumption of rape. Doesn't look like she put up much of a fight at all."

"Everybody's saying she was passed out drunk."

"Very possible." Pyle was paged on the overhead sound system. "I'll be interested in what comes back from toxicology. End of the week on the report. I'll state an official cause of death then."

McDaniel's phone rang. He stepped away and took the call, then nodded at Washington.

"Sewell. He, Shawn's parents and someone else from Atlanta are at a hotel on County Line."

Washington was already moving toward the door. "Keep us posted, Gomer."

"Will do, fellas."

* * *

The trek from Rankin Medical Center took thirty minutes in rush hour traffic. The upscale hotel was a block from the interstate, but the decrease in noise as one entered was as dramatic as power windows sealing off the interior of a car. The air-conditioning in the lobby ran full-blast, and soothing classical music played on overhead speakers. McDaniel and Washington entered discreetly and took an elevator to the second floor. The detectives paused and shared a look at the door of the suite before McDaniel knocked. This encounter wouldn't be pleasant.

Sewell let them in. The suite was spacious, with two bedrooms flanking a living area. Two leather-covered sofas sat at angles to a mahogany coffee table. The scent of fresh coffee was in the air. Sewell stood, quietly introducing the consultant from the Colonial corporate office. She was an ordinary-looking woman of perhaps fifty, clad in a pink business suit. The detectives stepped forward and shook her hand. Then Sewell introduced Jack and Leigh Forrest. Jack was a tall, stout man of fifty with perfectly styled gray hair, every bit as broad as Washington. He wore an expensive charcoal suit. Grim determination was on his face, a sharp contrast to the tears in his wife's eyes. Leigh was tall and matronly and dressed in black. Shawn was all over her face.

"Our deepest sympathies, Mr. and Mrs. Forrest," Washington said softly. "We are very sorry for your loss."

Jack Forrest leveled a finger. "Let me tell you something: You and your department drag your feet on this, and you won't know the meaning of torture once I've gotten my hands on you. Do you understand me, Detectives? We want answers!"

"Jack, stop!" Leigh Forrest cried. She placed a hand on her

husband's shoulder and stepped forward. "Who would do something like this?"

"We don't know yet, and frankly, we're not sure she was even murdered at this point," Washington said. His warmth ebbed after the threat, although he'd learned many years ago that mouthing off to relatives of the victims was unwise no matter the situation. "We're questioning the people around your daughter the night of her death. We're contacting anyone who might be of help. Nobody is dragging their feet, I assure you."

Leigh looked at her husband, started to speak, then covered her mouth.

"What is it, Mrs. Forrest?" McDaniel said gently.

Forrest bared his teeth. "I think my wife wants to know if our worthless son-in-law was one of those people."

"From what we understand, sir, your daughter had dinner with her husband and two other couples Saturday night," Washington said. "There was apparently a spat between them. Shawn went with the other couples to the home of Jim Yarbrough, the news director."

"We've met him," Forrest said tersely. He didn't add anything else.

"Shawn apparently had too much to drink and couldn't drive."

"Impossible!" Leigh Forrest said, her jaw tightening. "She hardly ever drinks! She would never, ever be out somewhere and intoxicated!"

"Jim Yarbrough drove Shawn back to her apartment in the Lexus. Gayle Kennedy met him there and helped get Shawn inside."

"I met her last time we were here," Leigh said to her husband. "A little blond girl."

"They were the last people to see your daughter," Washington said softly.

"You think they did it?" Leigh said in horror.

"Where was Darren, for God's sake?" Forrest said angrily.

McDaniel edged forward. "Did Shawn ever hint that Darren was having an affair?"

The words hung in the air. Sewell excused himself discreetly; the consultant had already backed away and was at the far end of the suite. Jack Forrest looked so angry both detectives feared he would fly into a rage. He gnashed his teeth, his large hands balled into fists. Leigh looked at the floor, tears dripping from her eyes.

"That lying, conniving bastard!" Forrest said, veins standing out on his forehead as he struggled to maintain control. "I knew it!"

"What did you know, sir?"

"He didn't know anything, Detective," Leigh said. "Who is it?"

"We're still looking into that, ma'am."

Forrest glowered. "While our daughter is here in this one-horse town, working her butt off trying to get to network, he's in that house we bought them screwing around!" He paused, his voice echoing through the suite. "Was he in on this, Detectives—yes or no?"

"Again, sir, we don't even know it was a murder. We're investigating it as such until we hear otherwise from the medical examiner," McDaniel said. "Mr. Clarke says he left Jackson Saturday night and went back to Hattiesburg. We can neither confirm nor deny he was telling the truth at this point. It would be premature to hazard a guess before then."

"So the person or people who did this are either our son-in-law or folks Shawn worked with?"

"Possibly, but there's no way to know yet. Believe me, sir, we want to see whoever is responsible for this brought to justice as much as you do."

"Don't give me that. Do you have kids, Detective?"

"Both of us do."

"How many?"

"Two," McDaniel said.

"Two. We had three," Washington said, looking Forrest squarely in the eye. "My oldest was killed in a drive-by shooting five years ago. He was walking an eighty-year-old woman home from church and was mistaken for someone else."

Forrest lowered his head. A long moment passed, and his voice was a whisper when he spoke. "Please, Detectives, find who did this. Shawn was our only child."

"We will, sir," Washington said softly, his adrenaline pumping. "We need to ask some questions. Please have a seat."

Leigh Forrest got her husband comfortable and nodded at Washington. Jack stared into the distance.

"We understand that your daughter didn't spend much time in Jackson on weekends."

"She hadn't planned to be in Jackson more than two years, although she'd just signed for two more," Leigh said. "Rick Sewell will tell you that Shawn did everything asked of her."

"Who was Shawn close to?" McDaniel said, poised to write. "People out of television? High school friends? An old boyfriend?"

Leigh smiled. "Shawn and Laci Gwynn were practically sisters growing up. They're the same age, graduated high school together. She's an attorney in Atlanta, private firm. Tax work, mostly—she's a CPA. Married, twin boys. Shawn's best friend."

"How often were they in touch?"

"At least twice a month. I'll put you in touch with her."

McDaniel extended his pad. Leigh dug an address book from her purse, flipped pages and scribbled out an Atlanta phone number. She eased forward.

"It's not that Shawn didn't have friends. Laci would do anything for her. But Shawn knew what she wanted and went for it." A long pause. "I just can't believe the similarities. Do either of you know who Jessica Savitch was?"

Washington nodded. "A national news anchor. Died in a car

accident under mysterious circumstances about twenty years ago."

A firm nod. "Jessica Savitch paved the way for Katie Couric, Jane Pauley and all the other women you see on television, Detectives. She started an entire movement by herself. Shawn met her six weeks before she died, when she was just eight years old. After her death Shawn vowed to be a network news anchor. It was what she lived for, just like Jessica Savitch." A pause. "And both of them were taken long before their time."

*   *   *

Tracey didn't hear from Parker Ford Saturday night. She was sick Sunday morning and bailed on church with her parents, and she was still sick by afternoon. Her mother looked in on her, assumed a twenty-four hour bug and assured Tracey that she would be fine the next morning. By then Parker had called, but she felt too weak to see him. Another wave of nausea awakened her in the middle of the night. She was due at the hospital in several hours, and she was considering calling in sick when cold sweat appeared on her forehead.

She threw on clothes and rushed to the grocery for an emergency pregnancy test, trying not to burst into tears in front of the droopy cashier. The test was positive, although she didn't trust it after one attempt. She slept fitfully, worked her shift with her mind miles away and raced home to test again. Another positive. She went for a long walk, crying much of the time, then ate nearly as much junk food as she had Saturday night. Then one final test.

She was pregnant.

Telling her parents wasn't an option. Her mother would faint and her father would scream—and this was before they had an inkling of the man whose child she was carrying. Sure, she was on friendly terms with the people she grew up with in church. Could she level with any of them? No. Ditto for the nurse who had befriended her and introduced her to Parker, and the neighbor with whom she walked occasionally. This was the price, she realized, of having a controlling mother as a best friend. On the verge of a nervous breakdown after work the following day, she assumed an air of calm and called Parker. She felt better, she said, and yearned for his touch. She rehearsed what to say and was so preoccupied she didn't notice the police tape over Shawn's door as she labored up the stairs. She paced around her small living room, eventually spotting the Ford Probe in a visitor's spot. He was in a Hawaiian shirt and jean shorts and reeked of cologne.

"Only woman I know who looks sexy in hospital scrubs," he said, liquor on his breath. He helped himself to her curves. "What'd you think about Shawn Forrest? Creepy, huh?"

"What are you talking about?"

"You walked right by the damn crime scene. Put the news on."

Jeff Parker and Gayle Kennedy were revealing the shocking news, as they had done at five o'clock. Rick Sewell joined them on the set and commented on the death in grave tones. Several background pieces ran, including a montage of comments from fellow newsroom staffers and influential community types. Gayle advised viewers with information to contact the police department. A phone number was displayed on the screen. Tracey was transfixed and paid no attention as Ford opened wine coolers and slipped a pill into hers. He shut off the television with the remote and pulled her into his lap. He clinked her drink, waiting for her to imbibe.

"No alcohol tonight, baby. There's a Sprite in the 'fridge."

Ford muttered to himself, then retreated to the kitchen and found a dark-colored stadium cup. He poured the soft drink and slipped in another pill, fortunate to have several extra in his pocket. He watched it dissolve and brought the drink to Tracey. This time she drank.

"We need to talk, Parker."

"We need to do a lot of things, darling. Got a lot of making up to do for Saturday night. I say we start here on your home turf. Then we adjourn to my place and frolic in the waterbed. Then we head up the Natchez Trace to our little spot under all those pines and get back to nature." He grinned, touching his tongue to her neck. "The hat trick. All Parker, all night. Let the fun begin."

He rubbed her shoulders. She put off the announcement, sipping the soft drink until it was gone and closing her eyes. She began to feel lightheaded and succumbed to his touch. When she opened her eyes he was smoking a cigarette, something she strongly opposed in her apartment, but it took too much energy to voice the complaint. Her head, which felt three feet thick, rested in his lap. She didn't remember getting undressed, but she was naked in her bed and noticed that his tin ash tray was resting on her belly. Some time later he was pulling her to her feet.

"Put your clothes on, babe. Off to my place so I can take 'em off again. The night has just begun."

She could hardly stand, let alone dress herself. Ford led her to the bathroom. Steadying her, he turned on the tap and threw water in her face. He did it a second time, rousing her toward consciousness.

"I'm pregnant," she said softly.

Ford was wetting a washcloth, which he planned to hold against her forehead in an attempt to jump start her central nervous system. His blood ran cold. He dropped the cloth and grabbed her shoulders, looking directly at her.

"What did you say?"

A weak smile through her haze. "That's why I was so sick."

He started to challenge her, but it was no use—he had deflowered her, and he knew there had been no one else. It was definitely his. He tightened his grip on her shoulders in rage. She was too high to register the pain, but ugly purple marks would form.

"You listen to me, Tracey . . ."

"I love you," she said, eyelids flickering.

"No!" He shoved her backward. Her head snapped back, blasting the medicine cabinet and leaving a web of cracks. Dazed, she pitched forward as blood dripped from the back of her head. He thrust her away in anger, realizing too late that she was all but asleep on her feet and wouldn't catch herself. She pitched into the bathtub, hitting her head solidly on the porcelain. Blood splattered. She lay motionless and didn't respond when he tried to shake her awake.

Heart pounding, he threw on his clothes, grabbed his keys and ran.

* * *

Washington reached Jeff Walker in the newsroom after leaving the hotel and confirmed a visit after the six o'clock news. James Norris let them in the back door of the newsroom and explained that a brief meeting was in progress. The detectives lingered near the door, listening as Sewell recounted his visit with Shawn's parents. Yarbrough said that coverage would be gradually scaled back, but the station would go live at a moment's notice in the event of breaking developments.

Walker was a handsome black man in his late forties. He strode up with a handshake and suggested they talk outside. He proved Yarbrough correct—although a pleasant, polite sort with a dry sense of humor, he was careful with his words and offered little about Shawn. The only helpful tidbit was a recent opening in Denver which sparked Shawn's interest for several days. She discovered the position in a trade publication just before the contract extension with Channel Five. The station wasn't part of the Colonial chain, however, and Walker sensed that Jack Forrest and the consultant leaned on her to stay in the family.

Assistant news director Rod Faber was outgoing and brusque

with New Orleans all over his voice. He was horrified that Shawn was dead but identified her as a prima donna and cited instances where she refused assignments, such as her duties with the station's adopted school. She seemed to know what buttons to push to inflame Yarbrough, he said, and likely spread the word about the salary hike herself.

"Gayle Kennedy sure got the hell out of Dodge," McDaniel said, watching a Ford Explorer weave around parked cars and disappear from sight. "That's one cage I'd like to rattle some more."

"She's working the late show," Washington said, climbing into McDaniel's Taurus. "The wife made a great big pot roast, Mac. Let's eat, then revisit the crime scene and come back out here."

* * *

The dark-haired man kissed the blond's neck and worked a hand under her cotton top. She sighed and rolled away.

"I don't feel like it right now."

"Okay. Let me know if you change your mind."

A harsh laugh. "Just once I'd like to be held instead of pawed at, you know?"

This smarted. He thought of himself as her mentor, an older, worldly sort who was giving her the kind of education she couldn't get in a classroom. The sex was great, and he admitted to a certain fondness for her. But the comment had reduced him to an overheated adolescent who lacked subtlety and charm. Nothing suave and sophisticated about that. He internally thumbed through a series of retorts, all of which would level her emotionally but wouldn't be worth the crying jag which was certain to follow. In the end he chose silence, hoping she would let the moment pass. No such luck.

"But that's far too much to ask, isn't it?"

"You've made your point," he said quietly. The more he was pushed, the harder he was to hear—the calm before the storm.

"Oh, and that's the end of it, huh?" She jumped to her feet and began dressing. "Since I don't want to put out, no point in me staying, huh?"

"Who just started taking her clothes off?"

Tears filled her eyes. "I'm scared!"

"Come here."

She crawled into his arms and cried. He held her, kissing the top of her head.

"There's no need to be scared, sweetheart."

"You keep saying that, but . . ."

"Trust me."

*　*　*

Shawn's Lexus was still in its parking space. The suitcase had been removed from the back seat, which meant Bernie had gotten it to the crime lab. The contents would be analyzed, and the detectives would be alerted if there was anything suspicious.

The landlady, who was still in the office but dressed for an evening out, plucked a spare key from a rack and told them to drop it in the mail slot when they were through. They displayed their badges for the crusty rent-a-cop at the foot of Shawn's stairs and entered the apartment. The techs had done their best to control the odor without disturbing the integrity of the crime scene, but it still smelled foul. Washington closed the door and flipped on the overhead light, keeping his hand in his jacket pocket to avoid adding prints. McDaniel stopped near the coffee table and furrowed his brow.

"I know that look," Washington said. "Watch, ladies and gentlemen, as Detective McDaniel solves the crime before your very eyes."

McDaniel bent over. "The earring fragment was found here, and Shawn's head was down there. Gomer thinks two people may have done this, based on the bruises. Heavier bruising on the shoulders, lighter on the calves. If this was a male and female, the man had the shoulders and the woman was basically along for the ride making sure Shawn couldn't get up."

"Okay, but what about the third wine glass? Did someone else hold the cushion in place?"

"Maybe. But let's assume a female is holding Shawn's calves. Shawn can't do much, but she flails here and there and a leg catches the female in the head and knocks loose part of an earring. Maybe the third wine glass got knocked away in the struggle." He wrinkled his nose. "Probably pointless to speculate until we have prints."

Washington moved to the wall unit. It had a cherry finish and housed a twenty-seven-inch television and stereo components, including a DVD player. The remaining shelves housed hardback novels, framed pictures and half a dozen Beanie Babies. A built-in cabinet was below the television and stood open. Washington nosed close. Several stacks of videocassettes were on one side. All were news tapes based on the labels, and many were Shawn's own work. Washington glanced through them. McDaniel leaned in and perused a stack of movies on the opposite side.

"*Broadcast News.* What a great flick."

Washington started to reply, then stopped. Between the videocassettes and DVD's was a red and white University of Alabama stadium cup. Tiny university flags hung over the front edge. A pair of what appeared to be candy cigars, handed out by friends and family upon the arrival of a newborn, stood at the back. The clear plastic seal had been broken off both cigars.

"What is it?"

"Get me a paper towel, Mac."

Carefully avoiding leaving prints, Washington lifted the cup into plain sight. "Look at the tips of those cigars."

McDaniel's eyes widened. "That what I think it is?"

"Somebody's DNA, my man. Wonder how long its been here."

"Did Bernie even look in here?"

"We'll sure find out."

McDaniel rummaged around and returned with a box which had housed a pair of size seven flats. The packing was still inside, and Washington, using the paper towel, placed the cup in the box and arranged the soft paper around it.

"Wonder what else they didn't find."

"I wouldn't have seen it if the light wasn't right. I'll get this to the lab on my way in tomorrow."

* * *

Twenty minutes later McDaniel nosed the Taurus into a parking space near the back door of the Channel Five newsroom. He was behind an office which apparently belonged to Jim Yarbrough. Fluorescent bulbs and a table lamp lit the room, which was visible in the dusk through partially drawn blinds. They arrived in time to see a short, thin black woman point sharply at Yarbrough, who was behind a desk.

"You tell him," McDaniel said, chuckling. "She doesn't buy his smooth talk, either, Jerome."

The discussion lasted another minute. The woman started to leave, listened to something Yarbrough said, then walked out and slammed the door.

"I've seen her on the air."

"That's Carolyn Davis. Miss Davis?" Washington said, getting out of the car as Carolyn threw open the door and brushed by. She whirled and looked Washington over, then shot a glance at McDaniel as he emerged. Washington showed his badge and introduced them.

"We'd like to ask some questions about Shawn Forrest."

"If you insist. Awfully long day, Detectives."

"We'll be brief. What was she like to work with?"

Carolyn rolled her eyes. "The viewers sure liked her, but the second the camera was off she was a different person—a poor little rich kid who got where she was because her corporate-level daddy pulled strings. I wouldn't wish what happened to her on anyone, but she was a back-stabber and didn't have a friend in that newsroom."

"You ever cross swords with her?"

"I stayed away, and she never started anything with me. But she picked fights all the time."

"Example?"

She lit a cigarette. "Our morning anchor is a sweet young white girl named Claire Bailey. We're friends, and I'm reluctant to be critical because she's such a nice person. But you'll never see her in a big market." Plumes of smoke wafted into the air. "Anyway, Claire thought Shawn was practically God and treated her like a celebrity. But instead of being flattered, Shawn made jokes behind her back. And Claire has gained weight, so Shawn took it upon herself a few weeks ago to e-mail the newsroom that the piglet on the morning show was embarrassing the station. And someone printed the damn thing and put it on a bulletin board. By the time Claire saw it, half a dozen people had added comments and drawn pictures of pigs. She was in tears, and I don't expect her to stay much longer, even with Shawn gone. She was humiliated."

Washington glanced at the office before him. The blinds were now closed.

"Mind if we ask what you and Jim Yarbrough were arguing about?"

Her poker face. "Let's just say we had a difference of opinion. Will there be anything else? I really need to get home."

"How well did Yarbrough and Shawn get along?"

"Not very. Yarbrough's funny when he gets ticked off. All red in the face, gripping his desk real tight so he won't lose control."

"He get ticked off at her a lot?"

"Oh, yeah. Then he made excuses for her and tried to play it down. We all saw through it."

"Could you ever see them together socially, like at a party?"

"That's an odd question." Another drag. "I went to a barbecue at his place once. Food was great, I'll give him that. But the last thing I want to do in my free time is hang with my boss. I'm sure that went triple for Shawn. She wouldn't give him the time of day at work, so I can't believe she'd socialize with him off the clock."

"With her out of the picture, where does that leave you? A promotion?"

"When hell freezes over." A friendlier smile. "I may anchor one of the night shows, so yeah, that would be a promotion of sorts, but I'll still get paid food stamps. The general public assumes that we television types are made of money. Nothing could be further from the truth, I assure you."

"Do you want to anchor every day? That sounds prestigious."

"I'd much rather report. That's what I do best. And the more I'm out covering stories, less I'm in the newsroom putting up with the crap. That's why I wasn't around Shawn much."

"We're told Gayle Kennedy will replace Shawn temporarily. She want the night shows?"

"I'm sure she does. But she doesn't have a daddy at corporate. The final nail in her coffin was mouthing off to the consultant. Gayle knows she's doomed."

She gave them a polite smile and left when they said they had no further questions. Washington climbed the short flight of cement steps and peered into the newsroom, then knocked sharply.

"Miss Kennedy!"

Gayle was walking through and glanced up. She frowned in recognition, then came to the door and opened it a crack. "Yes, Detective?"

"Need to speak with you again. Won't take long."

Gayle stepped outside and signaled for them to follow. She didn't slow until they were at the rear of the property, completely out of sight of the newsroom. The last light of day illuminated them, and the red beacon at the top of the transmitter tower was visible in the distance. Cigarette butts and soft drink cans littered the area.

"If this is going to take any time, please speak to Jim. He's in his office trying to help us get ready for the news. We're really crunched."

Washington ignored her. "You told us you wanted to anchor the night shows, right?"

"Somewhere, if not here. Why?"

"Who would you speak to about that? Yarbrough?"

"And the consultant."

"What's your take on her?"

Gayle frowned. "She's a consultant, Detective. She's based in Atlanta and works with the talent at each station in the chain. She's a little brusque for my taste, and she ought to lose weight if she's going to wear tight slacks. Now can I please get back to work?"

"Are you missing an earring?"

"Am I missing an earring? What kind of question is that?"

Washington stepped forward and confirmed that Gayle had an earring in each ear. Small gold diamonds were in both—far from cheap.

"A small piece of an earring was found at the crime scene this morning."

"So what?"

"Here's what we're thinking: A male and a female did Shawn, based on the bruising on her body. A large set of identical bruises was on her shoulders, which gives us the impression the man was at that end. A smaller set of identical bruises was on her calves."

Gayle glanced at her watch, then the building. The detectives got a clear look at her when she turned her head. Alarm was in her eyes now.

"The interesting thing was where on the carpet that piece of earring was found—almost exactly where the female would have been if she held Shawn's legs. Something broke that earring, made that little piece fall to the carpet. Maybe it was Shawn trying to get away. What do you think?"

Gayle looked Washington in the eye. She had regained her self-control and wore a steely facade. "I went over everything that happened Saturday night. If you insist on talking to me further, you'll have to do it after the news, sir."

Washington didn't budge. "Is there anything you'd like to tell us, Miss Kennedy? Now would be the time."

"Yes: I have to get back to work." She spun and started away. "If you want to talk after the news, please let Jim know. He's at his desk."

McDaniel watched as she disappeared from sight. "Wound tight, isn't she?"

"I smell fear, Mac."

"You and me both."

*   *   *

Carolyn heard Washington's attempt to get Gayle's attention. She stood near her car and faked a conversation on her cell phone, watching as Gayle led the men out of sight. Gayle wasn't pleased, and Carolyn's curiosity grew as the minutes passed. It was impossible to hear any snippets of conversation, but it sounded like an animated discussion was taking place.

Carolyn glanced around before returning to the building. There was no one in sight, and Yarbrough's blinds were still drawn. She entered the newsroom discreetly, noting that Yarbrough's door was still closed, and sat at her desk. She opened a drawer which was loaded with field tapes and pretended to be looking for one, wanting an alibi in case Yarbrough emerged and asked what she was doing. He didn't, and Gayle appeared ten minutes later. Her face was flushed as she strode rapidly through the room. Carolyn spoke as casually as she could.

"What's up with you?"

"Freakin' cops," she hissed. She paused, her jaw tight. "God, that pisses me off. I'm wearing earrings, so they think I killed Shawn."

"What?"

"They found part of an earring at the crime scene and asked if it was mine," Gayle said, leaning close. "Yeah, you're wearing them, too. Plan on having your chops busted. I've worked all freakin' day, and the thanks I get is a grilling by those bozos who don't know their asses from a hole in the ground." She exhaled and started away. "Let me get ready for the freakin' news."

A minute later Yarbrough emerged from his office. Carolyn rummaged through her desk and kept her head down, and he said nothing as he passed through and turned down a hall. She got to her feet, intent on slipping out before he returned and engaged her in further discussion. Then she felt the earring fragment in her pocket.

They found part of an earring at the crime scene and asked if it was mine.

Carolyn glanced around, her antenna up now. She slipped out the door and trotted to her car. She drove around the curve and pulled into the industrial park just down the street. She retrieved the earring fragment and looked it over, her heart speeding up.

WEDNESDAY

An above-the-fold, front page story about Shawn's death in *The Jackson Times* greeted the city the next morning. The reporter added nothing the detectives didn't already know, although a series of maudlin comments from Rick Sewell was printed. Washington leaned back at his desk and cackled, extending the paper to McDaniel as he arrived.

"Top of the morning, Mac. Dig these comments from Sewell. The station got two hundred calls? Please."

"Wife read it to me. Goes with the goddess image they're perpetuating, I guess."

Cowan called the morning staff meeting to order. McDaniel and Washington got the department spokesman up to speed on the Forrest case. The spokesman asked why the cup with the potentially crucial DNA sample was only found last night, and Washington patiently explained that it was inside a cabinet twelve feet from the body and barely visible. When Cowan pressed further, McDaniel snapped that he could take it up with the crime lab. Cowan glared, then moved to the other investigations. He took them aside afterward and said the chief was chomping at the bit for an arrest—no other case mattered for the time being.

McDaniel flipped through his notes and dialed Laci Gwynn's law firm in Atlanta. Laci picked up after a delay of ten minutes and spoke with the self-assured drawl of a successful southern belle. Yes, Leigh Forrest had alerted her that a Jackson homicide detective might call. No, she couldn't come to Jackson—a big trial was underway, and she would do well to break for Shawn's funeral. McDaniel rolled his eyes at the self-importance.

Laci added little to what they already knew. Shawn had worked at Colonial affiliates in Tuscaloosa and Chattanooga after interning at their Atlanta station during college. The Jackson job was her first shot at evening shows. She wanted to move to a bigger market when her contract was up, but none of the large Colonial stations had prime-time positions open. Jack Forrest and the consultant both felt Jackson was the best option for the time being.

Laci disliked Darren Clarke and found him insecure, but Shawn had once loved him—especially in the beginning when Darren waxed philosophic about doing weather on *The Today Show*. The plan was for both to rise through the ranks to broadcast glory, but somewhere along the way Darren decided he liked Hattiesburg and crippled their future by signing a long-term deal. This was before it came to light that he was bedding down with a coed half his age.

Laci shed remarkably little on Shawn's personal life. She was a regular at the athletic club, since maintaining her appearance was vital to her career path. She played tennis when she had the chance and enjoyed old movies. Returning to Atlanta, relaxing with her mother and catching up with old friends took place whenever possible. Regrettably, their marathon phone visits were down to once or twice a month in recent years. Laci claimed they never e-mailed—since their history was to stay in touch by phone, cyberspace just didn't cut it. McDaniel thanked her and hung up.

Washington's cell rang midway through the call. Seeing that McDaniel was off, he sidled over and pressed his thumb on his partner's notes. This was Washington code for fingerprint information.

"Prints on two of the wine glasses are a match to Darren and

Patti." A pause. "No prints on the third glass."

McDaniel stared in surprise.

"Rush job on the football tumbler, so we'll know late this afternoon." He lowered his voice. "I was told the chief went right to the top. Left for a meeting with the Public Safety Commissioner about the DNA."

"Meaning they're big-time serious about cracking this one fast."

"Got that right, my man. Hell, it's usually six weeks on DNA with the backlog at the crime lab. Now it could be a matter of days. Anything useful from Shawn's buddy?"

A snort. "Might as well have put her comments in press release form and faxed them here. The same crap about Jessica Savitch. Oh, and she said they never e-mailed because of a long-standing tradition of girl-talk phone marathons."

"They're best friends, live four hundred miles away and never e-mailed? Ain't buying that."

"Makes two of us. And we'll know when the disc from Shawn's e-mail program is ready." Washington's desk line rang. He took a seat and whipped his pad open. McDaniel watched as his partner scribbled, his face a twisted mask of emotions. He hung up and exhaled.

"One of our guys remembered us mentioning Parker Ford in the meeting. He's working a case with a couple of cops in Precinct Five who were called to Boardwalk Apartments last night."

"Where Shawn lived."

Washington nodded. "A twenty-four year old girl named Tracey Walton was found in her bathtub last night by her mother. Here's how that pertains to us, Mac: She dates Parker Ford and just found out she's pregnant with his baby. Sounds like he beat her up and left her for dead. She spilled her guts to her parents, and they told the cops. Turns out Ford has a record—a couple of minor drug felonies. Light jail time, small fines. But he sounds like a player, which makes me wonder what really went on at Yarbrough's house the other night."

"Will she talk to us, or can she?"

"She's at U.M.C. Let's see if we can at least talk to her doctor."

* * *

University Medical Center occupied several city blocks at the corner of State and Woodrow Wilson and was across the street from Veterans Memorial Stadium. The Mississippi Crime Lab was a quarter mile back up Woodrow Wilson. It was a straight shot from Spring Center to the hospital once McDaniel was on State, although morning congestion slowed the trek considerably. The day had dawned cloudy and humid, and light rain was falling as they arrived.

They were directed to the nurses' station in the intensive care unit, where a doctor was summoned over the intercom. Seconds later a fortyish man in wire-rimmed glasses and green scrubs emerged. He ushered them to a waiting room and explained that Tracey was expected to live, although she had lost an eight-week-old fetus and would be hospitalized for at least a week. She was on suicide watch, and psychiatric evaluations would take place when she was stronger. He consented when Washington asked if she was up to answering questions, although he reserved the right to stop the proceedings if Tracey became upset.

The doctor introduced them to the parents and family lawyer before leading them to Tracey's room. A can of air freshener stood alongside a trio of floral arrangements, and classical music played softly on a boom box. Tracey was a tall, big-boned red-head in her early twenties. She was conscious, although her face was ashen and her green eyes were glazed. The back of her head was bandaged, and a purple welt the size of a quarter was visible just above her left temple. Her breathing and heart rate were monitored while fluids were pumped into her veins. The parents hugged her and left the room.

Washington placed his tape recorder on a bedside table. He caught Tracey's eye and tried to smile. She stared blankly. He started the tape, introduced himself and his partner and described the occasion. The lawyer told Tracey to tell the detectives everything she'd told him. She nodded.

"We're very sorry, Miss Walton. We know you've been through a lot. We just have a few questions." A pause. "Tell us about Parker Ford. Start at the beginning, and take your time. There's no hurry."

The lawyer patted her hand. The doctor smiled from ten feet away. Tracey didn't acknowledge either of them. Her eyes were devoid of emotion. She began speaking in a soft, eerie monotone, and there would be no inflectional change during the interview.

"A nurse I work with took me to his club. He tends bar, plays in a band. I'm very inexperienced with men—never had a boyfriend before. But he seemed to like me."

She pointed at a pitcher of water. The lawyer poured a glass and slipped a straw into her mouth. She drank, then found Washington's face. Her eyes were still blank.

"He made me a drink—a screwdriver. First alcohol I ever had. Danced for the first time, had my first cigarette. First hangover the next morning. Flowers were waiting at the hospital when I got to work. His band played in Yazoo City that night, and we all shared a joint."

Washington started to speak, but there was a faint movement from McDaniel. Washington caught it and kept his mouth shut. McDaniel was right; fragile as this girl was, best to let her talk without interruption.

"I told him I was a virgin, but that was gone a couple of nights later. We were drinking on his couch, and I woke up bleeding in his bed."

McDaniel scribbled *date rape?* on his pad and flashed it discreetly.

"The more I fell for him, the more I resented my parents. Big mistake was telling him I've been on Ritalin since high school. Soon he was giving me stuff, like speed. We went dancing one night, and I felt like I could fly. Could hardly work the next day, but I was with him the next night."

Washington leaned closer. "Miss Walton, tell us about Mr. Ford's drug trade. Does he keep stuff at his apartment? And did he make you take drugs and sell them for him?"

She nodded. "The back bedroom is where he keeps everything. A loaded gun and a huge wad of cash are in the dresser. In the closet there's a hollowed-out amplifier; pot, pills, coke—you name it. One night he told me what to find in the amp, where to take it, and what I was supposed to bring back. I didn't want to, but his look scared me. I began seeing it if I balked at anything he said. There was pressure to do stronger drugs, drink more and do really weird things with him in bed. I knew he was trouble but didn't want to be alone and didn't know who to talk to."

The doctor stepped forward, then held back. The lawyer gave him a discreet thumbs-up.

"I was supposed to go out with him Saturday night, but he said his band was playing at some out of town dump that wasn't safe and didn't think I should come. So I sat home all night and waited for him to call."

Washington and McDaniel exchanged a glance.

"By the time he did—late the next afternoon—I was sick as a dog. Thought it was my body finally betraying me for all the drugs I took with him, but it dawned on me that my period was late. Took a home test, confirmed I was pregnant and planned to tell him last night." She paused, sipping her water. "We were at my place. He had a wine cooler, and I told him I wanted a Sprite. But it was so weird. Suddenly my head was all thick and I couldn't keep my eyes open."

"Did he slip you something, Miss Walton?"

"He must have. I was fully clothed on my couch, then I was

naked in bed. Then we were standing in my bathroom. I could hardly see him but I remember blurting out that I was pregnant and that I loved him. Next thing I remember was Mother and the police."

"How did he react when you said you were pregnant?"

"He was angry. He grabbed me."

The lawyer stepped forward and pulled Tracey's paper gown back far enough to reveal the purple marks on her left shoulder. Impressions of four fingers and a thumb were visible.

"Did he throw you into the bathtub?"

"I don't remember. But he shoved me—I hit the back of my head on the medicine cabinet."

"Last question," Washington said, acknowledging the desire of the doctor to wrap up. "Did he ever mention the name Shawn Forrest to you?"

"She was my neighbor. Found out she was dead yesterday when Parker said to put the news on—said there was tape across her door. I'd missed it." She glanced at the lawyer, then Washington. "I forgot all about this: I met her once in the parking lot and knew where she lived. I was waiting for Parker to call Saturday night and getting something to eat, and I happened to look out my window and saw two people coming out of her apartment."

The detectives stared at each other. Washington eased closer. "What time was this?"

"Just before midnight."

"Can you describe the people?"

"A man and a woman, both white. I couldn't see the man very well. Dress pants, I think, and dark hair. Average size. The blond was short—younger than him. Looked like she called out to someone over her shoulder."

"Would you be able to identify either of them?"

"Maybe the woman. The man was hard to see. My phone rang then—wrong number, of course—and when I got back they

84

were gone. I could see the taillights of a car leaving the parking lot, but that was all."

"Could you identify the car?"

"No, sir."

"Did you see anything else?"

"No, sir. I assumed they were friends of Shawn and didn't think twice about it."

* * *

McDaniel opened a file on his computer which contained an underlying facts and circumstances template. He filled in the blanks, typing Ford's name and address and other simple information. Calling Washington over, he worded an explanation of Ford's actions and the need for a warrant. The three paragraphs included Ford's record, his association with Gayle Kennedy, his involvement with Tracey Walton and the possibility that drugs were in his possession. It was noted that a cassette copy of Tracey's statement had been preserved for posterity, since Tracey was in grave condition.

McDaniel's cell rang as the pages were printing. He was off quickly. "The disc with Shawn's e-mails is ready, Jerome."

"Cool," Washington said, having recovered somewhat after the emotional wallop of the bedside interview. "Get them to dub Tracey to CD. I'll get our warrant signed and we'll go find this scumbag."

* * *

Washington drove the three blocks to City Hall to avoid the storm closing in on the city. It could take five minutes or two hours to catch a Hinds County Court judge, since all could be in court or have people in their offices. He caught a break when a portly old judge came out of the bathroom in the midst of a recess. Washington was on a first-name basis with him and got him to look over the warrant. He signed without hesitation.

McDaniel was on the phone when Washington returned. He gestured at a small stack of discs. There were two copies of Tracey's statement and a pair of CDs which contained Shawn's e-mails.

"The wife. Air-conditioner went out last night, and she met a repair man at the house. It's fixed and didn't cost as much as I thought." A pause. "Her mother just got back from the doctor. Maybe a couple of weeks. She's going downhill fast."

Washington groaned, then pledged his prayers.

"Thank you, Jerome. We knew this was coming. What about the warrant?"

"Caught the Michelin Man in a recess. Let's go."

The same bottleneck of traffic was along State Street, but the interstate was clear. McDaniel radioed and asked for backup. They reached the apartment complex and parked three buildings away. A patrol car with a pair of officers eased into the lot minutes later and parked alongside the Taurus. Washington described Ford and the circumstances, and the quartet strode the hundred yards to his door under threatening skies. McDaniel knocked, Washington at his side. Both men were ready to draw weapons. The patrolmen flanked them from behind.

Washington glanced around as the seconds passed. The first droplets of rain hit the ground. Lightning flashed close. "He may be in that back room."

"I don't think he's here. I'll get the manager," McDaniel said. He returned with a maintenance man, who calmly brandished a ring of keys and unlocked the door without comment.

It was eerily quiet, the bottom about to fall out of the sky. Both detectives drew their weapons. Washington nudged the door open and stepped into the foyer. He flipped on the light.

"Parker Ford! Police! Come out with your hands up!"

McDaniel eased into the tiny kitchen, which was to the right. Stale smells emanated from a stack of dirty dishes in the sink. He crept past Washington and flashed into the living room, gun pulled. It was a mess, but empty. The cheap plastic blinds were open, revealing a patio with an elderly grill and bags of charcoal. Washington crept down a short hallway. The door to the left bedroom was open. He announced himself, gun pulled, then darted into the room and flipped on the overhead light. The smell of marijuana was heavy. A king size bed was unmade, and piles of clothes were on the floor and atop the cheap dresser. *Playboy Magazine* centerfolds were tacked up on the walls.

Washington signaled to McDaniel, then eased the louvered doors of the large closet open. Scads of jackets, shirts and jeans were hanging, with a smattering of dress clothes at the end. An aluminum baseball bat was in the corner. The door on the other side of the room opened to the lone bathroom. Washington whipped it open, but other than towels on the floor, a grubby toilet and a general air of messiness, it looked normal.

Washington approached the back bedroom, McDaniel right behind. This door was locked. Washington's heart beat faster. He wiped sweat from his brow.

"If you're in here, come out now with your hands up!"

Silence.

"Mr. Ford, come out right this minute or we kick this door in!"

Lightning flashed close by, and thunder exploded. Both men jumped. On the heels of the noise was the pounding of sneakers on wet pavement. A rush of profanity, growing louder as someone approached. The detectives heard guns being drawn outside.

"Are you Parker Ford? Hey! Freeze!"

The sneakers could be heard in hasty retreat. McDaniel leaped forward and kicked in the cheap door. Guns drawn, they determined the room was empty. Washington kicked open the closet door, finding no one inside. Then he dashed for the front, leaving McDaniel to guard the premises until Ford was apprehended.

Heavy rain was falling when Washington sprinted into the parking lot. Ford was cornered by the patrolmen and trying to escape by dodging between parked cars. His pony tail flapped as he hurled himself across the roof of a Toyota Camry. The maneuver got him around the cops and gave him a sliver of chance at escape, but he slipped on the wet pavement and sprawled between the Camry and a large Chevrolet pickup. The cops pounced on him. Ford resisted until Washington reached the scene, then backed down. Washington looked on as Ford was secured in the patrol car, then trotted over to McDaniel. He was now in the doorway of the apartment.

"Crime lab is on the way," he said. "Tracey nailed it, Jerome. The amp is the mother lode—he has enough crap in there to open a Walgreens. There's also a loaded .38 and at least ten grand."

"One of us needs to go with them in case he starts yapping," Washington said, accepting a paper towel and wiping his face.

"Go ahead. I just talked to one of Patti St. John's sorority sisters. Swears neither Patti nor Jamie was at the house all Saturday night."

"Oh, really?"

"She agreed to meet in Mendenhall, so I'm headed that way in just a minute. Come have a look at this stuff."

There was nothing on the walls of Ford's spare bedroom. The only furniture was a cheap dresser, a folding chair and a small computer desk which housed an expensive notebook computer and a laser printer. Two well-worn acoustic guitars were propped against the wall. A pair of electric basses in better shape stood alongside. Stacks of *Musician Magazine* were nearby, along with packages of picks and strings. Sheet music was on the floor. The smell of marijuana lingered.

Using a paper towel, McDaniel opened the top dresser drawer. There was the loaded handgun, along with a digital camera and wads of hundred dollar bills in rubber bands.

"Watch. I just pulled these out of the closet," he said, gesturing at a pair of amplifiers. Both were scuffed but appeared to be legitimate. Nothing happened when he tapped the first one. He nudged the second and caused the entire frame to collapse—the contraption was nothing more than a large shoebox with the appearance of an amp. In plain sight were bags of cocaine, marijuana and perhaps a hundred pill bottles. Washington yanked a paper towel from the roll and picked up a vial. The word *Oxycontin* and the number 50 were visible in tiny, typed print. The label had probably been printed in this room.

"What a surprise," he said, fishing a bottle of rohypnol from the pile. The labeling was identical, right down to the font size. "The date-rape drug. Ain't no telling what we'll find on his computer." He cocked his ear. "Sounds like a break in the storm. Let me get our pharmacist taken care of."

McDaniel nodded. "Off to Mendenhall. I should be back by the time booking is done."

* * *

"What's eating you?" Norris said as he and Carolyn rode to Fifth Street Elementary, Channel Five's adopted school. Carolyn would take part in a talent show and speak to the children about the importance of staying in school.

"Yarbrough could have said, 'We'd like you to take over Shawn's responsibilities at Fifth Street,' and left it at that. But he had to mention that Shawn was adored, so the kids might not be as excited to see me. And he felt it necessary to point out that I'd been selected because Jeff and Gayle are too busy."

"Other words, you're his first choice if the janitor is tied up."

"About the size of it. I'm firmly convinced, Norris, that when former anchors move into management, they get jealous of the attention their people are getting. If I had a nickel for every time Yarbrough has shown someone his own resume tape, I wouldn't have to work again."

"What were you guys fighting about last night, by the way?"

"Damn, word gets around fast." She cracked the window and lit a cigarette. "For fanning the flames of racial division."

Norris raised an eyebrow.

"My words, not his, but that's clearly what he was getting at. Wanted to know why the interview with the Reverend Warren Jefferson was so long in that live shot after the Cronin verdict. And he went on to imply that it wasn't balanced."

"Look, Jefferson is a major civil rights leader in this country, and giving him three minutes wasn't anything out of the ordinary. And you pointed out that he was there in sixty-four and lived to see justice in a place plagued with racial baggage, which was a great comment. Sure, he did some grandstanding, but he admitted that the races worked together and did the right thing. Why would Yarbrough have a problem with any of it? Hell, the other stations would have killed for that interview."

"I got the impression he was coached."

A grin. "And don't tell me—you told him so. Smooth, Davis. And you wonder why you're last on his list to entertain the kiddies. And who coached him? Sewell?"

"Maybe. He could have passed it along to Yarbrough as an oh-by-the-way, and Yarbrough decided to flex his muscles and make a mountain out of it." A sharp exhalation of smoke. "Okay, I've vented. This next item doesn't leave the car."

Norris nodded. Carolyn described finding the earring fragment, then last night's visit from the detectives and Gayle's subsequent comments.

"Washington went to Forest Hill, right?"

"You got me."

"I talked to my uncle last night. Bet that's the same Jerome Washington who played quarterback and middle linebacker at Forest Hill in the seventies. My uncle was a trainer and said Washington was a god. Set some state records that may never be broken, and there's an entire shelf in their trophy case devoted to him. NFL caliber but tore up his knee as a freshman at Jackson State and chose to be a cop just like his dad. Been on the force ever since. Just a story idea for a slow news day."

Carolyn nodded.

"I heard they talked to Gayle last night before the ten, and she was all pissed off and kept screwing up during the show. And you keep this to yourself: Jeff Walker, who never complains about anything, told me he'd rather work with anyone else. He and Shawn weren't tight off the air, but they worked well together. He said Gayle thinks she knows everything and is always fighting with the director and producer each night. He's petitioning Sewell and Yarbrough to let him do the shows by himself until they hire someone."

"Hmmph." She inhaled and blew smoke out the window. "So should I give the earring piece to the cops? Maybe I'm crazy, but I was wondering if it could have something to do with Shawn."

"Your call. Could you leave it in the same place you found it? Then you could keep an eye out and see if it disappears."

She shrugged and tossed her cigarette out the window. Norris pulled into a parking spot at the school and cut the engine.

"One more thing before we go in." A deep breath. "Eric Redding and I went out last weekend. He asked me to dinner out of the blue."

"Really?"

Carolyn peered up at him and nodded. A quizzical smile was on his face. She and Norris had worked together every day for five years, and the friendship developed quickly since they were already acquainted from her childhood. The only blip was an evening three years ago when Norris took her to a movie, which he did periodically. Without warning he tried to kiss her, and Carolyn, mustering as much poise as possible, patted his hand and straightened herself in her seat. After the movie she gently explained that she treasured their friendship and didn't want to risk it on a romance that might go south. Norris handled it like a gentleman; if there were ruffled feathers, Carolyn never saw them. But she didn't want to rub it in by gushing about someone Norris had to work with each day, and the cat was out of the bag before she'd thought that angle through.

"Interesting. You don't need my permission, if that's what you're asking."

"You're my best friend, James," she said softly. "Had to tell somebody."

"You were moaning and groaning the other night about not having a boyfriend, as I recall."

"I wasn't ready to talk about it yet. And I still don't have a boyfriend."

Norris smiled. "Eric seems like a good guy. If you like him, go for it. This isn't 1964 any more. I really don't think the folks at the station will care one way or the other. And other than being surprised, I don't think your kin would have a problem with it."

"I was thinking about that. We had a great time, and he's been nice around the station. But I thought I'd hear from him, and I haven't. I told him the Cronin trial would have me busy all week, and he knows it ended quick."

"So why not ask him?"

"The truth? I'm a coward."

"Because he's white?"

"And because we work together."

"Give him a few days."

"Then what?"

Norris laughed. "I don't know, Davis. Trust your hunches. You'll know what to do."

* * *

The air conditioning ran full blast in the Mendenhall Subway restaurant and circulated the delicious aroma of deli meats, vegetables and fresh bread. Ravenous, McDaniel ordered a foot-long sandwich and was filling his soft drink cup when a somewhat heavy young lady with the familiar sorority letters entered. She was older than Patti and Jamie and not as pretty, although she radiated warmth and confidence and was more down to earth.

"We have the place to ourselves," she said, shaking his hand firmly. "I'm Allison Shelton."

"Detective McDaniel. Thanks for coming—we'll make this brief." He joined her in a yellow plexiglass booth and dug into his sandwich. "Neither Patti nor Jamie were at the house at all Saturday night, huh? Tell me how you got involved."

"Another girl came to me. She overheard Jamie tell you guys that she and Patti were in their room." A sigh. "I don't want to call one of my sisters a liar, but Jamie gave you bad information. Their room was locked all night, and they weren't there, Detective. I know because my roommate and I are next door, and we didn't go out. The girl who talked to me is three doors down. She and her roommate also stayed in and will tell you the same thing, as will a couple of other girls." She paused. "My mother loved Shawn Forrest and is in mourning. Are they suspects?"

"Not at this time," McDaniel said. He reached the halfway point of the sandwich with another huge bite. "But what you're saying doesn't match their story. There's a critical window of time involved. Jamie told us she was in her room by ten-thirty and in for the night. Patti said she arrived a little after eleven, got some stuff and left."

"Impossible. My roommate and I were not only in all night, our door was open and several girls came by and hung out with us. We knocked on their door a couple of times trying to get them to come play Bunco, and nobody answered. We never saw anybody in or out of Jamie and Patti's room all night. I will swear to it, and so will half a dozen other girls."

McDaniel finished writing and looked up. "What's your sense of Patti?"

A shrug. "Nice but immature. Don't see much of her—she has an off-campus boyfriend."

"Jamie?"

"Stuck on herself, but nice enough. Jamie seems older than eighteen. In some ways Patti seems younger. I wouldn't have picked them to be friends, but they're inseparable."

"Has either been in trouble to your knowledge?"

"We had to get on Patti about cutting class, but that's a freshman tradition. Some guy Jamie went out with got drunk and caused a scene outside the house one night, but that wasn't her fault. As freshmen go, I've seen far worse—I'm one of our officers and have some say in who we take. But this is real life, not some made-for-television movie. I hope they aren't caught up in something and think they can outsmart everyone."

"That happens more often than you think."

She scribbled a name and a pair of phone numbers on a paper napkin. "My roommate. She's from Wiggins, half an hour south of campus. Said to call her if you need to."

* * *

"There he is, ladies and germs, all the way from Simpson County," Washington said, grinning up at McDaniel. Several other detectives played along. "I told these men that you were on official police business, Mac, but they're not buying it—every one of these eggheads think you're scoping these college women and want in on the action."

McDaniel absorbed the kidding with a grin, then described the meeting with Allison Shelton. "I think she's telling the truth, Jerome. I could be wrong, but now I'm thinking Jamie and Patti lied to our faces."

"You just missed Jessica. Found a partial thumb print on the cup in Shawn's apartment—she got the impression someone tried to wipe it off. She said it's obvious that whoever left the DNA on the candy cigarettes left the print. And since Ford has a record and is already in the computer, we may know something fast. Let's see him. Told him an hour ago we'd be right up."

The third-floor conference room had green cinder block

walls. The front wall was glass, and Ford was visible on a gray folding chair at a brown, Formica-topped table. A styrofoam cup of water was in front of him. He gave Washington a cold look. Washington ignored him and conferred with the detention officer, a bald man who had served the department for thirty years. Then he and McDaniel entered the room. They remained on their feet and flanked Ford. Washington spoke first, a coy smile on his face.

"Detective McDaniel and I have been partners for many years. We grew up together, so I know some things about him, like his musical tastes. He absolutely digs the Allman Brothers." He glanced at McDaniel. "I know you saw them at Zoo Blues, but where else? Woodstock?"

"The Fillmore. I was fifteen," McDaniel said with a grin.

"So we were in your pad yesterday, Parker, and I saw Mac staring at that picture of you and that long-haired dude. And Mac said, 'Jerome, that's Gregg Allman.' I nearly fell on the floor," he said, chuckling. "Memory serves me correctly, Mac worked security at Zoo Blues that day and posed with him. An enlargement of that picture hangs in his den."

McDaniel smiled bemusedly. "Parker, did you know that the original Allman Brothers bass player was killed in a motorcycle wreck nearly a year to the day Duane Allman died, almost in the same place Duane was killed on his hog?"

Ford said nothing.

"Name was Berry Oakley. One hell of a bass player. I tried my hand at bass guitar when I was in high school, had a cheap little thing I couldn't tune. Now, that bass you have is nice. You guys gonna break out, or are you destined to be a lifelong Jackson band, having to supplement your income with drug trade?"

No response.

"You guys play *Jessica?* Just curious—one of my favorite Allman tunes."

Nothing.

"Yo!" Washington said, slamming his hand on the table a foot from Ford's face. Ford nearly jumped out of the chair. "Detective McDaniel asked you a question! Least you can do is answer, after telling us your band is destined for the rock and roll hall of fame!"

"Yeah, man. We play it."

"I mention that because the director of the crime lab is named Jessica," McDaniel said. "What a coincidence, huh? And I admit your amp would have fooled me, had someone not given you up."

Ford's flinch was quick, but Washington caught it. He placed a sheet and pen in front of him.

"Before we talk any more shop, we'd like to go ahead and get your signature. This advises us that you've waived your right to counsel. That cool with you?"

Ford raised an eyebrow. "You tell me what this is about before I sign anything."

"You know a girl named Tracey Walton?"

"Yeah, I know her. Why?"

"We think you drugged her, slept with her and beat her up. Sign right here, and we can talk about it. Cool?"

"Wait a minute, man. That was consensual all the way. She begged for it."

"Then you won't mind if we get a rape kit from you. And you can sign right here."

"Ain't signing nothing, Big Man," Ford said, his eyes narrow. "I have a lawyer."

"Who? Gregg Allman?" Washington said, exploding in laughter. "He show you how to put that amp together?"

"Lay off Gregg," McDaniel said, feigning insult. "Keyboard player, doesn't fool with amps. And he cleaned up."

"My bad, Mac. And I'm here if you need a shoulder after the trauma you went through seeing this doofus posed with your hero." Washington pulled up a chair and sat across from Ford, daring him to meet his eyes. He could barely contain his laughter. "You just crack me up, cool breeze, thinking you're so smooth. 'I know what I'll do: I'll put all my pills and coke and everything in a freakin' shoebox and make it look like an amp. Take it from show to show and look like a real-life rock star,' he said in a passable imitation of Gomer Pyle. "Well, my brother, you don't look like no rock star. You look like Captain Kangaroo!"

McDaniel couldn't help himself, finally having a good laugh as well. Ford's anger was close to the surface, but he maintained his facade. Washington's grin disappeared.

"Don't sweat it, dude. We'll get a court order for your DNA. Don't need your permission for that," Washington said, again sliding the consent form toward Ford.

"I told you I ain't signing nothing!"

"You lawyer up, then, my man. That's certainly within your rights, if you want to go that route. Let's go, Mac." Washington nodded at the detention officer, then dropped a business card on the table. "You change your mind, Mr. Rock Star, look me up. Otherwise, enjoy the penthouse suite at Raymond."

* * *

A short, thin female tech in a white lab coat was waiting in the lobby of the Mississippi Crime Lab when McDaniel and Washington arrived. Jessica Hunter was the director, a divorcee in her forties and a fifteen-year veteran of the police department. Her short, jet-black hair had a purple tint, and she wore a navel ring.

"I hate asking you to print these," Washington said. "Paper jams, low toner, faxes coming in every two minutes and morons who treat the damn printer like a piece of furniture. I know you have a mountain of things to do . . ."

"Don't sweat it. Can't exactly say no after the big boss e-mailed and said this case takes priority over everything."

"That's true, Jerome," McDaniel said with a grin. "We're number one with a bullet, so we can cut the phony suck-up routine."

Jessica smiled. "You guys are the best. The department ought to let you teach a seminar on manners. Your colleagues could learn something."

"Flattery will get you everywhere with us. Speeding tickets we can fix?"

She laughed. "No, but it's bowling night. I'm out the door at seven no matter what. But we'll get these printed in no time. Done it myself if I'd known the case would be such a priority."

She led them down a cinder-block hallway into a large room. Lab equipment was at one end with several cubicles across the way. There were twelve full-time employees, all of whom were sworn police officers. Teams of two, including the men the detectives conferred with at Shawn's apartment, were sent out each day to do prep work which was brought back to the lab. Jessica and an assistant analyzed the results and often presented their findings in court. This was a full-service facility, with satellite labs in Batesville, Meridian and Gulfport.

Jessica inserted the disc into her hard-drive and opened the first e-mail. The printer hummed into life a moment later. "Fellas, I'm starving. I will be at your beck and call the rest of your lives if you'll hit a drive-through up the street."

"And you'll have all that printed when we get back?"

"I'll make a pretty good dent. The stuff she received was first, if I remember right." She removed a twenty from her purse and winked. "Supper is on me. Everybody's talking about Shawn Forrest. You can fill me in while your stuff prints."

* * *

The blond lay on her back and stared at the ceiling as the dark-haired man snored softly. Tears dripped down her cheeks as she thought of the future. Although he wasn't ready to set a date, he was all for putting an engagement ring on her finger. He spoke fondly of his years in the northeast and was convinced she would grow to love shoveling snow. At the other end of the spectrum was the brutal heat of Phoenix, where his first news director now worked. Then there was Chicago, where they would never run out of things to do. There was no pressure to have kids, nor would he demand that she work. She couldn't believe the words were coming from his mouth.

But here in the quiet, after the throes of passion, it hit her. Forget simply saying goodbye to the life she once knew—that horse had ridden into the sunset and would never return. There would be no going back, to anyone or anything. His grand plans sounded rosy, and it was everything she said she wanted. But life with him meant moving to a new place many miles away and starting completely from scratch. It was almost like being a witness in a federal protection program. And for all his wonderful qualities, could she trust every aspect of the rest of her life to him? And would she spend every waking minute in that faraway place awaiting a knock on the door?

She dressed quietly, fighting back a flood of tears. She said a silent prayer for him, then kissed the top of his head without disturbing him. Then she slipped out the door, tears sliding down her cheeks.

*   *   *

The detectives returned fifteen minutes later. Washington spread cheeseburgers, fries and soft drinks across a roll-away cart Jessica retrieved from a storage closet. She manned the huge e-mail file, opening each individually and instructing the printer. She nibbled on her cheeseburger, continually wiping her fingers on a wet rag.

Washington, whose lunch was a package of crackers from the office vending machine, dug in and said little as he sated his appetite. McDaniel, not eating quite as fiercely, summarized the investigation for Jessica, including his feeling that Allison Shelton was telling the truth. If this was the case, McDaniel surmised, Jamie Fontenot could have been in the apartment as well. Jessica piped up, her mouth full of food, and stated that Darren, Patti and Jamie were the guilty party, citing her bias against sorority girls after the hell they put her through twenty-five years ago at LSU.

"Truthfully, the impression I had of Shawn Forrest was a bubble-headed prom queen with a big, fake smile and a big, fake rack."

The detectives laughed. Jessica removed a stack of pages from the printer. "That's everything she received the last sixty days of her life, not including the six which had attachments. Those are all from anonymous mailboxes, by the way, and there's no subject line or body of text. Let's open one."

The hard drive beeped. A warning box appeared on the screen.

"Uh-oh," Washington said. "A virus?"

"No, it's telling me the paper isn't big enough." She dug through the supply cabinet and returned with a large, glossy sheet. She adjusted the setting in the printer. "Folks e-mail pictures to each other all the time now. My sister gave me a framed shot of her family, and she didn't tell me until later that it was printed from her hard drive. I never knew. My daughter is an art major at Belhaven and does the most amazing things with Adobe Photoshop." She grunted, then glanced at her watch. "Estimated print time is thirty minutes."

"Damn. You need to go, don't you?" Washington said.

"It wouldn't take nearly as long if we had half-decent printers around here. Anyway, I live off Riverside. I'll run home and change, then come back and lock the door behind you on my way to the bowling alley. That should give this enough time to print. Must admit I'm curious."

"Cool. We'll read the e-mails while you're gone."

She strode across the room and placed the pages in a large copier. "Give it a couple of minutes and you won't have to share. Back soon."

*　*　*

McDaniel read quietly, placing the pages in a neat stack. Washington grunted, sighed and laughed out loud periodically, underlining some passages in pen and others with yellow highlighter. He tossed his pages aside, making half-hearted attempts to keep them together. Without knowing it, Jessica had done the men a huge favor; McDaniel was a compulsive neat freak, and Washington was far from it.

Shawn received at least two e-mails a week from Laci Gwynn, which was no surprise. Nor did it startle them that Shawn was in close contact with her mother. She was on the weekly mailing list of a bookstore in Atlanta. She received monthly newsletters from a recipe group in Atlanta and heard periodically from the University of Alabama alumni association. The only other individual she heard from in that span was someone named Robert. He was in Atlanta, and it didn't take long to determine that he was a love interest. Washington looked up, having forgotten the print job in the corner of the room.

"Mac, I can't find a single e-mail from Darren."

"Neither can I. You think Shawn and Darren were even on speaking terms by the end?"

"No, and ditto for Papa Bear. I think Robert was a secret that Shawn, Laci and Leigh Forrest shared." McDaniel flipped back through the stack. "Get a load of the devoted, would-be wife when Robert was leaning on her to move to Atlanta: 'I'm not getting anywhere trying to force Dear Old Dad to fire anyone.' But it's funny how she never even refers to Darren. It's as if she can pack up and go whenever she wants."

"Notice that Jack Forrest didn't turn their Atlanta station

upside down to accommodate her. Like Jeff Walker said, you start messing with popular anchors and viewers reach for the remote. The advertisers follow, and the Jack Forrest's of the world are on the street."

"I sense some father-daughter issues, Jerome. She blisters Jack a new one every time she talks to Laci. May have realized she wasn't going to be the next Katie Couric without him."

"I'm wondering if the frantic climb to the top was his idea."

"You and me both. But she clearly thought she was better than this town. Confucius say, 'He who believes press clippings has swelled head.'"

Washington laughed. "Your boy Confucius didn't deal with egos like these."

Jessica arrived, now clad in a navy windbreaker with an emblazoned yellow team logo over a snug t-shirt. Below were tight, faded jeans with the knees mostly gone. She was already in her bowling shoes, prepared to run right to her lane and join the fray.

"Didn't peek, did you?"

McDaniel smiled. "We got so caught up in the gossip we forgot it was there."

She plucked the sheet from the printer and laid it in front of the detectives. The three of them stared at a smiling Shawn Forrest in a red dress layered against a background of tall pine trees, blue sky and flowing green fields. A lake was in the distance. Shawn had been shot from the waist up, and the print showed her standing behind a black Ford Probe of recent vintage. Although her posture was a tiny bit unnatural, the designer had gone to great pains to make it appear that Shawn was photographed while standing behind the car. The casual observer would have no reason to assume she wasn't.

The montage alone could have been an elaborate joke, perhaps a gag gift. But text boxes were included along the side margins of the print. Inside each was an innocuous publicity quote in quotation marks. Below the quotes were responses which were set off in italics, as if the author was personally speaking to Shawn. All responses were lewd, while some were more clever than others. A paragraph in a flowery font along the bottom detailed the author's desire for Shawn; car parts were used as metaphors in juvenile references to the animal sex he had in mind. The banner across the top was in large italics:

Have you driven a Ford lately, Shawn Forrest?

"Jessica, can you pull up the Channel Five web site?" Washington said, his brow furrowed. "Something about that dress looks familiar."

Jessica glanced at her watch, then typed the web address. "I trust you guys. Hang here if you want, and I can come back. We're usually done by ten."

"I just want to see if I'm right about that picture. Won't take a second."

The Channel Five site emerged seconds later. He clicked on the anchor team link, then the Shawn Forrest link. The same photo appeared, a biography alongside. Included was Shawn's birthplace, education, hobbies, previous broadcast experience and future ambitions.

"That picture is in their lobby," Washington said. "I knew it."

"I've seen it on television," Jessica said. She gestured at the bio. "This makes me want to gag: 'I love Jackson and have never met such friendly people.' Does anyone really buy that crap? The bottom part is funny," she said, breaking into song: "'Have you driven a Ford lately?'"

The detectives shared a look. "One last thing before you bowl: Log on to the department computer network," Washington said. "We'll find out real quick if that Probe belongs to who we think it does."

He typed in Ford's name and address with Jessica watching over his shoulder. A black 2003 Ford Probe with a personalized Hinds County plate came up:

P-R-O-B-E-U

Jessica howled. "Probe you? My dream date—gold chains and chest hair, right?"

"Pony tail and an attitude," Washington said. "Currently in lockup at Raymond after we searched his place and found a gold mine of narcotics and cash. We were tipped off by his girlfriend, actually a neighbor of Shawn Forrest. Ford drugged her, and she either fell in her bathroom or he beat her up. She lost an eight week old fetus which belonged to him."

"Ugh. So he's definitely looking at the inside."

"And that's without assuming he did Shawn. We're beginning to wonder."

Jessica checked her watch again and opened the Forrest e-mail disc. A moment later the printer whirred into life. "It'll take half an hour to print the rest of these. I can stop back by and we can work on the attachments, or we can save them until tomorrow. Up to you. Must admit I'm curious—that's some mighty fine art work, even if he is the scum of the earth."

"Touch base when you're through bowling. We're curious, too."

* * *

McDaniel printed the remainder of the e-mails with Washington standing over his shoulder. Most of what Shawn sent out was gossipy and harmless, but one note caught their eye. It was sent to Leigh Forrest in late February, which extended past the sixty day window. But since Leigh had chosen to reply rather than starting her own e-mail, the result was a series of replies as mother and daughter wrote back and forth. The entire discussion was represented, since the last reply—sent by Shawn— fell within the window.

> *"I'm a little worried that I'm being followed after work. It's a dark-colored sports car and seems to pop up every so often on the interstate. It's not every night, and it usually stays north when I reach my exit. But last night it went all the way down County Line Road, then was behind me all the way down Old Canton. By then I was a little scared. I was going to skip my turn and go back out to the interstate, but it pulled into the grocery. I didn't see it again."*

Leigh Forrest was alarmed by this turn of events and advised her daughter to alert station management and the police. Shawn's reply was sent the next day:

> *"I might if it keeps up, but I took a different way home last night and didn't see it. Last thing I want to do is get the cops involved like that girl in Chattanooga did. I told you about that—they finally pulled the car over, and it was a nurse who worked an overnight shift at a hospital."*

Five days later Shawn replied to the same e-mail:

> *"I haven't seen it any more on the interstate. I even started coming home the old way just to make sure. But last night it was parked by the pool. I ran up the stairs, locked the door and called the answering service, which rang the rent-a-cop. I told him what was going on, and he said he would check on the car and call me back. He called five minutes later and said nobody was in it. He said he would leave a report with the landlady. So this morning I went to her. She said the rent-a-*

cop left a note saying he'd made periodic checks, but the car was still sitting empty when he got off work. And when the landlady went to check herself, it was gone. This is all I need."

This resulted in an urgent plea from Leigh Forrest to get law enforcement involved. Shawn replied that not only was the rent-a-cop instructed to be on the lookout for the car, the crew at Channel Five was reminded by Rick Sewell to observe extreme caution when entering or departing the building late at night. There were no further references to the mysterious vehicle for two weeks. Then this reply to Leigh's follow-up:

"It's the strangest thing. It disappeared—it's like it never happened. Rick Sewell asked about it today and wondered if it was someone who lives at the complex and works at the manufacturing plant right off the interstate—that's where I first noticed the car when I was coming home. Anyway, no news is good news. I'll keep you posted."

McDaniel looked up. "Two things: The landlady didn't say anything about a strange car in the parking lot, did she? And do we know if Tracey and Ford had already hooked up by then?"

Washington grunted. "The landlady didn't mention it. We'll look her up in the morning. And I didn't ask Tracey how long ago they met, did I?"

"Let's run over there. If she's not up to talking, bet her folks or their lawyer would know."

Washington got to his feet, then paused. "I just thought of something: What became of the suitcase in Shawn's car? Jessica hasn't mentioned it."

McDaniel frowned. "Let's page her."

"Let's do this first. Once we interrupt, she's probably through for the night."

* * *

The duty nurse hung her head when the detectives asked about Tracey.

"She's been in a light coma since early afternoon. Is there something I can help you with?"

"Has to do with the man she was involved with. Are her parents still here?"

"They haven't left her side."

They were twenty feet from Tracey's room when the door opened. It was the lawyer from this morning. His suit was rumpled, and he looked weary.

"We just heard, Counselor. How are her folks?"

"I'm glad you're here. Follow me, gentlemen." He led them to an empty waiting room and shut off the overhead television. "Look, I've been a friend of the family for years. I'm going to turn evidence over to you that could implicate Tracey. But I think you know she's the victim here. She was trying to cooperate and will continue to do so when she comes out of the coma, and I hope you'll keep that in mind."

Washington raised an eyebrow. "What evidence are we talking about?"

"Tracey's mother went by the apartment a little while ago to get underclothes and nightgowns for her. She found cash and drugs in Tracey's dresser. You can only imagine how frightened she was."

"Great. The mother didn't touch it, did she?"

"No, no. Backed away, left the dresser open and hightailed it back here. Didn't even get the underclothes." The lawyer rubbed his temples. "We wanted to give Tracey the night and see if she woke up, then report it in the morning. You can only imagine how much the family wants to put this ape away, and this should be the final nail in the coffin."

"We understand. We'll get a warrant and send the crime lab out there," McDaniel said. "Do you have any idea how long Tracey had been seeing Ford?"

"They met right after Valentine's Day."

"Thank you. We'll be in touch," Washington said. He and McDaniel started away.

"Again, Detectives, Tracey is the victim. Please do everything you can to protect her."

"We'll do our best, Counselor."

* * *

They returned to Spring Center, where McDaniel typed a search warrant which would get them into Tracey's apartment. Washington reached the Michelin Man and was told to bring the warrant straight to his home in west Jackson. He paged Jessica once they were en route and left a message. She returned the call and spoke above the din of the bowling alley, reporting that Bernie was on his way and would meet them.

"We've had three tenants give notice already," the landlady said. She lived on the premises and opened the door with a drink in her hand and a scowl on her face. "Management decided it's my fault and is threatening to fire me."

"Your security detail reported a car that might have followed Ms. Forrest several months ago," McDaniel said, ignoring her. "She spoke to you about it, and the security officer turned in a report. Ring a bell?"

"I looked for that car and never saw it."

"Have the report on file? We need the license plate."

"Might be one in the office."

"Well, let's mosey down there and find it, shall we?"

The office reeked of cigarette smoke. The woman yanked open the top drawer of a filing cabinet and almost overturned a potted plant. She rooted around and emerged with a manila folder. She tossed it on the desk and folded her arms.

"Anything else?"

McDaniel stepped closer. "We're investigating the death of one of your tenants, and we expect your full cooperation no matter how much of an inconvenience it may be. So you sit down, go through that folder and find the report. If you can't find it, get the security firm on the phone, tell them that we're here and want to talk to the officer who wrote it. Otherwise we'll haul you downtown."

The woman plopped down at the desk and riffled through the folder. Several pages fell to the floor. Then she handed a sheet across the desk. The template asked for the time, date and a brief statements of facts, and the officer had printed neatly and described a black Ford Probe which had been spotted by tenant Shawn Forrest. The Hinds County plate read:

P-R-O-B-E-U

"Very good. I'll need a copy of that."

Without a word, the woman copied the page using the fax machine.

"And a key into Tracey Walton's apartment, please."

This time she looked as if she'd been slapped. "What on earth for?"

"Police business, ma'am," McDaniel said patiently. "We have a warrant to enter Miss Walton's apartment. That's all I can say at this time."

His cell rang. It was Washington, who told him that Carolyn Davis from Channel Five had called and wanted to talk. He added that Bernie had forgotten the suitcase from Shawn's car in his haste to get everything to the lab, and it was gone when he returned late in the day. McDaniel looked up at the landlady, who was watching intently.

"We're also looking for a suitcase which belonged to Ms. Forrest, ma'am. It was last seen in her car yesterday, and a technician with the crime lab came to get it yesterday afternoon and said it was gone. Did you or anyone on your staff open her car, or perhaps see anyone open it?"

"No one here has a key to her car," the woman said, lighting a cigarette. She blew smoke rings, not trying to hide her exasperation. McDaniel saw her expression change and followed her eyes. He walked to the corner of the room, still holding the phone to his ear.

"Jerome, I'm looking at a brown Samsonite piece here in the office, next to a dying ficus tree. There's an identification tag with Shawn's name on it. Let me see what I can find out and I'll call you right back."

The landlady was pale when he clicked off. "I swear this is the first I've laid eyes on it."

"It didn't just magically appear, ma'am—someone turned it in. You weren't here?"

"I had meetings with the owners. The girl that answers the phone at lunch might know . . ."

"Call her."

* * *

The Samsonite piece had been turned in by a groundskeeper who found it near the clubhouse, some fifty yards from Shawn's car. Bernie tagged it and loaded it in his van, adding it to the roll of bills and bags of cocaine and marijuana from Tracey's dresser. No other drugs were found, nothing which indicated that crystal methamphetamine or anything else had been manufactured in the apartment. Bernie took the bottle of Ritalin from Tracey's medicine cabinet on the chance that someone had tampered with the contents.

The detectives also had Bernie dust the unopened Dell boxes in the corner of Tracey's bedroom for prints. There wasn't another computer in the apartment, and McDaniel opined that Ford may have bought it for Tracey so he could watch her through his web cam. The other item of interest was a framed eight-by-ten photo of Tracey on her dresser. She looked healthy and attractive as she stood behind a Ford Probe of recent vintage, the same pines and blue sky behind her. It was obviously the original from which the Forrest hybrid was created.

"What do you think, Mac? Little Miss Innocent who got corrupted by the big bad wolf, or a willing accomplice who liked the fast lane?"

"I'm going back and forth on that. Maybe a little of both. I just wish she had walked away."

"Now we need her prints. I just hope she's alive when we take them."

* * *

Carolyn Davis lived in a tiny rental house just off Springridge Road in Clinton, several blocks from the Mississippi College campus. Washington arrived as the sun was setting and parked along the curb. She waved as she rinsed her Sunbird with a garden hose. She was in a t-shirt and gym shorts and devoid of makeup, giving her a youthful appearance.

"Don't know why I even fool with this," she said, wiping her brow with a soaked towel. "A coat of pollen a foot thick will be on it in the morning. Come in and have some tea."

The house was at least fifty years old and had cracks and water stains in the living room ceiling. A humidifier ran on the scuffed coffee table, partly masking stale cigarette smoke. House plants were everywhere, and family pictures dominated the walls. She poured tea and pointed to an old white couch. She curled up in a swivel chair, the look of the reporter in her eye.

"Cute little place."

"A rental. A friend and I fixed it up a little."

"Were you poor-mouthing, or do TV folks really get paid like cops?"

111

"They broke the bank to pay Shawn, but that was because of her daddy. Jeff Walker and the chief meteorologist have been there for years and make good money. But not us young folks. In fairness, I'm a reporter in Jackson, Mississippi. I'm not covering the White House for one of the major networks."

"My wife likes you, I know that. You enjoy it?"

She smiled. "Usually. Always enjoy hunting down a story."

"Big aspirations? Want to cover the White House?"

"Used to think so, but now I'm not sure. My father died when I was little. Mama died of cancer three years ago. My sisters and cousins are in Port Gibson and Magee, and I made a vow to stay current with them. But I work so much I never see anyone. What about you? Want to be police chief?"

He snorted. "I hate politics. Running the homicide division is something I might want to do down the road, but I got no beef with the guy doing it now. Wouldn't trade my partner for anything. We grew up together, both took some college courses before joining the ranks like our fathers did."

"I understand you were quite the football star in high school before you got hurt."

"Many years ago, Miss Davis," he said with a grin. "Be honest, tearing up my knee was probably the best thing that could have happened to me. Made me get serious about my life, since I knew my career was over." He leaned back. "So what's on your mind?"

Carolyn removed a plastic container from behind her chair. It was lime green and approximately the size of a package of Silly Putty.

"You called me out here to hunt Easter eggs?"

Without a word she knelt next to the coffee table and opened the container. The earring fragment dropped into sight. Washington's grunt was barely audible, but she caught it.

"This mean something to you?"

"No games. Where'd you get it, and how long have you had it?"

"Found it yesterday on our newsroom floor, under Gayle Kennedy's chair. Her cubicle is next to mine. Frankly, I don't know how the cleaning crew didn't get it when they vacuumed." She paused, her eyes twinkling now. "So, Detective. This mean something to you?"

"Not at liberty to say."

She moved back to her seat. "We had a bomb of a newscast the night you guys talked to me. Gayle screwed up from start to finish and had a meltdown after the show—I'm told she was screaming at people. Memory serves me correctly, you wanted to speak with Gayle. You put the fear of God into her?"

"Not at liberty to say."

"I'd forgotten something and was back at my desk when she came inside. Pretty hyper. I asked what was up, and she said you guys made an issue of part of an earring being found at the scene. Should I presume that this is the other part?"

"Not at liberty to say."

"Is she or anyone in our newsroom a person of interest?"

He held up a hand. "Tell me about Gayle. Level with me— what's your opinion of her?"

"Professionally, she's an average talent who won't get to the next level. Nothing more than a pretty face on camera, pedestrian writing and presentation skills as a reporter. Personally, I like her okay. I've partied with her, and when you get her away from the folks she's trying to impress, she's a lot of fun—a chain-smoking, beer-guzzling, down-home girl with a good sense of humor."

"Who's she trying to impress?"

"The money crowd. Shawn was always getting calls from the movers and shakers around the city, and she didn't want a thing to do with them—didn't want a thing to do with Jackson. But I've seen Gayle kiss up to those folks as if her life depends on their acceptance. She told me that her father was mayor of her hometown. Found out later it's true—but her hometown is this tiny little place in rural Arkansas, and her father owns a hardware store. She drives that huge Explorer she can't afford to impress people, and she doesn't want anyone to know she lives in a shoebox of an apartment."

"Hmmph. Any chance at all she'll get Shawn's job, or would social status rule that out?"

"It doesn't work like that, Detective. It comes down to talent, and unless corporate is trying to save as much money as they possibly can, Gayle's merely filling in until they hire someone. But she apparently thinks it's hers and is acting accordingly—talking down to folks and not listening to anyone, and already bitching because she isn't being promoted as much as Shawn was. So there was no sympathy the other night when the wheels fell off. That's what I'm hearing, anyway."

"Sounds like you're clued in."

A wink. "I don't volunteer much, but I'm a good listener."

He gestured at the earring fragment. "So why give this to me and not to her? You sure you guys get along?"

"We get along fine. I don't expect you to understand, Detective—just the way my little brain works. She was bitching and moaning Monday about losing an earring, then the meltdown after the late newscast, which was right after you guys talked to her. As a reporter you learn not to rule anything out."

He gazed. "Very interesting. Do you have anything else to share?"

"Not at this time, Detective. What are you going to do with that earring?"

"I'm not going to wear it, if that's what you're asking. I'll do my best to get the egg back to you." He got to his feet. "Keep in touch."

Carolyn walked him to the door. "You, too. If any media breaks this open, I'd like it to be me. You probably understand that. And I'm sure the chief of police is all over you guys to find who did it. Maybe it'll help you knowing someone in our newsroom."

* * *

Jessica cut bowling short and returned to the lab. McDaniel and Washington joined her. She began printing the second attachment from the Forrest e-mail disc, then donned synthetic gloves and spread the contents of Shawn's suitcase on a stainless steel counter in the evidence room down the hall. Everything pertaining to the investigation was in sight, including hard drives belonging to Shawn and Ford. She retrieved a binder from a metal shelf.

"According to Bernie's notes, he left the scene at ten-twenty Tuesday morning. Got back just before five that afternoon and said the car was locked and the backseat empty. When was the last time you guys saw the suitcase in the car?"

"When we left for Hattiesburg, which was before Bernie left the scene," Washington said. "We asked Darren if he had a key to his wife's apartment, but I didn't think about him having one to her car."

"Could anyone else have access to it?"

"I suppose her parents could. We'll certainly ask." He glanced at the contents of the suitcase. There were jeans, casual tops and shorts, running clothes and a pair of paperback novels. Dress pants and blouses sat alongside an iron and a can of spray starch, and there were several pairs of shoes. "Looks like she planned to be gone several days."

Jessica hoisted a tube of lubricating gel. "You guys read her e-mails. Why would she need this?"

Both men burst into laughter.

"I'm serious. Women hate this stuff, fellas. She have kids? Some need it after childbirth."

"Not to our knowledge," Washington said.

"Interesting. I'm not condoning her husband's cheating, but I wonder if this was part of the problem. She wouldn't use it unless she had to." Jessica held a small pill bottle aloft and pried it open. "Ambien, commonly known as sleeping pills. Prescribed by a doctor in Alpharetta, Georgia, and just one left."

McDaniel glanced at Washington. "I'm thinking she was on her way to Atlanta for good."

"With ratings about to start?"

"You know she didn't want to stay in Jackson, Jerome, and Robert was leaning on her to move home and marry him. The plan may have been to drive to Atlanta Saturday night, then fly back here and put her stuff in a U-Haul. I sure wouldn't rule out walking away from the station without notice."

"Next is prints," Jessica said. "The partial on that stadium cup is a match to Parker Ford. And speaking of which, the e-mail attachment should be ready."

The designer had obtained a black and white photo of Shawn Forrest in a girl scout uniform. She was perhaps fourteen and mugged happily for the camera, a trophy in one hand and an armful of cookie boxes in the other. She was pretty, and there was already a camera presence about her.

Next to the picture was a carefully-edited image that the detectives studied closely. The body belonged to an adult male in a muscle shirt and jean shorts. He was holding a plate of brownies in front of him. But the man's head was Parker Ford in his early teens. The spliced image of Ford was also in black and white and would have given the impression that he posed with Shawn, although the adult body was clearly a joke. The banner across the top was the same as last time:

Have you driven a Ford lately, Shawn Forrest?

Along the side margins were tiny replicas of what the detectives now knew was Ford's license plate: P-R-O-B-E-U. They were rendered with impressive attention to detail, looking remarkably like actual license plates. And the banner across the bottom laid to rest any chance that the author—now indisputably Parker Ford—was merely attempting to be clever in his cyberspace communication:

I've never tried a Girl Scout,
but I've eaten a whole lot of brownies.

"This is one sick bastard," Washington said softly. "How do we prove he sent these, since it's from an anonymous box?"

"Start with a subpoena to the server," Jessica said. "A little legwork and you'll trace everything right to him. Some of these self-appointed computer geniuses don't realize there's software which traces deleted e-mails and that the cops have it. And dig into his background and see if he was an art major. I hate to keep harping on this, but he has a way with graphic design."

"Shawn e-mailed her mother about the car that was tailing her, but she didn't say a word about this stuff," McDaniel said.

"She probably didn't open them, Tim. I get an e-mail with an attachment from a box I don't recognize, I delete that sucker as fast as I can. Last thing I need is a virus wiping out my hard drive. She may not have put two and two together."

Washington glanced at his watch. It was after ten. "Let me get home before I'm locked out. Another day or two on the DNA?"

"I hope. You'll be the first to know."

"I think he's the guy. We have him stalking her. We have him creating this garbage and sending it to her. We have him in her apartment. The DNA is his—that stunt with the cigars is about his speed. And his alibi is a drunken haze."

"I'd love to know how he got that girl scout picture of her," Jessica said. "That e-mail was sent weeks ago, so he may have been in her place more than once. Was it on the station web site?"

McDaniel shook his head. "Had to come from a family

album or yearbook. That's a Leigh Forrest question. Ditto for the sleeping pills, and whether or not they expected Shawn last weekend." He turned to Jessica. "You should have heard that woman. Daughter isn't even cold in the ground yet and already comparing her to Jessica Savitch."

"Never heard of her."

"Another story for another time. It's after eleven there. Might as well wait until morning to pick a fight with her."

THURSDAY

Washington and McDaniel were front and center at the staff meeting, getting Cowan up to speed and helping prepare the spin the spokesman would deliver to the media. Cowan again took them aside and reiterated that no other case mattered.

McDaniel sipped coffee and tried unsuccessfully to reach Jack and Leigh Forrest, then dialed Rick Sewell's direct line at Channel Five.

"Good morning, Detective. Anything new?"

"I need a couple of things. First, did Shawn receive e-mail from her colleagues?"

"Yes. We have an internal e-mail program, and our chief engineer has already printed the contents. There's very little of interest, to be honest, but I'll be happy to fax copies to you."

"Please do. And I noticed on your web site that the general public can e-mail your anchors."

"That's true, although it wasn't the case with Shawn."

"Why not?"

"Quite frankly, she refused to open them."

McDaniel sat up straighter. "Why? Was there someone she was avoiding?"

"Not to my knowledge. She said she had a bad experience at a previous station and didn't want to fool with it—she claimed some strange guy sent her pornographic material and links."

McDaniel wrote quickly: *Could Ford have e-mailed Shawn at previous stations?*

"She wouldn't budge, so I didn't push her."

"So there are hundreds of e-mails to Shawn piled up in cyberspace waiting to be opened?"

"No. I told the group that handles our web site to shut down her e-mail. The link stayed up, but if you had e-mailed her, it would have been returned. All of them were."

"Going back how far?"

"We had that discussion six months after she got here. So a year and a half, I guess. Sorry about that. What else?"

"Leigh Forrest gave me six different phone numbers to reach them, and I'm getting voice mails, maids and receptionists who claim not to know where they are. I'm sensing reluctance to talk to us."

Sewell grunted. "The funeral is tomorrow. You can only imagine what they're going through."

"I don't doubt that, sir. But you can't tell me Jack's personal secretary has no idea where he is. Everyone is a suspect until ruled out. Let them know that if you speak with them."

The words hung in the air. "I will. And I trust you'll keep us informed. We're anxiously awaiting an arrest, as are many in the community."

McDaniel poured coffee and recounted the discussion with Washington, who had also been on the phone. Washington laughed.

"'Yes, Detective, we've looked everything over with a fine-toothed comb, and there's nothing here of consequence,'" he said, doing his best to imitate Sewell. "'Nothing we're sending you, anyway.'"

"We can subpoena her computer at work if we need it. Hell, we'll subpoena the server if it comes to that."

Washington cocked an eyebrow. "Didn't Carolyn Davis tell us about an internal e-mail that made fun of one of the on-air people—something supposedly sent by Shawn? We'll see if Sewell faxes that over." He sipped coffee. "Jessica just called. There's a partial on the sleeping pill bottle from Shawn's bathroom kit; she'll hopefully know whose later in the day. And the rape kit on Ford paid off—the DNA is a match. For you reasonable doubt enthusiasts, odds are a million to one that it isn't his." Washington's grin broadened. "I didn't break the news when he called just now. He wants to talk, Mac—without a lawyer."

McDaniel's jaw fell. "Which one of his drugs is he on?"

"He was mumbling about exorbitant legal fees. They'll have him here within the hour. This ought to be fun."

The detectives notified Cowan, who summoned the chief for a strategy session. McDaniel's cell rang midway through the meeting.

"This is Leigh Forrest, Detective. I understand you've been trying to reach me. Have you made an arrest?"

McDaniel sat at his desk and flipped open his notebook. "Not yet, ma'am. I realize this is a very difficult time, but it's critical that you and your husband give us everything you can about Shawn which might be pertinent to the investigation. Is there anything you haven't told us—anything at all you can think of?"

"Not that I'm aware of."

"I have some questions, then. Did you know that someone was following Shawn after work a couple of months ago?"

"Yes, I knew. But she reported the car to security and didn't see it again."

"And you didn't think that was worth mentioning?"

A harsh sigh. "You're right, I should have mentioned it. But to be honest, it sounds like you're grasping at straws. Jack was afraid this was going to happen—since she's being buried here, it's easier to bury the investigation in Jackson rather than . . ."

"One of the people at dinner Saturday night was Parker Ford. Did Shawn ever mention his name?"

"No."

"We think he was the one following her. He had her e-mail address and was in her apartment at least once. He put together a collage on his computer using a picture of Shawn selling girl scout cookies. The picture is black and white and looks like it came from a photo album or yearbook."

"Why the hell didn't we hear this yesterday?"

"We didn't have the information until last night. Why didn't you tell us about Robert?"

A pause. "Who?"

"We have Shawn's computer, Mrs. Forrest. We've printed every e-mail she sent and received going back sixty days. Laci Gwynn told me that she and Shawn didn't e-mail because they preferred phone visits, but we have over forty notes they sent to each other. So we know all about Robert. It goes without saying that Shawn's extra-marital involvement is critical to the investigation since one of the last people to see her alive was her husband. So please tell us everything you know. We can't help you if you don't."

A long pause. For a moment McDaniel thought the cell connection had gone dead. "There are issues of privacy here, Detective, and I will be speaking to my husband about them," Leigh Forrest said, her voice a growl. "You need to be searching for the person or people responsible for my daughter's death instead of using it as a means to snoop through her garbage!"

"Let me repeat myself, Mrs. Forrest: We are trying to help you," McDaniel said patiently. "I realize your daughter's reputation is important, but everyone close to Shawn is a suspect until ruled out. I suggest you and your husband think hard about everything which might help us, rather than making veiled threats and huddling to determine the right spin. That won't help us."

Leigh Forrest gasped. "The nerve of you to talk to me that way. Our daughter hasn't even been buried yet. Now show some respect! Or you'll get none from us!"

* * *

Ford wore an orange jumpsuit with Hinds County Sheriff's Department stamped across the back. He sat at the conference table, an untouched cup of water in front of him. McDaniel and Washington were on their feet and flanked him. Cowan listened through a speaker outside the door.

"You know the drill, my man," Washington said, a waiver in hand. "You want to talk, sign the piece of paper. You do that and you're waiving your right to counsel."

"Hand it here."

Washington placed the sheet and a felt tip pen alongside the cassette recorder in front of Ford. Printing in all capitals, he wrote Parker Garrison Ford at the bottom of the sheet and signed the name just below. Washington took a seat across from him. The differences in technique the detectives employed was striking. Washington used his intimidating physical presence and deep voice to advantage, sitting close to those he interrogated and talking almost intimately before turning up the heat. McDaniel was sharp-witted, and his sarcasm often had his partner on the brink of laughter. But what helped McDaniel extract more than his share of confessions was perpetual motion—he slowly paced around the table for hours if necessary and drove defendants crazy when he handled the interrogations. Which detective asked the questions was often decided at the last moment and based on instinct.

"That was quite a stash we found. Ain't too cool considering you're a repeat offender."

"It's all good, Big Man," Ford said, a smug grin on his face. His pride had taken a hit yesterday, and he was determined to regain the upper hand in this battle of wits. "Maybe I can help you. And maybe there's something you can do for me."

Washington smiled. "You know we don't make the deals. But you help us, we'll try to help you with the D.A." A pause. "Let's start with Shawn Forrest. We know you had a thing for her."

Ford raised an eyebrow in mock surprise.

"We have a signed affidavit from a security guard at Boardwalk Apartments whom Shawn spoke to after seeing your Probe in her rear-view a few times. You were e-mailing her, too—went to town with that girl scout picture. The manager of the crime lab even wanted to know if you have an art background. Looks like you're pretty handy with a camera, too."

"Look . . ."

"It's all good, Parker, my man. Just want to make sure we're on the same page," Washington said reassuringly. "We can prove you sent the e-mails, and that's your DNA on those cigars, by the way. We thought we'd seen some weird stuff over the years, but that really flipped our wigs. Problem is, Shawn's dead. So this goes beyond weird. You got some explaining to do, and we're all ears—just know we can't help you with the D.A. unless you tell us the truth."

Ford sipped his water and panned the room. His poise looked no worse for wear.

"An old flame used to live at Boardwalk. I was in the neighborhood one weekend and thought I'd pay her a visit. There was a U-Haul backed up to the stairs, and this really hot, really uptight chick was barking orders at these poor dudes moving the furniture. Walked up and asked where my ex was. The hot chick told me to get lost. So I'm tending bar one night and running the channels on the big screen before it got crowded, and I saw the face. Realized it's the chick who moved into my ex's place."

"Shawn Forrest?"

"Sure enough," he said, shaking his head. A twinkle was in his eye. "You dudes need to understand something: I don't watch the news—I make the news. I got plenty on my plate and ain't got time for the politics and the needy and all that crap. But that face—oh, mercy. Went home fantasizing about her and logged onto their web site, which they're always babbling about. I know where Channel Five is, and I was thinking about how cool it would be to stake her out when something dawned on me."

"And what might that be?"

"I had a key to that apartment. The ex and I didn't part on good terms, and she must have forgot I had it in her haste to get me out of her life."

Washington couldn't hide his surprise. Ford's grin broadened.

"Now, having a key didn't mean anything, right? Hell, it had been at least six months since I'd been in the damn place, and I figured the locks had been changed. But it was worth a try, right? So I went by there one night about ten, when I knew she would be on the tube. Made sure no one was watching and gave it a shot. Opened right up."

"How long ago was this?"

"January. Went back a couple of weeks later. That time I left with the yearbook, found what I wanted and scanned it. Took it back a few nights after that. That time I found a letter she'd written. It was on Channel Five stationery and had her e-mail addresses. I copied them down."

"Did she write back?"

"Hell, no. Nor did I expect her to."

"Tell us about Saturday night."

"Gayle Kennedy and several other chicks walked in one night. We struck up a conversation, and it turned out she worked with Shawn and didn't like her. She laughed when I said I had the hots for her—said she played second fiddle to Shawn at work and wasn't doing it in a bar. I took that to mean she wanted some action, but I didn't see her again until last week. Some television types were having dinner and she needed a date. It was for Saturday, and I was supposed to work. Then she said Shawn was going to be there, so I got out of it. She picked me up Saturday afternoon—found out then we were neighbors—and made a very interesting offer."

Ford paused, enjoying himself. Washington nodded for him to continue.

"I'll admit we shared a joint the night I met her at the club, and she asked what I would give Shawn to make her relax if I thought I might get lucky with her. She was dead serious, so I told her. She said she didn't want to bore me with details, but she and her boss had a problem with Shawn and wanted her out of the station. That was all I needed to know, but I could plan on getting five hundred bucks if I did my part to relax Shawn, and another two grand if she and her boss judged that I'd passed the test."

"What exactly are we talking about, Parker?"

A snort. "First, Big Man, I told her she was full of it—she didn't need to kid a kidder. 'You don't believe me?' Gave me this look and pulled five twenties out of her purse and stuck them in my hand. 'Four hundred more as soon as she's good and relaxed.' So I asked what would happen after that. She said it would be up to me, but I would be in a position if I played my cards right to have all the fun with Shawn I wanted, and make some money, too. She said I might want to call some friends and see if they wanted to get in on the action, maybe make a video."

"Something pornographic, I take it."

A big grin. "You got it, dude. Said I'd go a long way toward that two grand if there were pictures to prove Shawn was a bad girl. And I told her I just happened to have a state of the art digital camera. She called her boss with me sitting right there, and a second later she gave me another four hundred."

"Then what happened?"

"We went to Que Será Será. She warned me to bide my time—if all went well, a scene between Shawn and her husband was going to take place. By then I was confused. How the hell was I going to score with Shawn if her husband was there, right? But Gayle just said to trust her. So we're walking up to the door, and there was Shawn Forrest talking to this couple. Gayle said it was her boss and his wife—Jim and Samantha. This other dude walked up, and Shawn was immediately pissed at him. That was Shawn's husband, and he wouldn't talk to anyone. Shawn ignored him completely at dinner.

"So dinner finally wound down, thank God—that was an hour of sheer misery. Shawn's husband tried to pay his check and split, and Shawn went after him. Couldn't hear what she said, but every head turned. Chased him out in the parking lot and slapped the hell out of him. He got in his car—this nice Mitsubishi—and she started pounding on the hood," Ford said with a chuckle. "Then Jim's wife, who's no spring chicken, went lumbering out to play peacemaker. Next thing I know we're going out to Jim and Samantha's for drinks, and Shawn's coming. Samantha and Shawn did the girl talk thing and I was ready to bolt. But Samantha made daiquiris, and Gayle whispered that we ought to stay longer."

Washington smiled. "You doctor up Shawn's drinks?"

"Didn't touch the first one. Second round, yeah, I spiced it up. Samantha asked if anybody wanted another daiquiri, and Gayle pulled me into the kitchen and pointed at Shawn's glass."

"What did you put in it?"

"Rohypnol."

"Did Gayle tell you to spike it?"

"Not in so many words. But it was clear what she was getting at. She caught my eye and had this little smile. Then Jim and Samantha set up their ping-pong table in the garage. I brought Shawn's drink and challenged her to a game. First time I'd spoken to her, since she wasn't exactly bending my ear."

"What kind of shape was she in by then?"

"Drunk, but not incoherent. She drank that second glass down, and the stuff kicked in and she was wobbly. About then Samantha went to bed. I wasn't aware of her being that drunk, but it was like all at once she could hardly stand up."

Washington and McDaniel exchanged a glance.

"Jim and Gayle disappeared for a few minutes, and I put a

couple of moves on Shawn and found her receptive. Then Gayle comes walking up with my camera and starts taking pictures."

"Describe them."

A humorous shrug. "Just your average lewd scenes, Big Man. She was in my lap for some of them. Let's just say it's stuff you wouldn't see on the station web site."

"What did you do with them?"

"You have them, if you took my camera and computer. Jim downloaded them."

"Go on."

"By this point all I needed was a bed, but all of a sudden Gayle said we were leaving. I asked how I was gonna score with Shawn—she had the giggles and looked like easy pickings. But Gayle just said to trust her. She said Jim would be driving Shawn home in Shawn's car, and that we would help get Shawn into her apartment."

"Implying that you would be left alone with Shawn."

"What I figured, and that was cool. So she dropped me off and told me to get my car, because she was taking Jim home. I told her I'd be over in a few minutes. She got ticked off—said she wasn't a taxi and to come on if I was coming. Wasn't about to tell her I had a key. I gave her a kiss on the cheek and said thanks for a nice night. She stared at me a second, then said the two thousand dollars was off the table if I didn't go with her."

Washington laughed. "Come on, man. What the hell are you doing turning down two grand?"

Ford shrugged, his smirk gone for the moment. "Don't know, dude. Something told me I'd better get control of the situation, and I didn't have it following their lead."

"You didn't trust Yarbrough and Gayle? You thought they were playing you?"

"Maybe. Herding us out of Jim's pad was awfully abrupt. And I liked the idea of quietly slipping into Shawn's place alone, rather than barging up there with two other folks and getting some unwanted attention, you dig? So I went inside and freshened up, checked messages and went to Shawn's place."

"Approximately when was this?"

"About eleven-thirty. I parked down the street and walked."

"Who was at Shawn's apartment when you arrived?"

"Just her, or so I thought. Took her a long time to open the door, and I was getting ready to use the key. She could hardly stand. There were candles lit, wine glasses . . ."

"How many wine glasses?"

"Three, because I remember wondering if she and Jim and Gayle had a glass. But I never got around to asking. I said, 'Wanna play ping-pong?' And she started giggling. She closed the door and kissed me, and I had her right there on the couch. Afterward she was laying there, breathing heavy with her eyes closed. I looked around the apartment some more, stuck my nose in the cabinet and found those cigars." A sheepish grin. "You dudes can use your imagination."

Washington didn't crack a smile. "The cigars were in a cup, and the cup was in the television cabinet. Do you remember if the cabinet door was left open?"

Ford nodded. "The idea was for her to see the cigars. She wasn't going to remember anything, so I thought I'd give her a riddle to figure out. Anyway, she was out cold. Sweet dreams— no worse than a hangover the next day. Turned to go, and . . ."

"Hold it," McDaniel said, looking at his notes. "She was wearing a yellow and orange plaid dress. No undergarments were found. Did you take them?"

"No, man. Look, I admit I had sex with her. You got proof of that. But I didn't take her panties." A pause. "Anyway, I turned around to leave and a guy cold-cocked me."

McDaniel couldn't quite hide a smirk. Washington glanced at him, then faced Ford with his poker face. "And what did this mysterious man look like, Parker?"

"I just saw him for a nanosecond, because everything went

fuzzy. Let's see—dark hair, older than me, maybe. Looked pissed."

"Jim Yarbrough?"

"No. I don't know why I remember this, but Jim had a funny nose. Like he got it broke playing football or something. This guy had a small nose. All I remember is the nose and hair—not a freakin' hair out of place. But I couldn't tell you a thing about what he was wearing."

"A big man?"

Ford concentrated. "Shorter than me, a little huskier, maybe."

"Would you be able to identify him?"

"Possibly. Anyway, when I came to, I was lying in the hall-way! My head was up against the door of Shawn's bedroom. And the pain was so intense I could hardly move. But I clearly remember hearing this: 'Jamie, let's go!' Urgent, like let's get the hell out of here."

Washington and McDaniel exchanged another glance, but this time the skepticism was gone. Washington eased closer. "'Jamie, let's go.' Who said this?"

"A female. Not a voice I recognized—definitely not Gayle. And remember, I could hardly move my head, it hurt so much. Got my eyes opened and sat up. I was still out of sight of the living room. Then the front door slammed. I'm thinking somebody's really about to beat my ass now. But I heard feet on the stairs—somebody was getting the hell out of Dodge."

"How many people on the stairs?"

"Just one, far as I could tell. By then something smelled funny. And you know how it is when you drink—everything's a little out of kilter. But this was pretty noticeable, now that I was functioning again. Came out in the living room, and Shawn was all messed up."

"Explain as completely as you can."

"I didn't touch her—didn't get within five feet of her. She'd puked all over herself, and she wasn't breathing."

"Did you call nine-one-one?"

Ford snorted. "Hell, no. I wasn't sure she was dead, but I wasn't about to stick around and find out, then have to admit I'd been with her."

"Do you have any idea what time it was by then?"

"I bolted right then—tried to jog down the street without looking too conspicuous. When I got in my car, it was exactly midnight. I almost wrecked on the way home, my head hurt so much. Got home in one piece, crawled in the sack, and the next thing I knew it was twelve noon."

"Did you try to call, maybe check on her?"

"Please. I didn't know her, and I ain't stupid, man. I saw on the news that she was dead, and I wasn't surprised. Wasn't about to do anything that would tie my name to it."

"What about Gayle? Did you hear from her, or look her up?"

"Nope. I figured she'd come ask why the hell I made so much noise about getting with Shawn, then bail out. But I didn't hear from her, and I damn sure wasn't looking her up when I heard her on television talking about Shawn being dead." He paused. "Look, I didn't kill her, man. Yeah, I slipped something in her drink, and yeah, I slept with her. But she was passed out asleep and breathing just fine when that guy turned my lights out. That's who you ought to talk to."

"I'll tell you someone we have talked to," Washington said, his eyes hard. "Tracey Walton. Thought she was your girlfriend. Thought you had a date with her Saturday night. She sure thought so."

Ford said nothing, but the remaining swagger evaporated.

"Did you slip Tracey something before you slept with her the first time?"

"No, man. Consensual all the way."

"Ain't what she told us. Said you were her first—and she doesn't remember a thing about it."

Ford slapped the table with his palm. "No way, man! That lying whore begged for it!"

131

Washington raised his voice. "And you beat the hell out of her when she told you she was pregnant, didn't you? She lost the baby, by the way."

"I didn't beat her up. She fell," Ford said quietly. "She was out on her damned feet. Hit her head on the side of the tub."

"After you drugged her. What did you put in that soft drink?"

Ford heaved a sigh. "Mexican Valium."

"More date-rape drug, Mac! Ever been with a woman you didn't have to drug, Parker?"

Ford's jaw tightened. "Look, I ain't saying I didn't spike her drink. But Tracey said she wanted to loosen up and fly after being under her parents' thumb her whole life. If she told you I was forcing anything on her, she's lying."

"We found cash, pot and coke in her dresser. Yours, I assume?"

"The merchandise is mine—which she's been happy to partake of. Some of the prize money was hers as thanks for running some of my errands." He snickered. "I suppose she told you I planted every bit of it. Well, you just see if her prints are on it, Big Man. And ask her if that diamond necklace she's worn the last couple of weeks fell out of the sky. She spent some bucks on that."

Washington smiled. "So your story is that she liked doing drugs with you, volunteered to be your mule, was happy to perform any sexual favor you wanted and spent drug money on jewelry for herself? This from a girl who was a virgin, grew up in the church and is a registered nurse, and never even had a boyfriend before meeting you? I find that a little hard to believe."

"I swear it, man. I know how this looks, and I'm sure Tracey is calling everyone in her church and begging them to give a good account of her."

"She's not talking to anybody right now, actually. She slipped into a coma several hours after we talked to her. We decided to get her statement on tape in case she doesn't make it. Glad we did."

Ford lowered his head. A long moment passed. "Just check the freakin' bills, man. Had her hot little hands all over them. And she damn sure didn't object when I suggested we park some of my merchandise with her. Quote: 'I like feeling stoned.'"

"I'm with you. So you're saying you don't put your entire estate in one spot."

"No, dude," he said with a smug smile. "I'm spread out all over the place. And believe it or not, I'm just a small part of the empire. You tell the D.A. I can give him names that will get him reelected the rest of his life. One of them is the ex who lived in Shawn's pad."

Washington got to his feet. "We'll make sure he knows. Couple more things: We'll have this conversation transcribed, and we'll get your signature on it. And we'll have a narcotics officer pop in on you over in Raymond and hear about your big connections. That cool with you?"

"That'll work, Big Man. Now what are you gonna do for me?"

Washington grinned. "For right now we'll get you back to Raymond."

Ford made a face. "Don't forget me, dude. I know all about getting a speedy trial."

"We won't forget you, dude. Don't worry about that."

*　*　*

Another trip to Hattiesburg. This time Darren Clarke's garage door was open, his Mitsubishi in plain sight. He opened up and led the detectives to the dining room. McDaniel eyed the living area as they walked through the foyer. The curtains were open, and no one was pool side. Clarke was in a t-shirt and jeans with a dust rag in hand.

"Make an arrest?"

"Not yet," Washington said. "You told us that you and Patti

were in Shawn's apartment between approximately nine and nine-thirty Saturday night, correct?"

"That's right."

"Tell us again where you were at midnight."

"Right here."

"Can someone besides Patti verify that?"

"It was just the two of us. Why?"

"Does the name Jamie Fontenot mean anything to you?"

"Patti's roommate. Why?"

"What about Parker Ford?"

"No."

"He was at dinner the other night."

Clarke frowned. "The long-haired guy? I never got his name. Why? Does he have something to do with it?"

"He claims to have been in Shawn's apartment just before midnight and got beat up." Washington took a long look at Clarke. Not terribly tall, with a medium build. Dark, styled hair and a relatively small nose. "He said when he came to, Shawn had gotten sick all over herself and wasn't breathing. Said the guy who hit him was about your size and dark-haired. That ring a bell?"

Clarke stepped closer. "Listen to me: The last time I saw Shawn was in the Que Será Será parking lot. This was before eight. Patti and I were here at midnight. Now is there anything else I can help you with?"

McDaniel spoke, startling him. "Did you have a key to Shawn's car?"

"No, Detective."

"Someone did. Shawn had packed a bag with clothes for several days, and it apparently sat in her car all weekend. It was taken from the car sometime Tuesday, after her body was discovered. It was found by a maintenance man on the other side of the complex."

Clarke spread his hands. "Like I told you, I didn't speak to Shawn about where she was going that night. Check with her parents and see if they were expecting her."

"Was she on any medication that you were aware of?"

"Sleeping pills. Found it hard to unwind after being on the air. Like that from the beginning."

"Ever have a problem with it?"

"You're asking if she was a drug addict? No, Detective. Prescribed by her family doctor. Now will there be anything else?"

"Would anyone have had a key to her car?"

"Nobody off the top of my head. Her mother, possibly, but I wouldn't know why."

"Are you planning to go to the funeral?"

"Yes, I am."

"I'm not sure that's a good idea."

Clarke's jaw tightened. "She was my wife. May I ask why?"

"No, you go ahead, Mr. Clarke," Washington said, pretending to upstage his partner. He and McDaniel had rehearsed the mock disagreement, and McDaniel looked up in surprise.

"Jerome . . ."

Washington ignored him. "You just keep your cell phone on in case we need to reach you. When are you leaving?"

"Late tonight or very early tomorrow. Haven't decided."

"And when will you be back?" McDaniel said loudly, stepping forward.

"I don't know yet. I'm back on the air Monday."

Washington caught Clarke's eye. "You call us tomorrow, then, after the funeral. Let us know what your plans are. We don't want to have to hunt for you in case we need something. That clear?"

Clarke glowered at him. "Yes, Detective."

* * *

The detectives reached the sorority house before noon. Girls were scattered around the front yard, some with books or lunch and others in the company of a young man or two. More were in the first floor lobby and recreation room. McDaniel got the attention of a wispy blond who was starting up the stairs with a large Burger King bag in her arms.

"We're looking for Jamie Fontenot."

"Haven't seen her."

"Allison Shelton around?"

"Haven't seen her, either. Sorry," the girl said, resuming her trek. They were glancing around when Allison entered with her roommate. Washington asked about Jamie and Patti.

"I'm not sure when they have class," Allison said. "But we can take you to their room."

They climbed two flights of well-worn, squeaky stairs. The scent of perfume was heavy. Loud chatter and music ranging from rap to alternative could be heard. Small clumps of girls passed. Some spoke to Allison and the roommate; others eyed the detectives. Allison stopped at an open door on the third floor and knocked. Jamie stuck out her head, as did a pair of shorter girls. One was the blond the detectives encountered on the stairs when they arrived. She flinched the tiniest bit. Jamie groaned.

"I told you everything, but come in, I guess. Cheeseburger?"

"No, thanks. And we'd like to speak to you alone, Miss Fontenot."

Jamie's eyes narrowed. She looked at Allison. Something the detectives couldn't read passed between them. Allison started away with her roommate and signaled for the other girls to follow. McDaniel saw them out and closed the door. There were two unmade twin beds and television sets as well as stacks of textbooks, compact discs and magazines. Clothes were everywhere. Posters of Britney Spears and Jennifer Lopez were on the walls.

"Where's Patti?" Washington said, glancing around.

"She has a noon class on Wednesday. Why?"

"You guys went to a movie Saturday night, correct?"

"Yes, sir."

"What did you see?"

A frown. *Fifty First Dates.*

Washington turned to McDaniel. "That's not playing at the mall theater, is it?"

"Yes, it is! Or it was," Jamie said, an edge in her voice.

"Anyway, tell us again what happened after the movie?"

"I drove straight back here in my car and got in about ten-thirty. Patti was with him. She got in about eleven-fifteen, was here a few minutes and went to his place."

McDaniel gazed. "Problem is, two of your sorority sisters dispute that you were here."

Jamie's jaw tightened. "And one of them is Allison, that red-head who just brought you here, right? Well, let me tell you something: That lying, two-faced witch has had it in for me since my first week on campus because I went out with a guy she had a crush on! Fact, I'm going to settle this once and for all," she said, starting past the detectives. Washington put a hand on her shoulder.

"You sit tight. We're not interested in hearing you argue with Miss Shelton. We'd like you to find at least one person who'll confirm that you were in this room Saturday night."

Jamie picked up a cordless phone and punched numbers, pacing around the room. "Eileen? It's me. Come down here, please."

A minute later the blond from the stairs knocked on the door. Washington displayed his badge. "We're homicide investigators with the Jackson police department. What's your name, young lady?"

"Eileen Drake," the girl said quietly, looking at the floor.

"Were you here Saturday night, Miss Drake? Here at the house?"

Her eyes bounced from Washington to McDaniel. She swallowed hard.

"Eileen, this is no time for games," Jamie said, menace in her voice. "Tell them."

"Tell them the truth, Eileen," Allison Shelton said, appearing from behind and slipping an arm around the younger girl. "Tell them what you told me."

"I wasn't here," Eileen said, shaking with adrenaline and on the verge of tears. "I went out with some friends. I have no idea if Jamie was here, or Patti."

Jamie stepped forward, but McDaniel blocked the way. Washington was well over a foot taller than Eileen, and he eased closer and leaned down. He spoke softly.

"Listen carefully, Miss Drake: Did Jamie ask you to tell anyone who asked that she and Patti were here Saturday night, here in this room?"

Eileen looked everywhere but at Jamie, who was ready to pounce. Then she faced Washington. "Yes, sir."

"Did she ask that of anyone else?"

"My roommate."

"Thank you. That's all we need." Washington closed the door behind Allison and Eileen. Jamie leveled a finger, but McDaniel stepped on her words.

"Were you in Shawn Forrest's apartment with Patti and her boyfriend Saturday night?"

Jamie looked at him in disbelief. "Was I in her apartment? You can't be serious!"

"We're quite serious. Someone in the apartment heard a voice frantically call out, 'Jamie, let's go!' That someone—who'd been beaten up and was lying in the hallway—saw Shawn seconds later and said she looked like she was dying. This was right before midnight, which is the estimated time of death. Allison Shelton and her roommate told us that they were here all night, and that you and Patti never made an appearance. So you need to find someone who can confirm you were here."

"Allison Shelton is an alcoholic slut who has been out to get me since I set foot on this campus! Everybody in this house will tell you she's a liar! Did you ask how much she had to drink that night? Probably can't remember who she was with, either!"

Washington got to his feet and announced he was going to make a call. He was gone five minutes. Tears were dripping down Jamie's cheeks when he returned, and for a moment he thought McDaniel had extracted a confession. But McDaniel said nothing, his poker face in place. Washington cleared his throat.

"Come with us, Miss Fontenot."

"Are you arresting me?"

"Not at this time. But we'd like to ask you some questions. We will do that in Jackson, and your parents will meet us there."

She backed away and aimed a finger. "Not until I've talked to them will you take me out of here. You have no idea who my father is, do you?"

McDaniel sighed. "You can come quietly, or we can put cuffs on you and march you out to our car right in front of your sisters. Up to you."

* * *

Jamie's parents and the Fontenot family lawyer were waiting at Spring Center. The lawyer, an all-business sort in an expensive suit and a gold Rolex, swiftly ordered Jamie not to say anything and demanded that she be released to the custody of her parents unless she was being arrested. The father was clearly a lawyer, a coiffed, stout man who dropped names and implied a suit against the police department. Washington stepped away from the fracas to take a call from Jessica. He signaled to McDaniel and Cowan as the meeting broke up.

"There's a partial on the sleeping pill bottle in Shawn's bathroom bag which isn't hers. We've put it through AFIS, and about thirty possible matches came up. Freddy is looking as we speak."

AFIS was an acronym for the Automated Fingerprint Identification System, a database which was utilized by all forms of law enforcement around the country. Each set of prints taken by Washington and McDaniel during the investigation had been entered, giving them a basis of comparison for the partial on the Ambien bottle.

"That could take all day," Cowan said, frowning. "Great."

"I don't know about that, Sam," McDaniel said. "It's not like all thirty are going to be right here in Jackson. And you know Freddy—he can look at a print and know if it's a left thumb or a right middle finger in half a second."

A nod. "Keep me posted, and let's get this put to bed."

* * *

Carolyn and Norris were sent before lunch to cover a fire which destroyed a house in a poor area of the city. The good news was that the infant boy and ninety-year-old wheelchair-bound woman inside were rescued without serious injury. Norris set up in time to catch the flames billowing into the sky and shot the dramatic rescue of the old woman. Carolyn interviewed neighbors and learned that the family had been lifelong residents of the community and was active in their small church. She did a live shot from the church at noon with the minister, and helped promote a hastily-coordinated food and blanket drive for the family.

Now, at the afternoon news meeting, followup coverage was being discussed. Yarbrough was behind his desk, Faber alongside at the assignment blackboard. Carolyn and several other reporters were in the room as well as the trio of evening producers and the promotions producer, who would write teases for the evening newscasts based on the meeting.

"Carolyn on this morning's fire. Live in the studio at five and six, package at ten," Faber said to Yarbrough. Yarbrough nodded and gave Carolyn a thumbs-up.

"I second that emotion. We own this story, by the way," he said, panning the group. There were nods all around. "In case you didn't see the noon, Carolyn did a nice live shot and James did his usual exceptional job. A tragedy to be sure, but we kicked butt." He looked at the tease writer. "Talk to your boss about a P.O.P."

This was promotions code for "proof of performance." A thirty-second promotional ad would be put together, utilizing the dramatic video and compelling sound bites. It would saturate the air for several days before being replaced by one which detailed equally outstanding coverage of the next big event.

"She's already on it. Said to tell you she made her own copy of the noon show in master control, so she won't have to borrow yours." Yarbrough nodded his approval. The tease writer, a young man of perhaps twenty-five with an earring and goatee, cocked his head toward Carolyn. "What I'd like to know is why a ninety-year-old woman in a wheelchair was responsible for a six-month-old."

There was an uncomfortable silence. Carolyn caught Faber discreetly shaking his head from the corner of her eye.

"That's a good question," one of the producers said mildly. "And you're welcome to go back out with Carolyn this afternoon and ask the family yourself."

Several people stifled giggles, some more successfully than others. The young man looked at the floor and didn't respond.

"I'm sure there will be a time and place to make that inquiry," Yarbrough said at length, a bemused smile on his face. "The focus right now—and you correct me if I'm wrong, Carolyn—is to make the community aware of this family's loss. I think that's what our coverage needs to center around."

Carolyn glanced up from her notes and gazed at Yarbrough. One of the things she disliked most about him was his smug embrace of certain, politically-correct issues. He couldn't care less about the plight of this poor family; what mattered was saying the right things in front of his staff and conveying that he really gave a damn.

"For the time being, Jim, but that question needs to be asked at some point," Carolyn said. "Might make for a good followup package."

Yarbrough nodded. "Let's run our fire safety graphic, and you have that great bite with the fire captain."

"I just heard from the pastor. People are coming by in droves, all saying they heard about it on our news. How about we run out and see if we can catch folks handing out food and clothing?"

Faber pointed at the door. "You and Norris get right on it. Keep us updated."

*   *   *

Washington and McDaniel had begun their case summary and were describing Jim Yarbrough when Washington's desk line rang. It was Ben Pyle, the medical examiner.

"Gomer, my man. What's up?"

"Hi, Jerome. Shawn Forrest's toxicology is complete."

Washington grabbed his pad and flashed McDaniel a thumbs-up. "I'm taking notes. Go."

"Blood alcohol content of point-three-two . . ."

"Damn!"

". . . as well as a large quantity of Rohypnol in her blood-stream. That's the date-rape drug, which I'm sure you know. A heavy dose, but not lethal. But a possibly lethal amount of Ambien—sleeping pills which are commonly prescribed by a physician."

Washington's eyes widened. He scribbled *Ambien,* then *unknown print.*

"And it should be noted that she suffered cardiac arrest."

"Really? So the suffocation brought on a heart attack?"

A long pause. "No official cause of death yet."

"But Gomer, I thought you said the other day . . ."

"Off the record, Jerome, this one is awfully complicated. That's all I can say right now. I'll have an official report in a couple of days."

Washington frowned. McDaniel was watching. "Can we quote you on the contents of her bloodstream for right now? It's critical to the investigation."

"Certainly. And you'll be the first to know when it's official."

Washington summarized the discussion in Cowan's office.

"Too complicated? Is he already getting that much pressure, Sam?" McDaniel said. "Two days ago he sounded sure she was suffocated."

"It may be a close call, Tim. Call the D.A.'s office and have them fax a subpoena to her doctor. If they prescribed sleeping pills, they'll know what kind of shape she was in."

*   *   *

Two hours later McDaniel was put on with a nurse who worked closely with Shawn's physician. The nurse had gotten the subpoena and had Shawn's medical records in front of her.

"I haven't talked to Leigh, but Dr. Fisher has. Dr. Fisher's father, who passed away last year, was Jack's doctor for thirty years. We saw Leigh and Shawn last winter when they got their flu shots. Are you at liberty to say anything?"

"The investigation is ongoing, so I can't. But anything you can tell me about her medical history would be helpful. We know she had a prescription for sleeping pills."

"That's correct. Shawn took five milligrams of Ambien nightly. Ambien is a commonly prescribed medication for mild sleep disorder. We put her on it about six years ago."

"Which matches up to her time in television."

"That's correct. Dr. Fisher put her on it when she left for Chattanooga. Shawn had a history of tossing and turning, and you can only imagine the stress which goes with her line of work. She said it helped." A heavy sigh. "You'll have to forgive me, Detective—this is hard to take in. Anyway, I know Shawn put a lot of pressure on herself to succeed, and sleep difficulties are very common for that personality type."

"Anything else of note?"

"Nasty bout with the flu four years ago, which prompted the shots. And she was diagnosed with an irregular heartbeat in high school."

McDaniel raised an eyebrow. Washington, watching his partner, eased closer. "How serious?"

"Not enough for medication, just something she noticed occasionally. She took a physical each year and nothing surfaced. We told her to be aware of lightheadedness or dizzy spells, but she never said a word. I have no doubt she would have taken herself to the hospital if she thought she was in trouble. Other than that, healthy as a horse."

A pause. "The toxicology results just came back. Shawn was at a party which got out of hand, ma'am. There were large amounts of alcohol, Ambien and Rohypnol in her bloodstream."

"Oh, my God. First of all, Detective, Ambien is never to be taken while the person is drinking. Shawn knew that. And Rohypnol? What in the world?"

"We know her drink was spiked with Rohypnol and possibly the Ambien. How would her body react with all of that in her system?"

"Alcohol, Rohypnol and Ambien all slow the central nervous system," the nurse said quietly. "Heavy amounts would very possibly begin to shut it down. The human body is a remarkable piece of machinery, Detective—it senses danger and tries to compensate. In this case, it would have gone into fight-back mode, with accelerated heartbeat and adrenaline flow. And although

she didn't have heart trouble per se, Shawn's heart was potentially defective. It very easily could have given out under those
circumstances."

The nurse was crying when McDaniel got off the phone. He
was relaying the information to Cowan when Washington's desk
line rang.

"Sam, it's Jessica," Washington said, his voice carrying the
room. "I'm transferring to you. Hit the speaker."

Jessica said hello and handed the phone to Freddy, the ancient
fingerprint expert. He had a heavy drawl and sounded like he'd
taken in his share of Grateful Dead concerts, but he knew his
stuff.

"I was able to throw out twenty-eight of your thirty-three
possible matches right off the bat. You're looking at a left thumb
on that vial, fellas. Of the remaining five, three are from out of
state. That leaves two, and one of those belongs to a man in
Tunica."

"Nobody in this investigation has anything to do with
Tunica," Washington said, panning the room. "So are you going
to make us beg, or what?"

"It's Gayle Kennedy, Jerome. I like as many as ten points of
comparison on a partial. I can live with seven. This only has
five. But the more I look at it, the more I like it. Yeah, I'll get
on the stand and say it's hers."

"Damn. How many people were trying to kill this woman?"
Cowan said rhetorically. He dialed the District Attorney's
Office and spoke with Linda Carman, D.A. Blair Bennett's top
assistant. He hung up a moment later.

"Go pick up Gayle Kennedy."

* * *

It was after four when Carolyn hustled into the newsroom.
She had trained herself long ago to block out the clamor when
under the gun, and her fingers flew as she scripted the two-

minute fire package at her computer. She closed herself in the sound booth to record the audio track, then turned the tape over to Norris with a list of b-roll shots and sound bites. Then she wrote the introductions to her in-studio appearances and added them to the show rundowns at five and six. She would join Jeff and Gayle on the set early in the first block of each newscast. After they introduced her, she would read the intro from the Teleprompter before the package rolled. The package would be included at ten without her on hand.

She checked on Norris, who was putting the finishing touches on the package. He was a craftsman, and the edits were clean and the sound quality was good. She stepped outside for a cigarette, relishing the adrenal rush that came with humping it to finalize a strong report just before deadline, then plopped into her chair. It was twenty minutes until five. Gayle caught her eye and eased forward.

"If I get any more attitude out of the director, I'm kicking his balls into his throat."

Carolyn allowed a smile and waited her out. She got along fine with the man who directed the evening shows, an easygoing sort who'd manned the chair for a decade.

"All I did was remind him to tell his camera people how I like to be shot, and I got this lecture about how I need to focus on my job and not theirs. Everybody on the damned crew is a smart-ass." She lowered her voice. "Even Jeff Walker is on me. That's all I need. I mean, who elected him king?"

Carolyn was tiring of the diatribe and hoped it didn't show on her face.

"Anyway, want to do dinner if I can sneak away after the six?"

"Already have plans," she said, lying. "But I'll do a rain check."

"A hot date, huh? Find me one," Gayle said, grinning over her shoulder as she started away. "Let me go so I can put on my game face."

Carolyn sighed, glad to be rid of her. She glanced up a moment later when someone tugged on the locked back door. Detective Washington's large frame filled the doorway. His partner was behind him. Their faces were grim. The promotions producer, on his way to Yarbrough's office, let them in. Washington stepped forward and glanced around. Then he spoke, his voice booming through the room.

"Gayle Kennedy?"

Yarbrough stepped into view. He didn't look pleased. "What is it now, Detective?"

"Is Miss Kennedy on the premises?"

Yarbrough glanced at her cubicle. The detectives followed his eyes.

"She's putting on makeup," Carolyn said, panning the men.

"Why don't you go get her, Miss Davis."

The newsroom had quieted. Faces poked out of cubicles to watch what was unfolding. Heart beating faster, Carolyn stepped out of sight and into the hallway. She grabbed her cell phone from her jeans and speed-dialed Norris. She lingered a few feet from the bathroom, praying he would answer quickly. The tension couldn't be felt out here yet, but there would be a stampede once everyone realized what was happening.

"Norris."

"Where are you?"

"Parking lot. Hey, cops just showed up . . ."

"James, roll tape," she said, pitching her voice down. "You hear me? Stay where you are and roll tape—now! Something's going down!"

She clicked off, took a deep breath and stepped into the bathroom, trying her best to appear casual. Gayle was spraying her hair.

"Your friends from the police department are here."

Gayle slammed the hair spray can onto the counter. Without

a word she stalked back to the newsroom, which was almost completely still. Carolyn followed at a distance, positioning herself so she could see through to the back door. Norris was white-balancing his camera. He would be ready in seconds.

"Well, now," Gayle said with a sneer. "What a surprise, Detectives. Long time, no see."

Washington stepped forward. "Gayle Kennedy, you are under arrest for the attempted murder of Shawn Forrest."

There was a collective gasp. Gayle's jaw fell.

"You have the right to remain silent. What you say can and will be used against you in a court of law. You have the right to an attorney . . ."

"What the hell do you think you're doing?" Yarbrough said, attempting to get between them. "We have a newscast in twenty minutes, Detectives!"

"Back off, Mr. Yarbrough, or you're coming, too," McDaniel said, admonishing him with a glare.

"You have the right to an attorney," Washington said, towering over Gayle and boring into her eyes with a sullen stare. "If you can't afford an attorney, one will be provided for you. Do you understand these rights?"

Tears of anger streamed down Gayle's face, smearing her makeup. Her eyes circled the room until she found Yarbrough. Something passed between them, but he stared back helplessly.

"Miss Kennedy! Do you understand your rights?"

Gayle spun and started back toward the hallway, but Rick Sewell trotted in and unwittingly blocked her way.

"What the hell is going on here?"

"Gayle Kennedy is being arrested, Mr. Sewell. Cuff her, Mac."

"What on earth for, Detective?"

Washington stepped closer. "For the attempted murder of Shawn Forrest."

Sewell looked as if someone punched him in the stomach. He

sagged and stepped aside, watching as McDaniel slapped hand-cuffs on his young anchor.

"Get your hands off me!"

"Let's go," McDaniel said, snapping the cuffs into place. "And not another word."

Gayle glanced over her shoulder and found Carolyn's shocked face. Carolyn couldn't read what she saw. Then Gayle was led away.

* * *

The newsroom was frozen for several seconds. Then Faber clapped his hands and barked that they had a newscast to do. Sewell signaled for Yarbrough to follow, and they disappeared down the hall. Faber and the five o'clock producer hustled to Jeff Walker and readied him to go solo. The camera sequencing with a lone anchor was different, and there was more copy to read.

Carolyn headed to the bathroom to freshen her makeup, now in dire need of another cigarette. Norris caught her in the hall and whispered that he had video of Gayle being forced into the police car, complete with a close-up of her extended middle finger. She finished her face and strode to the set. Jeff Walker was going over scripts. He smiled when Carolyn sat next to him.

"You okay?"

"I think so. What about you, old-timer?"

"Hopefully the show won't be nearly as eventful as the last few minutes." He turned to her. "Nice live shot at noon. You're rolling, Carolyn. Put that and your Cronin packages on your resume tape."

Faber hustled up and pitched his voice down. "Mandatory staff meeting as soon as the show is over—we'll do it right here. Five minutes, Jeff. Got everything you need?"

"Good to go."

"Carolyn?"

"I'm fine."

He started away. "Yell if you need me—I'm helping produce."

Walker was unflappable under pressure, and Carolyn's package was compelling. She unclipped her microphone and strode from the set once he was reading the next story. She stepped outside and lit a cigarette, trying to digest what had happened. Her cell rang as she stubbed the butt on the asphalt.

"Hey, it's Claire Bailey. What's this from Faber about a mandatory staff meeting? I have to get up at two-thirty for morning show, remember?"

"I'll call you back and hit the high points." She stifled a laugh as she remembered Gayle's dinner offer. "Or we can have dinner. You and your husband have plans?"

"He's at the church. Try this on for size: A mouth-watering, home-cooked meal will be waiting on you if you'll drive out here."

"That'll work, child. I'm in the studio at six. Look for me about seven."

*   *   *

Gayle's tailored purple suit and smudged mascara raised eyebrows when she was marched through Spring Center, although her clenched jaw and foul language was responsible for much of the attention. Her lawyer was a youthful, heavyset man who arrived during the booking procedure. He told her not to say another word, promising to find a judge and establish her bail in short order. He assured Gayle that she would be driving home in minutes.

"Do you want to give us a statement, Miss Kennedy, now that your attorney is here?" McDaniel said.

"Not at this time, Detective," the lawyer said.

"Works for us," Washington said. He signaled to the detention officer. "Get her out to Raymond."

Gayle looked up. "What's in Raymond?"

McDaniel grinned. "The county jail."

She frowned and turned to her lawyer. "Why do I have to go out there? I can't wait here until my bond is set?"

The lawyer tried to maintain an air of control. He looked at the detectives. "Can't you give me a few minutes to find a judge who can set her bond?"

Washington held his laughter more effectively than McDaniel. He glanced at his watch, then the lawyer.

"If you can find a judge this time of night, be my guest. For the time being, Raymond is her home away from home."

* * *

Claire Bailey and her husband lived in Crossgates, a sprawling, tree-lined Brandon neighborhood twenty minutes from the station and a stone's throw from Eric Redding's apartment. Claire welcomed Carolyn with a hug. She was Carolyn's height but twenty-five pounds heavier, a full-figured, blue-eyed blond with a soft voice who barely looked legal when not dressed for work. She wore an apron over a t-shirt and gym shorts, and her thick glasses were a sharp contrast to the contact lenses she wore on the air.

Claire was one of the more interesting people Carolyn had met in broadcasting. Born into a wealthy Memphis family, she graduated high school at fifteen and finished college three years later. A promising writer, she published a dozen poems in regional publications as an undergrad and became interested in broadcasting after a newswriting course. She worked as a gopher in a Memphis newsroom after college and was hired at Channel Five to produce the morning show, but several weeks later the incumbent anchor quit and Claire was offered the job. Woefully inexperienced, she did her best to make up for her lack of training with the excitement of a young child on Christmas morning.

Her enthusiasm was gone now, however, as the hardness and

cynicism of the newsroom had worn her down over time. Viewed as a poor little rich kid after showing up her first day in a BMW, she felt picked on in the newsroom and slighted by Jim Yarbrough. A contract extension hadn't even been mentioned as her two-year deal wound down, and whatever spark remained was crushed when Shawn Forrest sent a group e-mail which made fun of her size. Eric said she talked daily about quitting, and he feared her poor morale would get her fired before that happened.

"Smells good in here," Carolyn said, inhaling as she glanced at family portraits on the paneled walls. A projection-screen television in the living room was tuned to Channel Five. It was muted, and Top 40 music played on an overhead sound system. A stocked china cabinet was on display across the way. Carolyn was convinced that part of Shawn's spite toward Claire came down to one rich kid being jealous of another. It was a shame, since she was such a kind-hearted person and still very much a youngster—she would turn twenty-two this fall.

"Buttermilk chicken," Claire said, emerging with a casserole dish. "One of Mother's finest. And a pecan pie is in the oven. We'll get these salads out of the way, then the fun begins." A grin. "I eat one meal a day on the Slim Fast diet, so I make it count."

Carolyn revealed the events of late afternoon. Claire dropped her fork and stared.

"Did you have the news on at six?"

"No."

"We teased it at the very end. Didn't mention Gayle by name, but Jeff said that there was shocking new information in the Shawn Forrest case. That way, none of the other stations know what's up until it's too late."

Claire laughed. "Gosh, that's cold. We're talking about one of our own maybe killing one of our own, and our station is still trying to own the story."

Carolyn grinned. "You got it. And you, young lady, will

have the privilege of reading the story tomorrow morning. Everybody else will have it by then, and it'll be front-page news in the paper, I'm sure, but we had it first."

"And a big deal will be made out of that, too."

"Probably. Stick a fork in her, baby—she's done."

"I guess even if she makes bond they can't put her back on, can they?"

"Claire, would you watch an anchor who had been arrested for murder?" Carolyn said with a chuckle. "So tell me about you, kid. Its been ages."

Claire's husband was the youth minister of a large Jackson church, and he had gotten caught up in church politics and was being blamed for the collapse of a highly-anticipated youth trip to the Bahamas. This made for tension around the house, as did the fact that they weren't expecting a baby after months of trying.

"He wants me to quit the station. Talks about it every day. Says I need to be home baking cookies and doing the things a minister's wife does to support him. Wants me to take a job at the church day care, maybe start teaching Sunday school. Something that fits the image."

Carolyn frowned. She liked the husband well enough, but it hadn't taken long around him to determine that he controlled the household. She started to tell Claire to stand up for herself, but she wasn't sure it was her place.

"Does he enjoy what he does?"

"He says so, but he stays stressed out and is a different person when he's climbing the social ladder. I wouldn't tell him so, but that seems to trump what he does for the youth."

A dubious smile. "So should I try to talk you into staying or not?"

"I don't know. My ego wants an offer, but I'm sick of the place, to be honest. And I'll share something with you, Carolyn: I've been on anti-depressants since I was fifteen, and I take Xanax for panic attacks. There are days I don't want to get out of bed, let alone be on television and interact with the public. But at least I can function. Flip side is that I have no energy and struggle with my weight, which I've always had trouble with. I wanted to tell Shawn, 'Anything but that.' It's bad enough that my husband stays on me about it, and having a memo posted at work nearly sent me over the edge."

Carolyn sipped her tea. Her own marriage hadn't lasted long, but at least her husband was civil as they realized they had little in common and no desire to stay together. This sounded like a nightmare, and she didn't know how much Claire would put up with before leaving—or snapping.

"What do you want to do, sweetie? What's your dream job?"

"The truth? I'd love to stay home and start writing poetry and short stories again, maybe work on a novel or screenplay. I'd probably put on fifty pounds and go for days at a time without leaving the house, but I'd sleep regular hours again, and I might even relax enough being out of television not to need those damned pills. And I could bake all the cookies and have all the babies he wanted. The last thing I want to do is work at a day care. Might as well go ahead and plan on having a nervous breakdown with all those screaming kids."

"You sure you want kids yet? You're only twenty-one."

A heavy sigh. "He does, so it's final."

Claire's voice was shaky. Not knowing what else to do, Carolyn embraced her. A flood of tears came. Eventually Claire gathered herself, and they ate in silence before conversation ensued. The topic soon became Shawn's death.

"Eric is convinced she was set up, Carolyn. He said people were fired for sending e-mails from other computers a few years ago, before Yarbrough got there. Maybe he's right."

Carolyn nodded. "I was sent on a story one day and forgot to log out. That's how that stuff happens—someone sneaks up and sends something and makes it look like you did it. If that's what went down, someone was out to get Shawn as much as you."

Claire disappeared into the kitchen and returned with the steaming pie and a gallon of vanilla ice cream. "Gayle, maybe? You know how mad she was when Shawn stole the five show from her. She's been nice to me, but that may not count for much." A dubious look. "You don't really think Gayle killed her, do you?"

"Hope not. Ain't the way to advance your career with Colonial Broadcasting." Carolyn's eyes narrowed in mock seriousness. "By the way, where were you Saturday night, young lady?"

"Some business leader in Jackson had a party, and we were invited. It was excruciating—I don't drink, and I wanted to start. And just where were you Saturday night?"

Carolyn blushed and gripped Claire's hand. "You are sworn to secrecy on this, my friend. This is as private as your medication."

A grin. "Ooh, something juicy. Between you, me and the pecan pie."

"I assume Eric hasn't said anything. We had dinner last weekend. This wasn't two buddies getting together for a Coke and a smile—this was a real date. A real kiss at the end. A real nice evening. I'm hoping for another one soon and thought you might put in a good word."

Claire's mouth fell open. She stared, then looked away. "Gosh. Sure didn't expect that." A long moment passed. "Always wondered if you and James Norris had something going."

Carolyn frowned. "No, no. James and my oldest sister dated a long time ago. I've known him since I was ten years old. He probably thinks I'm still ten." She smiled. "'Mr. James, I'm selling calendars to raise money for my school. Would you like to buy one?' He bought everything I sold, and it was obviously to impress my mama and sister. I still tease him about that."

Claire didn't respond.

"Anyway, your thoughts, now that the cat's out of the bag?"

"I'm not sure Eric is your type." She faced Carolyn, her warmth gone. "He has his quirks. He's a great friend, but he can be self-absorbed. I'm sure that comes from a bad marriage and having to reassert control over his life. I assume you know he's divorced. And may I be so bold to ask if you really want to date a white man?"

Carolyn frowned. Claire's smug tone bothered her, not the question. "We talked about that. He seems pretty open-minded. I like to think I am. I'll just come right out and ask: Do you think he'd have a problem going out with someone of color?"

Claire gazed long enough to make Carolyn uncomfortable. "No, but I'm not sure he'd date a co-worker. He went out with someone he worked with before he got married. Something happened and she tried to get him fired."

Carolyn finished her pie and kept her eyes on her plate. Claire knew Eric well and was playing devil's advocate, but the mood swing was noticeable. Was it a racial issue after all? Eric seemed fine the other night, but would Claire be uncomfortable with her white friend dating a black woman? The prospect sickened her, and she kicked herself for mentioning his name at all.

"Anyway, I'll put in a good word if he mentions it."

"That would be appreciated."

There was an awkward moment, then Claire excused herself to the bathroom. The phone rang as she returned. She took the call in the kitchen. It was her husband, who was apparently going to be in meetings for hours. Claire said she would join him and hung up.

"This is what you get for thinking you know everything, dearest," she muttered, clearing the dishes. "Of course I'll be a good spouse and drive all the way into Jackson and sit alongside while you're chewed out. Then we can come home and you can take your bad mood out on me. Then we can have sex again and try to get pregnant. Then I'll sleep for three or four hours, take my crazy pills and be a perky television host."

Carolyn already had her purse over her shoulder. Claire gave her a quick hug. It was half as warm as the first one.

"This has been an awful day, Carolyn. Please forgive me. At least the food was good."

"The food was delicious, and the company was fine—you have a lot on your mind. Tell Eric hello, and think hard about writing full time, Claire. That sounds terrific."

A disinterested shrug. "Maybe. Good night."

* * *

Eric Redding's apartment was on Crossgates Boulevard. Carolyn would have been tempted to surprise him but was shaken after the visit with Claire. She circled through the parking lot and noted his Saturn, then headed home.

Ten minutes later Claire parked her BMW next to the Saturn. She stomped up the steps and rapped on Eric's door. He was shirtless, having just emerged from the shower after racquetball. His smile faded at her scowl.

"May I come in, Mr. Redding?"

He closed the door behind her. "What's the matter?"

"Let's fight about this now so I can sleep tonight. Carolyn Davis came over for supper, and I understand the two of you had a romantic evening last weekend. Care to explain?"

Eric grimaced and looked away.

"I realize I have very little standing here," Claire said, sarcasm and hurt seeping from her. "After all, I'm a married woman and you're a single man. But since we're sleeping together, Eric, the least you could do is tell me you're interested in playing the field."

Shame was on his face. He couldn't manage a response.

"I mean it when I tell you I love you," she said, tears welling in her eyes. "You mean everything to me—I live for seeing you

157

each morning and would have quit long ago if you weren't there. I was so repulsed at the thought of you kissing her I wanted to beat your face in, and it was all I could do to get rid of her without hitting her."

He tried to embrace her, but she pushed him away.

"You tell me every day that you love me, Eric. Is it a lie? I'm quitting tomorrow if it is, and you'll never see me again. And just who else do I not know about?"

"There's no one else, and that's the only time Carolyn and I have gone out." A heavy sigh. "I do love you, Claire. I try not to dwell on the fact that I'm a home-wrecker and we're sneaking around. Mornings mean everything to me, too. But weekends just kill me. I went out with Carolyn because I was lonely, not to hurt you. I want to wake up next to you, sweetheart. I want to make love to you the second you open your eyes and tell you how beautiful you are. You don't know what I'd give."

She took his face in her hands, tears streaming down her cheeks. "I'm leaving him, then. I have no choice—I can't live with the thought of you and someone else. Let me get some things in order, but it will be soon. I'll find a way to see you on weekends until then, I swear it. Just don't see Carolyn any more. I beg you not to see anybody, but especially not her. She's my friend, Eric—that's a knife in my heart. Promise me."

Eric smiled. "Promise."

* * *

Washington and McDaniel were at their desks when Cowan sent them to the conference room. He appeared minutes later with Hinds County Assistant District Attorney Linda Carman, a leggy brunette in her thirties. She was a graduate of Ole Miss Law School and D.A. Blair Bennett's top assistant.

"Hey, Blair, it's me," she said, projecting her voice as she leaned over a phone in the center of the table. "Detectives Washington and McDaniel and Lieutenant Cowan are alongside.

You're on speaker—update them on Patti St. John."

"Hi, fellas," Bennett said, his voice booming through the static. "Talked to Patti's lawyer. She's with her parents. He advised the family not to speak with you or anyone else about the case—I take that to mean she halted communication with Darren Clarke. Tell me where we stand on him."

The men exchanged glances. Washington summarized today's visit to Clarke and recapped Ford's description of the crime scene. Bennett cursed his cell connection, which wavered before strengthening.

"I know Ford is no saint, Counselor . . ."

A snort. "I need corroboration, Detective. I don't need the likes of Parker Ford as my star witness."

"But if he ID's Clarke . . ."

"His word against Clarke's? I can't take that to trial." A long moan, which was audible despite the acoustics of the cell connection. "Let me think about a photo lineup for Ford. I'm on my way to a meeting with the St. John family lawyer, and I'll get back with you as soon as it's done. Continue your case summary for me. I know we'll get an indictment on Ford, and possibly Gayle Kennedy." A chuckle. "I watched these women each night on the news and it never occurred to me that one would want to kill the other."

*   *   *

Darren Clarke sat in his living room and watched baseball with the sound muted. A bluesy Eric Clapton CD played on the stereo. He drank imported beer and brooded, wondering if he wanted to fool with the Atlanta trip at all. He barely knew Shawn's old friends, and it wasn't like he would get a hug from Jack and Leigh Forrest.

His cell rang. He muted the music and grabbed it, expecting Patti. He scowled when his news director spoke. He paced around the room, then stopped and hung his head.

"All right. If he absolutely, positively won't do it, I'll come in."

"Darren, I'm sorry. I know this is a horrible time for you and that you're trying to get away. But he has food poisoning—it isn't a matter of him not wanting to do it. Hell, I'd do it myself if I could run the equipment."

"Forget it," he said, slamming his empty beer bottle into the trash. "Let me finish packing and I'll come do the freakin' show. Then maybe I can leave in peace."

* * *

Still upset after leaving Redding, Claire drove aimlessly toward Jackson and spotted a package store just off Lakeland Drive as she reached the city limits. She sat in front of the store for several minutes, then went inside. She emerged with a fifth of Jack Daniels in a paper bag. The clerk asked for her driver's license, and he still wasn't convinced she was legal when he sold her the whiskey. Claire couldn't have cared less.

I have no friends.

Tears welled in her eyes as she drove across the spillway in Rankin County. The water was crystal clear, and sailboats dotted the horizon as far as the eye could see. On the other side of the bridge were the fishermen who inhabited the area nearly all year. Claire paid no attention. She was contemplating how her whole life revolved around two men; she was married to one and spent every waking moment thinking about the other.

She was talking to herself when she remembered a reservoir-area realtor, a girl from Jackson with whom she had a class in college. They crossed paths again when Claire and her husband were looking for a house, and plans were made to have lunch and keep in touch. The realtor didn't follow up when they bought from someone else, and Claire quickly forgot about her. She dug through her purse in the parking lot of a convenience store and found the girl's card. Her hopes were dashed when she reached the voice mail. There was no point in leaving a message.

She went inside the store and bought an oversized soft-drink cup and ice, filling it with Diet Coke. Talking to herself about the differences between Eric and her husband, she drove back across the spillway and wound along a parkway into a series of upscale subdivisions. One encircled a lake, with substantial lots and plenty of privacy for each family fortunate enough to be out there. The last lot was under construction and backed up to a dense expanse of woods, and Claire pulled off the road and cut the engine. It was quiet and peaceful, with the sounds of crickets and young children in the distance. She cracked the window and mixed the whiskey with the soft drink, taking a good, long drink. It burned her throat, but she sipped again.

*   *   *

Carolyn lit a cigarette and paced through her small house. Was it worth calling Eric? Maybe she should have dropped in on him after all. But they'd only been out once. Most men she knew fled if they perceived pressure, and she didn't need to push. Best not to worry about it. The phone rang, startling her. It was Jim Yarbrough.

"Hate to do this to you. I just heard from Claire Bailey. She's sick, so I need you to work tomorrow morning."

Carolyn scowled. "And report the rest of the day, I assume. Is there a backup plan in case she's out several days?"

"She thinks it'll pass pretty quick. I'm sorry, Carolyn. I wouldn't ask if we weren't in ratings—we need our best people on the air. I'll do everything I can to get you out at a decent hour tomorrow since you'll still have to anchor this weekend."

"That was my next question."

"Can't do that—we need our best people on the air. Hang in there. We'll get through sweeps and get you out of here for a week."

"Okay," she said quietly. "We'll make it work."

"Thank you—I mean it. And you've worked with Redding before. Good guy."

She frowned as she hung up. An hour ago Claire was happily shoveling down a rich meal, and now she was too sick to work? The food hadn't bothered Carolyn at all, other than eating too much. She did recall a trip to the bathroom, and Claire was in a bad mood when she returned. Maybe she was ill, but the venom at her husband was totally out of character. Carolyn now regretted the entire evening. In addition to muddling things with Eric, Claire had raised a sliver of doubt about her stability by mentioning the anti-depressants. Could a scene at the church have gotten out of hand?

Something else hit her. She would have the run of the newsroom depending upon how early she wanted to drag herself to the station, and there might be an opportunity to nose around Shawn's cubicle. Although Sewell and Yarbrough had certainly gone through it by now, perhaps something interesting had been left behind. Ditto for Gayle's desk—her adrenaline surged at the thought of finding something crucial.

She sat and thought. The overnight producer was supposed to be in at midnight, but the master control operator told Eric that she arrived anywhere from two to three each morning. Might be worth sneaking in around twelve-thirty. Wouldn't take long to poke around, and she could sleep several hours before beginning her marathon day. She changed clothes and stretched out on the floor of her bedroom, beginning a series of yoga exercises which would hopefully relax her enough to nap before her first visit to the station.

* * *

Cowan strolled out to McDaniel's desk. Washington was on his feet, giving his input as McDaniel worded a description in their case summary.

"Bennett just called. We need to set up a photo lineup for Ford. He's on his way from the lockup. And the St. John family and their lawyer will be here in an hour."

McDaniel booted up a networked computer and entered Darren Clarke's name and address. A moment later an image of his driver's license appeared. McDaniel cropped the picture until only the face was left and printed it. Washington mentioned an officer about Clarke's age with dark hair, and McDaniel followed the same procedure. He printed a picture of his cousin a minute later. Washington dug up a pair of men from open cases who fit the description, leaving one face for the six-person lineup. They agreed on Jim Yarbrough and mounted the images on a sheet of printer paper. Cowan and a desk sergeant escorted Ford to the conference room. He was in cuffs and an orange jumpsuit.

"Let's do better than that thing you guys call a bed," he said, panning the group with a grin. "Especially since I scratched your backs in such a big way."

No one responded. The desk sergeant pointed Ford to a seat and left with Cowan to listen over the speaker. Washington placed the lineup in front of him. McDaniel, who moments ago had placed fresh batteries in his tape recorder, set the unit alongside and nodded at Washington.

"All right, Parker," Washington said over his shoulder. "You're looking for the man that you claim attacked you in Shawn Forrest's apartment Saturday night, just before midnight. There's no hurry. Take a good look at all six and tell us if you see him. We want a positive identification. If he isn't in this group, let us know."

Ford glanced up a second later. "I told you it wasn't Yarbrough."

"Look at the other five, then."

Ford spent a long moment on the photo in the top right corner—McDaniel's cousin—then panned the page. He jerked back, then leaned close again.

"I'll be damned. This dude right here," Ford said, pointing to Clarke.

Washington shot a glance at McDaniel. "Take all the time you need. We can't help you if you aren't sure."

Ford turned. "He wore glasses at dinner, but he wasn't wearing them at Shawn's place." He tapped the picture. "That's him, man. Bet my life on it. Give me a couple of minutes with him and I'll wipe the floor with his sorry ass."

* * *

Patti St. John was clad in a purple Ralph Lauren button-down and faded jeans. Her eyes were on the floor as her lawyer led her into the conference room. Her parents remained outside the glass and stood next to Cowan, poised to listen over the speaker. Cowan huddled with Washington and McDaniel before Patti arrived, explaining that she would plead to an accessory after the fact to murder charge in exchange for her testimony against Clarke. The lawyer, a bearded man in his fifties, talked quietly to Patti and got her seated. He introduced himself to the detectives and sat next to her. McDaniel placed the recorder in the middle of the table.

"Tell us exactly what happened, Miss St. John," Washington said gently. "Start at the beginning, and take your time."

Patti spoke in a small voice and kept her eyes on the table. Jamie rode to Jackson with them in Clarke's car, and Clarke dropped the girls at the mall and went to dinner. The plan was to pick them up after the movie and meet up with Jamie's boyfriend at a reservoir club.

"We had an hour with nothing to do because he was still at work," Patti said. "Darren took us to Shawn's apartment. Jamie and I felt funny about being there, but he said not to worry about it. We all had a glass of wine—he said his wife was a drunk and didn't need it. He wanted to make love, and Jamie snooped while we were in bed."

Washington frowned. "You're saying you and Darren were in bed with Jamie in the apartment?"

Patti blushed fiercely. "Darren told Jamie to watch TV and shut the door. When we came out, Jamie was looking at this note. Darren grabbed it away and asked where she got it. She said it fell out of the phone book when she was looking up a number."

"What did the note say?"

"It was a love letter, basically. To Shawn, from the guy Darren thought was sleeping with her."

"You get a name?"

"No, but I heard Atlanta mentioned. He thought it was an old boyfriend. Anyway, we went to the reservoir, and Darren was in his own world and wouldn't talk. I wanted to go back to Hattiesburg and get his mind off her, but we were stuck with Jamie because she rode with us, and her boyfriend got mad because he only sees her on weekends and assumed she was staying over. Jamie argued with him and left with us. Darren went back to Shawn's place—wanted to find anything else which proved she was cheating. We pulled into the parking lot, and at that moment Shawn was being helped up the stairs by two people he'd seen at dinner. She was blitzed and couldn't walk."

"Describe them."

"The girl was short and blond, a few years older than me. Slender—tight jeans and a black leather jacket. The man had dark hair—Darren's age or a little older. He was in slacks."

"Would you be able to identify them?"

"Not sure about him, but definitely her."

"Then what happened?"

"We stayed in the car and waited. They weren't inside five minutes. Walked right past us, got in their car and left. Then we went up there. The wine glasses were still there, but now there were candles. Shawn was lying on the couch giggling, and you could smell the alcohol—I'm not sure she knew anyone was there. Darren went to her bedroom and started through the closet, and

Jamie and I followed. There was a knock on the door, and we all froze. Shawn was giggling her head off, but she got the door open and we heard some guy. It was obvious what he wanted, and Darren got this look on his face—he whispered that the guy had been at dinner. They went at it right there on the couch."

Washington frowned. "Who did what on the couch? I'm not following you."

Patti looked away. "The guy from dinner had sex with Shawn right there in the living room."

"And where were you and Darren and Jamie while this was happening?"

"In Shawn's bedroom." She glanced at her lawyer, who nodded. "I've never seen anyone so angry. Darren wanted a camera, but we couldn't find one. Then he walked out there. He motioned for me to stay back, but there was no way. Jamie was right behind me."

"Tell us exactly what you saw, Miss St. John."

She made a face. "They had just finished, and she was lying there on the couch mumbling to herself and giggling. He was this mangy, long-haired guy with a pony tail. Cologne from here to Hattiesburg. Had this little grin as he buttoned his shirt. Darren walked up behind him, and when the guy turned around Darren punched his lights out. He went down like a ton of bricks."

"Then what?"

"I thought Darren had really hurt him, but Jamie made sure he was breathing. Then Darren dragged him into the hall." A long pause, which ended when the lawyer placed a gentle hand on her shoulder. "Then he looked at Jamie and me. 'Jamie, you go keep an eye on him. Patti, come here.'"

"Explain as completely as you can, Miss St. John," Washington said. "This part is very important."

Patti closed her eyes for a moment, then looked up. "Shawn was trying to stand. She couldn't talk sense at all. She started to fall right onto the coffee table, and Darren caught her. She tried to slap him, but she was so drunk she couldn't have hurt a flea. Then she started to get sick—made these horrible noises—and was passing out right there in his arms."

"When he said, 'Patti, come here,' what did he ask you to do?"

"He laid her out on the couch and told me to grab her ankles." A long pause. "Then he took one of the couch cushions and told me to hold her legs. I turned my head—it was awful."

"Did you see Darren try to kill her?"

"No, I was looking away. That's what I assumed he was going to do," she said, tears forming in her eyes. The lawyer patted her shoulder. "It was so horrible. I could hear her getting sick. It seemed like it took forever, but I guess it was only a few seconds." She paused, taking a deep breath. "I can still see her face when I turned around. Her cheeks were stuffed full."

"Was she breathing?"

"No," Patti said quietly. "Darren said not to move until he was sure she was gone."

"Then what happened?"

"There was a picture of them in the shelves, and he broke it and put Shawn's hand on the edge of the frame. He told us to leave everything else like it was and get the hell out of there."

Washington walked around the table and glanced over McDaniel's shoulder. Without looking up, McDaniel wrote *Did she fight back?* Washington returned to his seat.

"How much of a fight did Shawn put up while this was happening, Patti?"

Patti looked at her hands. "Very little."

"Tell us about leaving the apartment."

"Jamie panicked when the long-haired guy started to wake up. She was looking for her keys, and by then Darren and I were in the doorway. I said, 'Your keys are in your purse, and it's in the car, Jamie! Let's go!'"

Jamie, let's go! Washington glanced at McDaniel, who nodded discreetly.

"Then what?"

"Jamie was crying and said she wanted to see her boyfriend. She swore to Darren she wouldn't say anything. He agreed to drop her at her boyfriend's place, and we drove back to Hattiesburg."

"Did Darren talk about what happened when you were alone with him?"

"He said the pony-tailed guy would take the fall—it would look like he raped and killed her. Darren said he might get the death penalty."

"So there was no stop at the sorority house, and Jamie didn't spend the night there?"

A sigh. "No, sir. She spent the night with her boyfriend, and he brought her down the next day. Darren drove me straight to his house, and we spent the night there."

"When was the last time you talked to Darren?"

She glanced at her lawyer. Another nod. "Today. He showed me their insurance papers—she was worth half a million dollars. That's when the light came on. I realized right then how much of a monster he is. I let him make love to me, then sneaked out when he was asleep and called my parents."

"We understand Shawn's funeral is tomorrow in Atlanta. Did he say if he was going?"

"Yes, sir. He said he needed to put in an appearance. We'd planned on going to Gulf Shores this weekend, but I didn't want to get near him after he told me about the insurance money."

The lawyer stood. "Anything else, gentlemen?"

"Last question," McDaniel said. "Did you, Darren or Jamie open Shawn's car at any point that night, or any time since then?"

"The Lexus? No, sir. The only time I saw it was late Saturday night. Nobody touched it."

*　*　*

Cowan spoke with Blair Bennett, then sent Washington and

McDaniel to Hattiesburg. He made a courtesy call to the Hattiesburg Police Department. Two uniformed officers met them at Clarke's house, arriving within minutes of the detectives.

"He isn't here," Washington said to the cops, glancing at the dark house and closed garage. "We've already been around back. No lights are on, and it's locked up tight. My partner just tried the TV station, and they said he got called in. You know where we're headed?"

The station was east of town in an elevated, rural area twenty minutes from Clarke's home. Transmitters and satellite dishes loomed in the distance. A red beacon shimmered from the top of the tallest tower and competed with the stars in the clear night sky. The older cop led them around to the back of the building, where a variety of station vehicles and other cars were in sight. A large, well-lit room beckoned. The glass door was locked, but Washington spotted a young woman passing through with a stack of papers in her hand and rapped on the door. Eyes wide, she approached and let them inside the newsroom. As in Jackson, television monitors were mounted high along a wall, and a sea of desks and computer terminals spread out before them.

"We need Darren Clarke," Washington said.

"We're in the middle of the newscast."

He displayed his badge. "Right now."

The woman trotted away. Two minutes passed. McDaniel became impatient. He walked around a corner and arrived at the set, where the late news was taking place. He snapped his fingers at Washington. An older white male and a young white female were reading from Teleprompters, and a husky man behind a studio camera got McDaniel's attention and stopped him—another ten feet and he would have made his television debut. Washington approached, as did the Hattiesburg cops. The male anchor was heard teasing Meteorologist Darren Clarke's precision forecast. The camera operator started toward them once the commercial break was underway, and the anchors stared in surprise.

"Two minutes, Darren. Mike check," a voice said over the speaker.

"Where's Darren?" Washington said, glancing around.

The female anchor glanced at the green chroma key wall, where Clarke would stand while doing his weather presentation. The director would key his maps and graphics from the control room, giving the illusion that Clarke was actually in front of them.

"Mike check, mike check—one, two, three," Clarke said, emerging and coming to rest in front of the green wall. He was in a dark suit with a white dress shirt. "Somebody gonna frame my shot?"

"You frame the shot," Washington said to the cameraman, who wasn't sure what to do. Clarke whirled and stared. "Hi, Mr. Clarke. You do your thing, and we'll talk when you're done."

Clarke stammered through the weather segment, repeatedly glancing off camera. The studio photographer tried to wrap him as his three minutes came and went, but Clarke continued with his presentation. His voice was tight as he finished, and he shook with adrenaline as he joined the anchors for several seconds of awkward banter. The male teased the sports segment, and the sports anchor, who didn't know what was happening, strode toward the set as the commercial break played. He stopped cold when Washington and McDaniel approached.

"Darren Clarke, you are under arrest for the murder of Shawn Forrest," Washington said, his voice carrying the room. There was a gasp. Clarke tried to maintain his cool and muttered that he needed to unclip his microphone. It was wireless, and he placed it on the set next to the hand-held clicker which operated his weather presentation. Then he sprang from the set and tried to dash across the floor. He plowed into the sports anchor, and

McDaniel got his arms around him. Washington grabbed him in a bear hug and forced him to the floor.

"Cuff him, Mac!"

The group stared with open mouths as Clarke was handcuffed while lying on his stomach on the studio floor. A local truck ad played on the studio monitor, then a commercial for a Chinese restaurant.

"One minute to sports," came the voice over the loudspeaker. "Mike check, please."

"You have the right to remain silent," Washington said, standing over Clarke. He was aware of the studio camera being pointed their way. "What you say can and will be used against you in a court of law. You have the right to an attorney. If you can't afford an attorney, one will be provided for you. Do you understand these rights?"

Clarke squirmed and said nothing. The anchors looked around nervously. The young sports anchor shrugged, then tested his microphone and announced that he was ready.

"Sports in thirty," came the voice from the loudspeaker. This time there was an edge to it. "We have a newscast to do, folks, and we're in ratings. I refuse to come out of commercials with dead air, so everybody get in position and let's go."

"Get him on his feet," Washington said. The Hattiesburg officers yanked Clarke into a standing position. His jacket had been torn in the skirmish, and there was dirt on his shirt and droplets of blood from a small cut on his chin. His makeup was smeared. "Do you understand your rights, Mr. Clarke?"

Clarke nodded. The sports anchor was narrating Atlanta Braves highlights as he was escorted from the building.

* * *

The long-haired Channel Five master control operator was smoking a cigarette on the back steps of the newsroom when

Carolyn arrived. He was a strange bird, a white college kid who wore nothing but black and rarely spoke to anyone. She forced a smile as she entered and found the cleaning crew in the final stages of their night's work. She walked discreetly down the hall and stuck her head in the break room, then passed through the studio before arriving at her desk. She booted up her computer and checked e-mails, wanting to look busy when the operator walked back through. Soon she heard doors slamming on the ancient van parked in front of the building. The cleaning crew was gone a moment later, and the operator was at his post in the control room. It appeared to be only the two of them in the building, and she had the newsroom to herself.

She stood, then frowned. Yarbrough's office, always locked when he wasn't there, stood open. The lights were off. She started to enter, then held back. She glanced over her shoulder and stepped around to Shawn's cubicle. Removing a paper towel from her jeans, she tried the desk drawers. All were locked. There were no personal items on the desk or in the cubicle. She accidentally bumped the computer, activating the station screen saver. She cursed herself and scooted back to her desk, hoping the operator wouldn't walk through and see that Shawn's computer was on.

Gayle's desk beckoned. She glanced around, then tugged on the thin middle drawer. It opened and revealed pens, pencils, paper clips and loose change. The station handbook and a Colonial calendar were the only items in the large tray.

The two drawers on the left side of the desk were locked, as was the top right drawer. But the bottom drawer almost opened. She jiggled it, again glancing over her shoulder, and felt something give. She tugged, and a second later it popped open. Her heart beating faster, she sifted through manila folders which contained story notes and media contacts. Nothing caught her eye. She pushed past the last folder and spotted a purse in the back. Glancing around again, she hoisted it out of the drawer and riffled through it. Standard anchor paraphernalia—hair spray, brushes, makeup and perfume. She inhaled and recognized the scent Gayle wore at work.

She replaced the purse and was closing the drawer when something in the last manila folder caught her eye. The folder had no label and contained one sheet. She found herself staring at a pair of book covers which had been mimeographed and sat side by side: Jim Yarbrough's head sat atop Bill Clinton's body on the book *Dereliction of Duty,* and Gayle's face had replaced Hillary Clinton's on the cover of *Living History.* Gayle's hair and smile matched those of the former first lady perfectly, while Yarbrough had a golf tee in his mouth and a grim look on his face. A copier had been used to create the finished product, and the words *First the newsroom—then the White House* were in red sharpie marker on the bottom.

Carolyn giggled and looked over her shoulder to make sure no one was in sight. Hardly a work of art, but it was clever and would have drawn laughs on the bulletin board. She wondered how long it had been in Gayle's drawer and if Yarbrough had a copy. She glanced toward his open door, then back at the sheet. Maybe it hadn't been displayed because the message implied that the two of them were a team—someone could interpret favoritism on the part of Yarbrough. If that was the case it wasn't getting Gayle far, since Shawn had asserted herself and claimed the five o'clock show a few weeks ago. If nothing else, it indicated at least a casual friendship. But Yarbrough tried hard to be liked and may have sold her on taking part in the concept.

She heard a stirring across the way and slid the drawer closed, easing back into her seat. A few seconds later the master control operator walked through and settled on the back steps for another cigarette. She took the opportunity to visit the engineering area and found a pen flashlight among the hard drives, tape machines and monitors. She had been at her desk less than a minute when the kid returned. He paused and spoke. His voice was soft and ethereal and would have disappeared in the ambient noise during the daytime.

"Why are you up here so late?"

"Claire is sick and I'm anchoring morning show," she said with a yawn. "Usually get to bed about now, so I thought I'd look through tonight's news and see what we're rehashing in the morning besides Gayle's arrest. That way I can come in at the last minute, since I'll report all day."

The kid snorted. "Claire doesn't get here until after five, so the producer's used to it. Of course, she doesn't have room to talk—she didn't get here until three the other day. Our morning show is a joke, and it pisses me off that they get away with not working half the hours they say they do. I told Eric he ought to tell Yarbrough what really goes on, but he's too nice to say anything."

He sidled away. Another cocky kid who thought he knew everything, just like the promotions producer. If he was taking cigarette breaks this frequently, she wouldn't have long to snoop in Yarbrough's office. She darted in and aimed the penlight across his cluttered desk. She doubted anything would be in plain sight and tried the drawers. To her amazement, all opened. She glanced around, certain the cleaning crew forgot to lock up after vacuuming the room. The previous crew was fired after Sewell's door was left open one night.

The middle drawer was loaded with office supplies. The other four were packed with files and videocassettes. Not knowing where to start, she swung the light across the desk again and spotted his planner. She grabbed it and crouched behind his desk, spreading it on the floor. She glanced through the calendar first, perusing his appointments in the spring months. She kept seeing JGKY, an acronym or initials she didn't recognize. *Que Será Será—6:00* was listed for last Saturday. Good thing Eric hadn't wanted to eat there. She could only imagine how quickly that would have gone around the station.

The back of the planner contained a notepad. Carolyn listened for sounds, then flipped pages. Yarbrough wrote in neat, capitalized block print, and notes from weekly department head meetings went back well into last year. What she would give for an hour at home with his planner. That would be far too risky—the producer could arrive and close his door, leaving her in an impossible position. A better option would be to read in her car, keeping an eye out for headlights in the distance. She would have enough of a head start to return the planner, although she ran the risk of being spotted by the master control operator. Her adrenaline flowed as she took in Yarbrough's notes from March 21:

- *February ratings to arrive next week*
- *February sales strong after poor January; March close to expectations so far*
- *Consultant considering new graphic look for all affiliates*
- *Consultant says Claire dreadful . . . wants new morning anchor for May . . . talk to Carolyn*
- *Jack wants Shawn to stay . . . offering eighty . . . Shawn taking five show . . . Gayle noon only*

Carolyn's mind spun. The last thing she wanted was to get up at three-thirty each day, and she wouldn't be able to face her friend. But it obviously didn't come to pass—Claire was still on board. And there was Shawn's huge contract in black and white. Who had blabbed? Shawn herself, or had one of the managers confided in someone with loose lips? Interesting to note that Jack Forrest himself engineered her stay. She wondered if he was in on Gayle being removed from the five.

She turned the page and brushed against something in a zipped pocket. She opened it and found a folded sheet of paper and a photograph. Her breath caught as she stared at a three by five of a nearly naked Gayle Kennedy. Wearing only black panties and a devilish smile, Gayle held a sign in front of her which obscured her breasts and read JGKY in bold lettering. An unmade king size bed with an antique canopy was in the background. Where the hell had that been taken, and what was Gayle doing? She took in the sheet, a mimeographed *Playboy* magazine cover with Gayle's head on a voluptuous model's body. It was reproduced the same way as the page Carolyn found in her desk. At the bottom of the sheet was a message in the same red sharpie marker:

Since I'm too short to model, this will have to do!
Love, Jackie

Jackie? That made no sense. Carolyn stared at the photo, trying to get an idea of where it might have been taken. She flipped back to the calendar and noted the JGKY entries. They dated back to last year, and it didn't take a genius to realize Yarbrough and Gayle were involved. She remained there, unsure what to do, then decided to copy the photo and the sheet. Then she would put the planner away and get the hell out of his office.

She cocked her ear and heard nothing, then got to her feet and crept through the newsroom. The copier was adjacent to the engineering room. She ran copies of the picture and the page, then retraced her steps. No one in sight. She put the duplicates on her desk and darted into Yarbrough's office. Kneeling down, she replaced the originals in the pocket and zipped it. She closed the planner and placed it exactly where she found it. All that remained was to return to her desk. She was starting out of Yarbrough's office when a voice nearly stopped her heart.

"Carolyn? What are you doing in here?"

* * *

It was Samantha Yarbrough. She flipped on the fluorescent light and looked at Carolyn with a quizzical expression.

176

"Looking for last night's scripts," Carolyn said, thinking fast. "I have to work—Claire's sick."

"I heard. And Taryn quit, so I'm producing the show. She just called Jim."

Carolyn stepped into the newsroom. She lingered ten feet from her cubicle, not wanting to call attention to the sheets which lay face up on her desk.

"What do you mean, she quit?"

Samantha heaved a sigh, nearly bringing Carolyn to her knees with bad breath. She was in tattered pink sweat bottoms and a Hard Rock Café t-shirt, obviously roused minutes ago from the depths of sleep. Her eyes were bloodshot, and her hair was hopelessly askew.

"She said she needed the rest of the week off and wouldn't say why. Jim told her they could talk in the morning but said she absolutely had to work tonight. She said she wasn't coming in and hung up." She shook her head. "I have trouble sleeping, and it really messes up my constitution to be awakened suddenly and have to run around and think. But here I am. And here you are." She gestured at Yarbrough's office. "How'd you get in?"

"It was open."

"Cleaning people been here?"

"Just left," Carolyn said, knowing they might be replaced. But she hadn't left the damned door open and wasn't about to take the fall for it. "Thought I'd get a head start on the show, since this is about when I usually crash. Planned to roll in around five, but I can get here as early as you need."

Samantha started for the cubicle shared by the team of producers. "Go home and get some rest. If you can get here by five-fifteen, we'll make it work. Jim said you'd be in the field all day."

Carolyn thanked her, then grabbed the pages on her desk and stuffed them in her purse. Her heart didn't slow down until she was off the property.

* * *

The last clear memory Claire had was of an older couple feeding bread crusts to ducks across the lake as the sun disappeared. There were hazy, distant images, including a snippet of angry car horns as she vomited. As she came to, the stench on her clothes and interior of her car brought her head and stomach to a boil. She got her door open and fell to the ground, heaving yet again. She caught her breath, then struggled to her feet and tried to get her bearings. The sky was as dark as coal, and the car was embedded in a thicket of brush and small trees adjacent to the north entrance of Eric Redding's apartment community. She glanced at her watch and couldn't read the dancing red numerals.

"Eric?"

She staggered toward the building closest to her. A chocolate lab came trotting up and sniffed, then followed her. Beginning to cry, she yelled for the dog to leave her alone, drawing sharp whistles from its owner across the way. She climbed a flight of steps, at one point nearly losing her balance and falling, and rapped on the first door she reached.

"Eric?"

Nothing happened. She knocked harder. A baby began crying inside, and a light came on. The door was opened by an old woman. A young woman stood behind her and glowered.

"Eric?"

Both women groaned. "You have the wrong apartment, miss. And you just woke up my sick daughter," the young woman said, slamming the door.

Claire sobbed and knocked again. "Eric? Help me."

The door flew open. The young woman stepped forward with an aimed finger, then flinched back at the smell.

"Eric doesn't live here, damn you! Now get out of here before we call the cops!"

*   *   *

"Norris."

"We have to talk. Right now."

A long, low moan. "Davis, do you realize what time it is?"

"This is important. Meet me at the Waffle House at County Line and the interstate in twenty minutes."

Norris laughed, which became a coughing fit. "Have you been drinking?"

A pause. "No, James. I know what time it is, and I need to talk to you."

"All right. I'll be there."

*   *   *

Carolyn was eating an omelet when Norris staggered into the diner. A plate of scrambled eggs, bacon, grits and hash browns awaited him. The smell of fried meat hung in the air, and country music played on a juke box across the way. The place was half-full and afforded a view of the interstate. A weary waitress forced a smile as she dropped off the check.

"Now, Davis. What couldn't wait until morning?"

She recounted tonight's escapades. Norris sated his appetite, drank milk and began to look and sound more like himself.

"I know Claire's your friend, but she's a kid and you've always mothered her. To the rest of us, she's a whiny, immature brat. I don't know how the hell Eric puts up with her each morning. Next time you see her, ask her point blank what happened at dinner. You'll know right away if it's race. And if it is, she's not your friend and you don't need her in your life."

He sopped up the last bit of egg with a sliver of toast and drained his milk. She slid the photograph of Gayle and the doctored copy in front of him. He nearly choked.

"Damn. Safe to say you weren't supposed to find this."

"If she's in bed with Yarbrough, he may have had something to do with Shawn."

"Maybe. But you kicked open an ant hill by getting caught. No way Samantha bought your noise about scripts—I guarantee she'll tell him. And it wouldn't be a big deal if he weren't in Gayle's pants. But he must be."

"You think Samantha knows about them? A lot of women put up with that, Norris."

"No, I don't. It's one thing to be in denial, but no woman in her right mind is going to knowingly let her husband sleep with one of his subordinates while she's working with both of them. She might as well pull up a chair and break out the camcorder."

Carolyn got to her feet and left a tip. Norris followed her out.

"Thanks for coming. I just needed an ear. Go back to bed."

"Get some sleep, kid. Drive safe."

FRIDAY

It was well after midnight by the time Clarke was booked. Washington's cell rang. He assumed it was his wife, with whom he'd touched base on the way to Hattiesburg.

"Detective, it's Carolyn Davis from Channel Five," she said, her voice shaky. "I'm sorry to bother you this late. I was going to call the police . . ."

"What is it? Where are you?"

"Parked in front of my house."

"Burglar?"

"No, sir. Something is on the door of my carport. I was going to call you tomorrow because we need to talk, but I'm afraid this has something to do with it. I'm sorry about calling so late—I know I woke the whole house. Could you send somebody out here?"

"I'm at the office—we've had a late night. Hang on a second." He conferred with McDaniel, who promised to coordinate Clarke's transfer to the lockup. "You sit tight. I'm on my way."

* * *

Washington radioed for backup. A Clinton patrol car pulled onto Carolyn's street seconds after he did. A lone white officer strode up to Washington. The men conferred and split up, searching the yard with flashlights and drawn service revolvers. An inspection of the house followed.

"Nobody," Washington said to Carolyn after sending the officer on his way. "Let's have a look."

A steak knife was jammed into the wooden carport door and held a post-it note in place. A message was displayed in jagged, handwritten scrawl:

WATCH YOUR BACK

Carolyn puffed on a cigarette and paced.

"Anyone you can think of who might want to hurt you, Miss Davis? A co-worker? A boyfriend? Somebody you did a story on who might not have taken a shine to you?"

"I'm divorced, and my ex is in Atlanta. We parted on good terms. I don't have a boyfriend. Could be some crazy who's following me."

Washington punched numbers on his cell phone. Jessica would return the page and awaken Bernie, who would bring the van. He explained that the crime lab was coming and that a police report would be filed.

"Let's walk through and see if anything has been disturbed. Then we'll sit down and talk."

Carolyn searched the house and found nothing out of order. She made coffee and lit another cigarette. Washington sat on the couch and took notes as she recapped the evening. He grunted at the photograph of Gayle, then stared at the superimposed photo.

"Nobody knew about them?"

She shook her head. "I'm amazed. If we worked as hard at news as we do at gossip, the competition wouldn't have a chance." A nervous titter. "I told you Que Será Será was on his calendar for last Saturday. Thank God Eric didn't want to eat there."

Washington gazed at her. "So I assume this photo is what you would have shared with me tomorrow. This is twice you've turned over potential evidence against Gayle Kennedy, and now there's a knife in your door. You're a reporter—who could have put it there?"

She took her time. "You took Gayle into custody. Has there been an escape?"

"No. She's been at Raymond all night."

"I'm sure Samantha told Jim I was in his office, and maybe he freaked. But he's my boss, Detective. All he has to do is fire me."

A long pause. "We're off the record now. You don't tell a soul what I'm about to tell you. You do, and your station can kiss goodbye any cooperation it gets from the department as long as I'm around. With me?"

"Yes, sir."

"An arrest was made tonight. Shawn's husband, Darren Clarke, was picked up in Hattiesburg."

Carolyn's jaw fell.

"You mentioned Que Será Será. Remember when we asked if Yarbrough and Shawn ever socialized? Six people had dinner together at Que Será Será Saturday night: Jim and Samantha, Darren and Shawn, and Gayle and a date who isn't in television. Strange, huh?"

She nodded, trying to picture the scene. Washington recapped Patti's statement and described Shawn's toxicology results. Carolyn sat in stunned silence.

"Ford raped her. Then Clarke beat him up, suffocated Shawn and tried to make it look like Ford did it—that's according to Clarke's girlfriend. But somewhere along the way Shawn suffered cardiac arrest. The medical examiner hasn't gone on record with an official cause of death, which might mean he's considering poisoning. And since she had a prescription for the sleeping pills in her blood, he can't rule out an overdose."

Carolyn's eyes widened. "Meaning she could have killed herself?"

A bemused smile. "I'm glad I don't have to make that call. But it appears that two different groups may have been trying to kill her. Darren's girlfriend said it was insurance money. Very believable—he gets rid of Shawn and gets rich, and he and his honey can get on with their lives. Meanwhile, Yarbrough and Gayle were taking home a drunk party guest. Very believable. But when you throw the affair into the mix, then add the mutual resentment they had of Shawn, that spells motive. Far as that knife is concerned, somebody may have had the wrong house. But I'm thinking it's someone you work with."

"But like I said, it would be a lot safer to just fire me."

"Not if you might talk. And I'm not convinced it's him. When did you leave the station?"

"Twelve-fifteen."

"You called me at one-thirty. That's an hour and fifteen minutes. Would that have given Samantha time to drive from the station to here and back?"

Carolyn gasped.

"We took fingerprints from all of them, so we'll know right away if we get something halfway decent. May not be either one of them, Miss Davis. But I wouldn't rule anything out."

Bernie's van rolled up then. Norris was right behind in his Toyota pickup. He and Carolyn watched as Bernie bagged and tagged the items. Washington sent him on his way, then made a call on his cell phone from her front yard. He stepped inside a minute later.

"We ran Gayle's address in the computer. I assume the first three initials of that acronym are Jacqueline Gayle Kennedy."

Carolyn raised an eyebrow. "She's Jackie? And could the last letter stand for Yarbrough?"

"Sounds like it. One mystery solved, plenty more to go. We'll be in touch."

She collapsed into Norris's arms, her facade crumbling. He squeezed hard.

"You're safe now. The Clinton cop will swing by every hour or so, and I'm staying. I can sleep on the couch, or I can sit in a chair in your bedroom doorway all night. And I'll follow you to work."

She groaned. "I'd forgotten about that. Of all the times for Claire to be sick."

"Get ready for bed. I'm going to heat some milk, and I'll hold your hand until you're asleep. I won't let anything happen to you. And don't forget to set your clock."

She smiled through her tears and kissed his cheek.

*   *   *

Carolyn slept ninety minutes before the clock radio came on. Norris checked the carport when she was ready to leave and found nothing. He followed her to the station, then returned to her house to grab a few more hours of sleep. He said to call him before eight to make sure he was up.

"There she is," Samantha said, a steaming cup of coffee nearby. She gave Carolyn a big smile. "I was hoping Claire would come in and I could tell you to stay home, but no such luck."

Carolyn looked Samantha over. She was energized after a night of caffeine but radiated nothing which sent up red flags. "I'll do the best I can. Never worked morning show."

Samantha held up a copy of *The Jackson Times*. Gayle's arrest was front page news. Carolyn gasped. Channel Five had broken the story last night, but seeing Gayle's picture in the paper drove the shock home.

"Rick is on his way to Atlanta this morning, and he and Jim have already talked. Jim just called me, and we updated our copy from last night. We can only assume all four stations will have it this morning, so we'll hit it hard."

Carolyn booted her computer and glanced over the rundown. The newscast lasted ninety minutes, but the top stories were repeated every half hour. The show was heavy on weather and guests, and Redding had volunteered to handle both interview segments. Didn't sound terribly taxing, other than the lack of sleep and obscene hour. Her desk line rang. It was Yarbrough.

"Just wanted to make sure you were up and running. I know the situation with Gayle is awkward, but there's no other way. Samantha probably told you that Rick is on his way to Atlanta for the funeral. The Colonial station there will have a crew and get a standup from Rick, then shoot it over here in time for the noon show. Plan on doing the noon, Carolyn, and some sort of package to update the story. I should be able to send you home after that."

Carolyn strolled out to the set, her mind more at ease. If Jim Yarbrough had malice on his mind, he was an awfully good actor. Redding was using the remote clicker to run through his weather presentation. He gave her a big smile.

"Eric, take over if I screw up too much or fall asleep."

"Just don't say on the air that Gayle hated Shawn's guts because she stole the five from her."

Carolyn laughed. "Ain't that the truth. So where's our buddy Claire?"

"She called last night and said she was throwing up. With folks dropping like flies, last thing we need is her making the rest of us sick."

He seemed as natural as he had last weekend. She tested her microphone and read over her copy a final time, preparing to tell the viewers that Gayle Kennedy had been arrested in connection with the death of Shawn Forrest.

* * *

A pine cone landed inches from Claire's face and roused her with a jolt. Her first sensation was a pounding in her head, as if a post-hole digger was loose inside her cranium. Her eyes widened as she realized where she was—in a fetal position on the ground next to her car, the door of which was open. She got gingerly to her feet, gasping at the sight of the BMW ten feet off the road in a clump of brush and trees. The sun was just beginning to rise, so maybe there was a way to get out before a tenant noticed or a cop drove past. She was apparently far enough off the road not to have been seen in the dark.

Vomit was caked on her jeans and shoes and was all over the interior of the car. She panicked as she realized she was missing the newscast, but there was a vague memory of talking to Yarbrough. What had she told him? She didn't remember a thing about getting here, nor did she remember getting sick on herself and wrecking the car. None of that rang a bell at all.

Her heart sank when she climbed into the car. The keys had been in the ignition all night, and the dome light was fuzzy. There was a clicking noise when she tried the engine, and tears immediately filled her eyes. She said a prayer and tried again. This time it coughed, and it turned over a minute later. She tried to back straight out and was almost to the road when her back tires sank in a muddy depression. She did her best to maneuver the car, then gunned it in frustration. The engine howled, but the car lurched backward and into the road, sending a spray of mud in all directions.

It dawned on her that she'd been out all night without a word to her husband—at least she didn't remember talking to him. He would kill her, if he hadn't died of fright. For that matter, the police might be looking for her at this moment. She needed a few minutes before she faced him, and she gassed up and went through a car wash. At least the exterior was clean, even if the interior stunk to high heaven. She would tell her husband she'd driven to Carolyn's house for dinner, gotten sick on the way home and felt too weak to make it the rest of the way. He wouldn't believe it for an instant, but it was more plausible than anything else she could come up with. She turned into her driveway and prayed before opening the garage with a remote. His car was gone. She dashed inside and found a note on the kitchen table.

Claire—

I don't know what's gotten into you, but I'm going to make us an appointment with a marriage counselor. I don't know if I'll ever get over the things you said last night. It sure sounded like you were drunk, which might explain your behavior, but if you were drinking, why? You know we don't drink. What's the matter with you? I'll be at my parents' house tonight. I'm under a lot of stress as it is, and this has only added to it. If you're this unhappy, I sure wish you'd said so, rather than let everything build up and go off on me.

Claire's jaw fell. His parents were in Memphis, so now her alibi might work since he'd left sometime last night and didn't know she hadn't come home. She had no memory of talking to him and shuddered at the possibility of having mentioned Eric. He certainly would have mentioned it in his note, but perhaps he was waiting to confront her in the presence of a marriage counselor. For a fleeting second she had an image of him divorcing her and Eric getting cold feet, but she forced it from her mind. If he had gone to Memphis for the night, it would be mid-morning before he was back. At least she had the house to herself.

She scrubbed the BMW's interior and sprayed air freshener, then showered and started a load of clothes. Already jumpy, she popped her last Xanax and headed for the refrigerator. No Slim-Fast this morning—she needed comfort food. She cut a huge hunk of pecan pie and added a scoop of ice cream, plopping down in front of the morning newscast. The idea was to get her belly full and catch up on sleep. Once rested, she would be in a better position to take stock of her life. The diet could wait.

"Hello, my love," she said, speaking to the television as Redding appeared. "Miss me? I miss you, too. How 'bout we run away and spend the rest of our lives together? You'd like that? Me, too. I'll be right over."

Redding finished his forecast and bantered with Carolyn, who gave him a big smile.

"Don't even think about it, girl. He's mine. M-I-N-E."

She ran the channels but couldn't get her mind off Carolyn and Eric. She finished her pie and flipped back in time to see them seated together at the interview seat. Why was she sitting so damned close to him? Might as well sit in his lap. She shut the television off and paced around the living room, cursing as her blood boiled. She stopped as a wave of nausea hit her, then dashed to the bathroom and lost her breakfast. She wiped her face and collapsed into bed, tears streaming down her cheeks.

* * *

Rod Faber arrived each morning at seven-thirty. He had been at his desk five minutes when the fax machine whirred into life. He sipped coffee and listened as the scanner simultaneously came alive—someone had gassed up at a north Jackson convenience store and booked without paying. Faber rolled his eyes at the wisdom of a drive-off at rush hour. They widened as he read the fax.

"Samantha! Press conference at eleven at Spring Center. An arrest in the Forrest case last night. Where's Carolyn?"

"Here I am," she said, entering the newsroom with a cup of coffee. "What's up, Rod?"

He repeated the information and gestured at the monitor near his desk. The network morning show was on the air. "Rewrite your cut-ins and lead with it—say that a second arrest has been made and that we'll have full coverage at noon, five, six and ten. Plan on going with Norris to the press conference, and maybe to one or both initial appearances in court, depending on when they are."

Carolyn nodded, poker face in place. This was obviously Darren Clarke. Samantha had kept an eye on the competing stations once their show was over and would have screamed if someone else had the story. *The Jackson Times* didn't have a mention of Clarke, either.

She updated her copy, then stuck her head in the weather office. Redding was eating a banana and perusing a major league baseball web site. He was difficult to read. He couldn't have been nicer or more helpful this morning, but nothing had been said which implied interest in a second date. She was coming to terms with the fact that there might not be one.

"Someone else was arrested in the Forrest case."

His eyes widened. He glanced around and lowered his voice. "One of our folks?"

"Press release didn't say. We'll find out in about an hour." A pause. "I'd ask where you were Saturday night, but I already know."

The words were out before she could get them back. She cursed herself internally and awaited his response. He smiled again.

"That's true. I have the receipt from dinner to prove it. Once your schedule settles down, maybe we can catch lunch."

"I'd like that. Let me get back to work."

She waited until she was out of sight before hanging her head. Sure, Eric. Let's do lunch sometime, which will be a nice transition from a date to nothing. That way you'll feel less guilty now that you've decided you aren't interested. Her cell rang then. It was Washington. She trotted through the studio and took the call where the detectives had questioned Gayle the other night.

"Nothing yet on the knife and note. The Forrest case is priority, but this may get a bit of a rush job since it could be connected. So we should know something within twenty-four hours on the prints. Anyway, keep your guard up. And I assume you know about the press conference."

"Fax just came in. We'll be there."

* * *

Carolyn and Norris reached the Hinds County Courthouse before nine. By now the lack of sleep was catching up with her, and she sipped yet more coffee to keep the energy flowing. Norris lingered, setting his gear down on the marble floor near the double doors of the courtroom and joining the banter between the photographers from the competing stations. Eventually they all went inside, and Norris set up his tripod near the back of the room. This was the first year cameras had been allowed in court.

The rows of wooden benches were almost completely devoid of onlookers, although representatives from media outlets all over the state were on hand. Carolyn nodded at several reporters and looked up just in time to see Gayle paraded through the room. She stared, caught in the unreality of watching someone she worked with every day with her wrists cuffed behind her back. Gayle wore no makeup and obviously couldn't fix her hair, and the orange jumpsuit made her look like a common criminal. She kept her eyes on the floor, painfully aware of the stares. Her lawyer stood alongside, a man who looked as young as Gayle.

The judge was an obese white male in his fifties. Sounding bored, he confirmed that Gayle understood why she had been arrested and had legal representation. Bond was set at two hundred fifty thousand dollars, which drew a pained look. Carolyn grimaced while taking notes, thinking of Gayle's father and his hardware store. She might be at the lockup a while. The judge banged his gavel and Gayle was led away, again keeping her eyes on the floor.

"I could have rolled on you and slipped it into a package," Norris said a few minutes later, startling her. Carolyn glanced around, then swore under her breath. She had dozed off with her head hanging backward, and she grabbed her notebook and tried her best to assume her dignity.

"Would anybody say anything if I napped in here until they bring out Clarke?"

Norris snickered. "The court wouldn't, but a photog or two would get it on tape."

She smiled. "Tipped off by you, of course."

"Least I could do, after not tipping them off just now. You'd die if you could have seen yourself, Davis."

She bought a Mountain Dew from a vending machine, desperate to spike her central nervous system for several more hours. She took her seat in the courtroom and tried to stay alert, wanting a good look at Clarke when he arrived. She had just looked up when he was brought into the room. She stared as Norris rolled tape over her shoulder, trying to imagine Shawn Forrest married to this man. Handsome but grim, with dark hair and a nice build. It was rumored that he was cheating. He was also in cuffs and the orange jumpsuit but stared straight ahead, paying no attention to the whispers. He had a lawyer with him, a middle-aged man in a pinstripe suit. The judge asked Clarke in the same bored voice if he understood why he was arrested and confirmed that the man with him was his attorney. The leggy assistant district attorney asked for no bond, and Clarke's attorney howled when the request was granted. The judge ignored him and banged his gavel. Clarke was led away. That was that.

The brief press conference at Spring Center was a touch self-congratulatory, as the spokesman called Washington and McDaniel by name and commended the Mississippi Crime Lab and the Hinds County Sheriff's Department for their cooperation and hustle. Little was said which Carolyn didn't already have after the discussion with Washington, and the barrage of questions from the assembled media largely went unanswered; since the investigation was continuing, further speculation could not be made.

Carolyn had a caffeine headache by the time she reached the station. She and Norris slapped together a ninety-second package which included a pair of sound bites from the police spokesman and a standup Norris shot of her outside the courthouse. Faber had acquired the still shots of Gayle and Clarke as they were booked last night, and he had come up with video of Clarke doing weather in Hattiesburg. The package was rounded out with video of Gayle on the set. It wasn't resume tape material, but it would do.

Yarbrough, Faber and Samantha put together the team coverage. After Carolyn's effort, there was a funeral package sent by the Colonial affiliate in Atlanta which included a gushy sound bite from Sewell. Next were the equally trite comments from members of the Junior League of Jackson, the Metro Jackson Chamber of Commerce and Fifth Street Elementary. Since an official cause of death hadn't been announced, Yarbrough was adamant that they take a female angle—a trio of on-the-street bites from single women were included, and coverage wrapped up with a graphic listing safety tips for single females who lived alone. The final tally was eight minutes of Forrest coverage, which comprised the entire first block of the newscast and easily outdistanced the competition. The other guys were backing away from the story now, and Faber said the approach made sense—after all, if one of the competing anchors had died, viewers would be watching his or her station for the latest information, not Channel Five.

Carolyn got through the show in one piece, thanks in large part to Eric Redding's vending machine run when her blood sugar plummeted. She wolfed down a candy bar while he did the weather and was buoyed enough to last the rest of the way. She considered asking him to lunch, but this wasn't the day—she was starving, not having eaten since meeting Norris at Waffle House, and she was focused on a carry-out plate from the grocery near her house and a long nap. Thoughtful analysis of the situation with Eric wasn't going to take place with her head buzzing from lack of sleep.

Carolyn dutifully recorded the four-second ID's which teased the newscasts at five, six and ten, then trudged to Yarbrough's office. She lingered in the doorway, hoping her body language would be enough to convince him to let her go for the day. The Forrest case would be the lead story all night, barring a breaking story of similar magnitude.

"Nice job," he said, giving her a big smile. "Come in and close the door. Have a seat."

She did, unable to stifle a yawn. He didn't acknowledge it.

"Before I forget, the folks in Hattiesburg told us that Clarke was arrested right there in the studio after he did weather," he said with a laugh. "They rolled on it in the control room and plan to use the footage in a promo if they can disguise Clarke's face enough. Rod mentioned using the video James shot of Gayle as the cops led her away—don't know if you've seen it, but she flipped off the camera. But I told him we had what we needed. Maybe we can play with the video and let promotions use it somehow."

Carolyn nodded, trying her best to remain casual. Did Yarbrough know that she knew about the affair and was trying to goad her into mentioning it? Something else to be analyzed after a long nap.

"Anyway, keep your cell on in case there's anything further about Shawn. Far as this weekend, both days as usual. I know you haven't had a day off in two weeks, but we're in ratings, and Rick and I just don't want Claire on the air any more than necessary. We'll make it up to you. Thanks again for the hard work."

At least she was done for the day, which gave her twenty-four hours until she was due back. She got to her feet, but he motioned her down. He came around and sat next to her. He was three feet away and almost too close—she could smell breath mints.

"Need to talk to you about something. Samantha said the cleaning crew left my door open last night, and that you were in here when she walked in. Mind telling me what you were doing?"

Carolyn's heart raced. She was so tired that she'd forgotten about the incident, and her guard was all the way down. She did her best to appear relaxed.

"Looking for last night's ten o'clock scripts. Like I told her, thought I'd get a jump on this morning's show."

"Why not look in your computer?"

A painfully obvious question, one she should have thought of when crafting the plan. Anyone with a log-in and password could access the newscasts in seconds.

"Easier to grab a handful of scripts, I guess."

"And you didn't bother to check the trash can behind the set? That's where just about every script I've ever seen lands after being read."

Yarbrough's smile was chilly. His outbursts in the past almost seemed rehearsed, something coordinated to curry favor with his bosses. But he was clearly on his own here, shooting from the hip and not likely to let the matter drop. She didn't respond, not wanting to guess whether the cleaning crew had emptied the trash cans behind the set. She hadn't looked there and didn't want to bury herself further by being caught in a lie.

"Look, I'm sorry. I was just trying to . . ."

"Samantha was told you were in Gayle's desk as well."

Great. The weirdo master control operator, slinking around and taking cigarette breaks with little to do, had spotted her and spoken up. And what had Yarbrough just said? *Samantha was told you were in Gayle's desk as well.* The last two words were crucial—did he know she went through his planner, or did he simply know she was in his office?

"Mind telling me what you were looking for?"

"Evidence," she said, thinking quickly. She trained her eyes on the floor, momentarily pleased with herself. Several seconds went by. Carolyn dared look up and found Yarbrough gazing at her. He made a sound, something between a laugh and a snort.

"Let me make something perfectly clear, young lady: You work the assignments we give you, within the understood boundaries of this newsroom. Creative expression is encouraged, and extra effort is appreciated. But you cross a line when you come up here on your own and snoop in the middle of the night. That absolutely won't be tolerated."

Carolyn's first thought was that Shawn Forrest was never chewed out for anything, and here was Yarbrough reaming her a new one based on secondhand information from a dubious source. But she realized he was in a corner. He couldn't go to Sewell, since he would be forced to own up to the affair. And since the affair was with a subordinate who had been arrested in connection to the death of the big boss's daughter, he might never work in television again. Thinking as quickly as her weary mind would allow, she surmised that he was limited to intimidation. She faced him, prepared to apologize and eat whatever serving of crow came her way.

"And this is off the charts," he said, startling her as he snatched a single sheet from his desk. It was a printed e-mail from the internal station program. She read the brief message, her eyes widening in horror. The name of the recipient had been marked out. The time stamp indicated that it had been sent at 5:22 this morning.

Hey ********
I cheered when the cops hauled Gayle away yesterday. Glad to get that cheap whore out of our lives. Yarbrough was pretty funny when it happened, wasn't he? He looked like he was going to go to the mat for her. Everybody sees right

through his pathetic song and dance. With any luck he'll be fired before long, and we'll get things back to the way they used to be when we ran this show. Anyway, let me go since it's showtime in just a minute because Fatso called in sick and I had to get up at this God-awful hour.

Carolyn

Carolyn looked up, already shaking from adrenaline. A glint was in Yarbrough's eye, a sardonic smile on his face.

"Where'd you get this, Jim? Who gave it to you?"

"You realize this is exactly what Shawn Forrest did to Claire Bailey, don't you? And as I remember, you were one of Shawn's most vocal critics. Called her a cancer, I believe."

This threw Carolyn. When the e-mail about Claire's weight circulated two months ago, Yarbrough confronted Shawn in front of the staff. Along with everyone else, Carolyn watched in stunned silence as Shawn fumed aloud and swore to get whoever set her up. She and Norris discussed the matter at length, but not in the presence of anyone else.

"Jim, I never said . . ."

"Rick and I are going to have a long talk. This is very serious, Carolyn. Trust is something that's a given in a small shop like ours, and we're all in big trouble without it."

She got to her feet and aimed a finger. "I didn't send this!"

He stood, never taking his eyes from her. "It has your name on it. Five-twenty-two is right before you'd head out to the set to do the news because Fatso, as you call her, couldn't come in. Talk is cheap, so I'm not surprised you and the others make comments about my job security. But the line about 'getting things back to the way it was when we ran the show' is intriguing. What way was that?"

She slammed her fist on his desk. "I didn't send that, damn it!"

He smiled and shrugged, spreading his arms in an intentionally exaggerated motion designed to drive her over the edge. It almost succeeded, as she came very close to attacking him. She turned away for an instant, willing herself to be calm, then faced him.

"Let me have it," she said, reaching for it. He drew his arm back.

"No way in hell am I going to let you drag an innocent person into this."

She exhaled. There had to be a way to print the e-mail and determine who received it, but she didn't know anyone on the engineering team well enough to risk an explanation. Word would go right to the chief engineer, who would go directly to Yarbrough and Sewell.

"That person's name isn't on it, Jim. Give it to me."

He gazed at her, then strode from his office. He returned a minute later with a copy and closed the door again. They were nose to nose.

"This will be dealt with, Carolyn. Expect a meeting."

Yarbrough opened the door. She stepped past and ignored the curious looks from several people nearby. She grabbed her purse and left without a word.

*   *   *

Eric Redding's apartment community was marketed to single professionals, the majority of whom worked an eight to five day. Since almost nobody was home when he arrived each day, Claire was comfortable with early-afternoon visits. She dropped in a couple of days a week, spending an hour or two before returning home to cook supper for her husband.

She pulled into a visitor's space as he checked his mailbox and casually followed him up the stairs. Once inside, she kicked off her flats and tossed her purse aside without a word, kissing him hard on the mouth. Needing no further encouragement, Redding took her to bed. Afterward he pulled her into his arms, aware that she coveted being held after they made love; she often cried quietly and whispered how much he meant to her. Not this time, however.

"Weren't thinking about Carolyn, were you?"

Redding opened his eyes. Claire's smile was brittle.

"I thought we settled this last night."

Tears welled in her eyes. "I was sick to my stomach watching you with her this morning."

"We were doing the news."

"What if she's interested after last weekend? I wouldn't blame her."

Redding sat up and took her hand. "I know you're hurt, honey. Now please forgive me. There won't be another date. I was going to take her to lunch and tell her I was seeing someone . . ."

"No, Eric!"

". . . but I won't even do that. I'll completely let it drop, okay?" He mussed her hair and smiled. "You have a jealous streak a mile wide, Chocolate."

This was Redding's pet name for her. Her real name was Elaine Claire, which Redding transformed into E. Claire and eventually Chocolate Eclair. She didn't smile.

"I can't share you with anyone. Now promise me again."

He pulled her onto his lap and assured her that there was no one else.

"What gives with you? Earlier you were on your deathbed, and now you're a bundle of nerves."

She sighed. "Took my last Xanax this morning, and it must have come up when I got sick. Earliest I can see my shrink is Monday, which means I have to anchor without it. God only knows how I'll do that. And my husband spent his lunch hour yelling at me. Said he's going back to Memphis to spend the weekend with his parents. He makes me feel so worthless, Eric."

Redding wiped away a tear. "At least you'll have a couple of days without him. Do some writing, and have some pecan pie."

"And see you, I hope . . ."

"Definitely. And call in sick Monday if you haven't seen your doctor, sweetheart. The station won't burn down."

She smiled through her tears. "May write a pair of poems about the men in my life. One about darkness, the other about light. You know which one is yours."

*   *   *

Washington's cell rang as he and McDaniel put the finishing touches on their case summary. It was Carolyn. She described the harrowing encounter with Yarbrough.

"I don't doubt what you're saying, but we can't act on any punishment you think he and Sewell will take against you."

"Detective, this isn't about being fired. He was menacing. It was like I'd found him out, and he was warning me not to come any closer. You said last night it makes a difference that he and Gayle are involved."

"But we have no reason to suspect him of a crime right now. We'll make sure Clinton police keep an eye on your house over the next few nights, but that's all we can do. We need evidence. If his prints are on that knife, he'll be in cuffs."

"Can you at least talk to him?"

"Let me see what I can do. But we can't bring him in unless we tie him to something."

Cowan strolled over and waited until Washington was off the phone.

"Company's coming, fellas. Jamie Fontenot wishes to make a statement. She'll be with her parents and lawyer. They've already cut a deal with Bennett." A pause. "She's getting probation."

"Oh, for God's sake," McDaniel said. "There are days I don't know why we even do this stuff. Why doesn't Bennett just go ahead and let her walk?"

"You can ask Carman yourself when she gets here." Cowan

paused. "And our pal Gayle Kennedy will be stopping by. She doesn't have a deal—just wants to talk."

*   *   *

Jamie admitted to Washington that Allison Shelton was telling the truth about their room at the sorority house being empty Saturday night. Her story with her attorney present matched what Patti told them, right down to the description of Ford's strut through Shawn's living room just before Clarke punched him out. Tears filled her eyes as she described the scene, and she insisted that she went along with him out of fear for her life.

"Tell me again what Darren wanted you to do?" Washington said.

"He dragged the guy he beat up out in the hallway, and he said for me to watch him."

"Did you see Darren try to kill his wife?"

"No, sir. I couldn't see from there."

"What could you hear?"

"I heard his wife get sick, then it was quiet. A minute or two later Patti asked if she was breathing. Darren told her she wasn't."

Jamie said she begged Patti to leave Darren the following day, and that Patti finally saw the light when Clarke revealed the insurance money. Cowan walked the parents and attorney to the elevator and returned with Linda Carman.

"What deal did you guys cut with her, Counselor?" McDaniel said.

"Probation, community service. You sound skeptical, Detective."

"We're not convinced she's the angel she made herself out to be just now."

"I'm not debating that. But this looks like Clarke's show. He takes the fall, and Patti gets three to five years for assisting. Best we can tell, Jamie was the lookout, and her testimony is crucial because it backs what will put Clarke away. I think Blair did the right thing."

Cowan was paged on the overhead system. Carman eased closer.

"Gayle Kennedy's lawyer caught me at the courthouse a few minutes ago. Hinted around, tried to see what I would give him. He doesn't strike me as knowing much law, Detectives—not much at all. Announced that she was holding a lot of cards."

"What did you tell him?" Washington said.

"That we'd see what she had to say," Carman said, grinning. "He was excited and trotted off to call Cowan. I don't know what's about to happen, but Clarence Darrow he ain't."

A minute later Cowan returned with the detention officer, who escorted Gayle Kennedy into the room. Her young lawyer was at her side. He sat next to Gayle and patted her hand. Gayle, dressed in her orange jumpsuit, stared into space. Devoid of the nice clothes and makeup she wore on television, she resembled a rock band groupie after a long night of partying. The rebel posturing was gone; she simply looked exhausted. McDaniel started the recorder and prepared to take notes. Washington sat across from Gayle and smiled.

"So what's on your mind?"

She fixed on a point in the distance and spoke casually, admitting to the affair with Yarbrough. She said he was fed up with Shawn's abuse and furious that he couldn't counter it because of her father. Jack Forrest had pushed to keep Shawn in Jackson, and Shawn's terms included a huge salary increase and the removal of the "little blond cancer" from the five o'clock newscast. Yarbrough had no choice but to acquiesce.

"Did he promise a promotion once you guys were involved?"

A benign smile, offered to the point in the distance. "There wasn't much he could do. He hired me to anchor noon and five, and that's what I did until March. He was livid when he told me

I was coming off the five—that was in private. Shawn walked by the next day and gave me this crap about how it was forced on her and that she hoped we were still friends. She made sure Jim heard it, and he told me that he was ready to resign. But that same night Shawn walked out abruptly after the six o'clock news and left her computer on and desk unlocked, as if she had to split because of an emergency. Jim kept an eye on her cubicle and waited until everyone had cleared out for dinner, then went through her desk."

Washington nodded for her to continue.

"He found a bottle of Ambien and copied the information, pretty sure that Samantha took the same thing. She does."

The detectives shared a glance.

"Then he wrote the e-mail about our morning anchor and sent it from Shawn's terminal. It was mean, but it was meant to get Shawn in trouble. He called a meeting the next afternoon and ripped Shawn a new one in front of everybody. There was a problem a few years ago with bogus e-mails, and it's supposed to mean instant dismissal. But since it was Shawn Forrest, Rick Sewell got involved, which meant not a thing in the world happened to Shawn.

"Anyway, word was already out that her husband was unfaithful, and Jim heard through the grapevine that Shawn was cheating with someone back home in Atlanta. His goal was to create an event where Shawn and Darren were together and had a scene. See, Detectives, Shawn got away with stuff in our newsroom that anyone else would have been fired for. Jim figured the best we could do was embarrass her publicly, and maybe Daddy Jack would move her to another station.

"She was loved at our adopted school—which she completely blew off—and Jim planned dinner under the pretense of brainstorming about promoting the school. He called Darren first. Darren initially said no, but he called back and agreed to come. Then Jim puckered up, called Shawn in and said he had a peace offering. She practically spit in his face, but Jim got Darren to lean on her. Finally Shawn said she'd make an appearance."

"Before we go any farther, tell us about Parker Ford," Washington said. "Start at the beginning."

"Couple of girls I went to high school with were in town, and we happened to pick the place where he tends bar. I sat at the bar while every guy in the room hit on my friends, and Parker introduced himself. Talked a lot of trash. Kept saying he'd seen me somewhere. I finally told him I was on television, and his eyebrows went up when I told him where I worked. Said he had the hots for Shawn. Made me a couple of drinks and started hitting on me, eventually asked if I wanted to share a joint out back. We did, and he said he could get me anything I wanted for the right price."

"Meaning?"

A sneer. "Use your imagination, Detective. Anyway, when Jim was describing his plans for last Saturday, I remembered Parker and told Jim about him. He got this look in his eye. His exact words were, 'You just found a date. I think he'll be a lot of use.'"

"Elaborate."

"Like I told you, Jim wanted to embarrass Shawn enough to get her moved to another station. He'd heard she drank a lot, so he was envisioning an evening at a nice place where she made a spectacle of herself. He said, 'You think if we paid off this guy, we could get him to help us?'"

"How, exactly?"

"He told me to tell Parker that if he played his cards right, he might be able to get in Shawn's pants. Not only that, we'd pay him twenty-five hundred dollars, depending on how successful he was in humiliating her publicly. Jim said he would cough all of it up."

"Did you make this offer to Ford?"

Gayle nodded. "Went by the club Thursday night. I told him that Shawn and her husband, my boss and his wife, and the two of us would all meet at Que Será Será, and that Shawn was being set up—she would hopefully learn that her husband was having an affair just before having to face him at the restaurant in front of a bunch of people. Parker said he'd do it, and I picked him up at his place Saturday evening and gave him five hundred in cash. Told him the other two grand was payable if things went like we wanted them to. And he said, 'Something about this ain't right. You're saying if I get lucky with Shawn Forrest, you're paying me two grand?' I said, 'Get her good and relaxed and think of her as your trophy. What do you do with your trophy? You show it off, right?'"

"Meaning what?"

An exasperated sigh. "Meaning I told him to bring his digital camera he bragged about and take pictures! Meaning I told him to use his imagination and think about what he might want to do to make sure Shawn was in the mood. He got it then. Disappeared into the back of his place and came out a couple minutes later. Had his camera with him."

"What else did he have with him?"

"He didn't say, and I didn't ask. But he had this little grin on his face. Took that to mean he was prepared."

"Prepared as in having a condom with him?"

A smug smile. "No, Detective. Prepared as in possessing a narcotic substance which would get her in the mood."

Washington glanced at Gayle's lawyer, who was as pale as a ghost and hadn't said a word. He swiftly nodded for Gayle to continue.

"Well, Jim has a friend in Hattiesburg who knows Darren and doesn't like him. He said Darren had a party which got a little wild a couple of weeks ago—everybody was drunk in the pool, and Darren's little girlfriend performed a certain act on him in front of a bunch of wildly enthusiastic onlookers. Not only that, someone else saw the little girlfriend leave Darren's house the next morning. Jim talked to his friend and made sure a card with a Hattiesburg postmark was mailed to Shawn's apartment in Jackson. It was timed to get there Saturday."

"What did the card say?"

A brief smile. "Described what the girlfriend did in bed with Darren. A snapshot of the act was included, so Shawn would know it was on the level."

"Do you know if Shawn got the card?"

"We assume so. She was talking to Jim and Samantha when Parker and I walked up at Que Será Será, and Darren was coming from the other direction. Shawn bared her fangs when she saw him. She whispered something, and he got this look on his face and whispered back. None of us could hear what was said, but they didn't speak again until he tried to leave. I've already gone over that."

"Let's talk about what happened at Yarbrough's house. Daiquiri's were made, right?"

Gayle nodded. "Samantha made them. We all had one. Then Samantha asked if we wanted another. I told you that Shawn and Samantha kept to themselves in the beginning, but Shawn had loosened up by the time the second round was being poured. I was next to Parker, and I told him that this might be his chance."

"You told him what, Miss Kennedy? To spike Shawn's drink?"

"Not in so many words. But he walked in the kitchen and volunteered to help serve drinks. And Jim went down the hall. I saw a light in the back of the house come on, then he came back through and went in the kitchen. A second later he appeared again and said, 'Anybody want to play ping-pong?' And he started setting up the table in the garage. Right behind him was Parker, with a huge daiquiri in each hand. Walked right up to Shawn and said, 'Hey, pretty lady. How about something cold to drink and a game of ping-pong?'" Gayle rolled her eyes. "Shawn treated him like he had leprosy at the restaurant—wouldn't so much as look at him. But by then she was drunk, and she gave him this big smile and went out in the garage with him. Parker looked over his shoulder at me and winked."

"What did that indicate to you?"

"That he had slipped something into her drink. Samantha went into the garage, and I heard Jim say he was going to get his high-eight and make a blooper tape of us. He came back in and took me aside, and told me he'd put sleeping pills in Shawn's daiquiri."

"Yarbrough?"

"Yes."

"How many?"

"He didn't say. He said he'd gotten them out of Samantha's vial and would need to replenish them."

"Did you tell Yarbrough that you were pretty sure Ford had also put something in Shawn's drink?"

"Yes. He said this would give Parker an even better chance to do his thing. I'd already told Jim that Parker had his camera with him, and he said, 'He damn well better use it if he wants the rest.'"

"The rest of the money?"

"Yes. Then he said he put two pills in Samantha's drink."

Washington frowned. "Who did? Yarbrough or Ford?"

"Jim. He said she takes one like clockwork each night to help her sleep, and two would make sure she slept more deeply. He said we needed to get some from Shawn and put them in Samantha's vial because she kept up very carefully with how many she had. At first he said we'd have to look in Shawn's apartment. Then he told me to join the ping-pong game. While I was playing he went through Shawn's purse and got her keys, then sneaked out to her car. There was a suitcase in the back seat."

Washington was aware of movement from McDaniel. This testimony was crucial, since a partial print allegedly belonging to Gayle was on the Ambien bottle in Shawn's bag.

"Then what happened?"

"Suddenly Samantha couldn't stand up. Jim put her to bed real fast. He told Parker to play ping-pong with Shawn and took me in the kitchen. Gave me the key to Shawn's car and told me to go through the suitcase. Shawn was pretty wobbly by then, but if she realized someone was in her car, he thought it would look better if it was me instead of him. And there was an Ambien bottle in the bathroom kit. It was almost empty. I took all but one."

Washington again noted his partner's body language, which was more relaxed. This matched the evidence and other testimony, which would hopefully make cracking the case a bit easier.

"How many did you take?"

"I didn't count them. Six or seven, I guess."

"Go on."

"I put Shawn's vial back in her bag and zipped the suitcase shut, and Jim put the pills in Samantha's vial and left it in the medicine cabinet where she would find it. Then Jim told me to get Parker's camera from my car. And then it got wild."

"Explain."

"Shawn was in Parker's lap when I got to the garage. Jim stood off to the side telling Parker what to do, and I took pictures." Gayle blushed and looked away. "Let's just say some x-rated pictures were taken. Anyway, Shawn was pretty much out on her feet by then. Jim took the camera to his computer and downloaded the pictures, then told me we needed to get Shawn home."

"Let's talk about that for a minute. You said Jim drove Shawn in the Lexus, and that you drove Parker in your car. Did you see Parker after you dropped him off?"

Gayle raised an eyebrow. "No. I pulled up next to his car and told him to follow me. He said he'd be over later. I asked him what the hell he was talking about, and he said he had some things to do. I said, 'Look, I'm not a freakin' taxi. I'm not sitting over there waiting on your ass.'

"He gave me a big smile, which pissed me off further. I told him he wouldn't see a penny of Jim's money. That didn't faze him a bit. He climbed out of the car and made no move to follow me. So I went to Shawn's place without him and got there right when Jim was pulling in. I told you what happened after that. She was breathing when we left. Purse was on the kitchen table, Lexus parked in front of her apartment."

"What was Yarbrough's reaction when Parker didn't follow you?"

"Figured we'd been played somehow."

"Elaborate. Was he concerned, upset or what?"

"He was irritated. Said Parker wasn't getting a nickel more of his money."

"Was he concerned about Ford exposing him somehow?"

"Not really, because he had video of Shawn and him doing all kinds of crazy things."

"Let's talk about Shawn's apartment. Did you light candles?"

Gayle frowned. "No. Jim flipped on the overhead light and turned it off when we left."

"About that suitcase," McDaniel said, looking up. "It was still in the car as of late morning on Tuesday, but it was found in the parking lot sometime Tuesday or Wednesday and turned in to the manager's office. Can you explain that?"

"No," she said slowly. "I have no idea. The only time I touched it was when the Lexus was in front of Jim's house."

"You said Yarbrough drove Shawn home. Did he have access to the Lexus—could he have gotten into it after the body was discovered?"

"I don't think so, but you'd have to ask him."

"What's Yarbrough's take on Carolyn Davis, if you don't mind?"

Gayle frowned again. "Carolyn? Thinks she has a big mouth, but considers her an excellent reporter. Why?"

"Axe to grind against her?"

"Jim? None that I can think of. What does she have to do with anything?"

"That's everything, I think," Washington said, ignoring her and getting to his feet. McDaniel followed suit, and Linda Carman and Cowan entered the room. "The detention officer will have you transported back to Raymond."

"What do you mean, back to Raymond?" Gayle said. She pulled her lawyer to a corner of the room and whispered fiercely, her voice easily heard across the way. "You said they would help me if I told the truth. I just told the damned truth, and I'm going back out there?"

"Miss Kennedy, you'll be released if you can post bond," Carman said.

Gayle whirled. "I don't have twenty-five thousand dollars! You think I'm made of money?"

"Then you'll be held until trial."

"Trial for what?"

"You've been arrested for attempted murder. Based on what you just told us, we'll let the grand jury decide whether or not you'll be indicted."

She spun and aimed a finger at her lawyer. "You said they would cut a deal!"

He wiped sweat from his brow. "I didn't say they would let you walk out of here after you told your story, Gayle."

"Not in so many words," she said with gritted teeth. She was led away. The lawyer trailed at a distance. Carman shook her head when the elevator door closed.

"Where'd she find that lawyer?" McDaniel said. "The gym?"

"You laugh, Detective, but that may come back to bite us. I can see an ineffective assistance of counsel claim down the road."

The men groaned, but Carman waved it away.

"We'll cross that bridge when we get to it. Let me call Blair. I'd be amazed if he doesn't want you guys to pick up Yarbrough."

* * *

Claire paced as her husband packed for the trip to Memphis. A short, thin, intense sort who regularly quoted scripture in conversation, he continued a diatribe about their church which began the second she stepped inside the house. Then he started in on her, criticizing her selfishness and lack of support. Her size was next. He was subtle, commenting that she needed to look her best when they were spreading the word out in the community. Then he announced that there was one question which couldn't wait until Monday, at which time they would be in front of a marriage counselor. Her heart raced.

Do you not want kids after all?

The tirade resumed as she breathed a huge internal sigh of relief; she was certain that he was onto her affair with Eric, but he apparently didn't know after all. God wasn't going to plant his seed inside her if she didn't have the right attitude, he continued, and hers had taken a nosedive. He was still complaining when he drove off, leaving without a hug, kiss or an indication of when he would return. Nerves jangling and temper short, she dashed for the refrigerator and raced through a wedge of pecan pie. She continued to pace, in dire need of a Xanax and Eric's touch. She would see him tonight and had every intention of spending the night with him, but the hours between now and then were going to cause a nervous breakdown if she didn't do something.

Her doctor had warned her not to imbibe after a drunken escapade with friends the night she turned eighteen. Genetics was a problem, thanks to the alcoholism of her father and grandfather, but the grave danger was the chemical imbalance in her brain—it did not take kindly to alcohol. She thought about the whiskey from last night. She would have to buy some more, since the bottle disappeared somewhere along the way. Just a glass or two—maybe a couple tomorrow and Sunday as well. Enough alcohol to calm her nerves and get her through the weekend, and she wouldn't drive. She would call in sick again on Monday and stay in bed until her appointment with the shrink, since he wouldn't approve refills over the phone. Then she would get her hands on her blessed Xanax and the panic attack would cease. Then she would sit calmly while her husband ranted in front of a marriage counselor. And when he was through, before the counselor said a word, she would tell him they were through.

* * *

Yarbrough chaired the afternoon news meeting, then left for Jackson International Airport to meet Sewell's plane. It was a task normally handled by Sewell's secretary, but Yarbrough told her that he had newsroom business to discuss before Sewell reached the station and went through his mountain of phone messages and e-mails. Classical music played softly in Yarbrough's Buick as they pulled away from Allen C. Thompson Field. Sewell, dressed in a navy pinstripe suit, aimed an air conditioning vent at himself and leaned back.

"Jack is holding up, but a friend whose name I didn't get said this is the calm before the storm," he said. "And Leigh is a mess, poor thing. She's talking about suing the police department. Ours, Jim."

"What did they do?"

"She's just upset, but she said one of the detectives went out of his way to be ugly. McDaniel, I think—the white one. Frankly, I'm not crazy about him, either."

Yarbrough allowed a minute of quiet, then recapped the station's coverage. It met with Sewell's approval. Then he delved into the problems with Carolyn. Sewell turned to him.

"Where was Claire?"

"Out sick. Too many trips to the feeding trough, I'm sure."

Sewell ignored the wisecrack. "She's done, Jim. We'll talk first thing Monday about replacing her. Like it to be a female—no preference on race. You find someone you feel strongly about who can start right away, we'll put her on and buy out the rest of Claire's contract. It's up at the end of June, so corporate won't yell too much. Especially with them pushing to get rid of her."

"Replace her in the middle of sweeps?"

"God, yes. Can't go out and report. Can't work morning and noon. Can't get along with the crew. Can't keep her weight under control. 'Mr. Sewell, may I speak to you about something? Mr. Sewell, I need your help. Mr. Sewell, do you have a minute?' Jack even mentioned her today—asked if she e-mailed herself and tried to make it look like Shawn did it. I wrote it off at first, but he may have a point. Someone that narcissistic might just do it for the attention."

Yarbrough almost laughed. He kept his eyes on the road.

"And maybe it's time Samantha produced the morning show. I'll tell corporate we have no choice—we have a mature woman with experience who's begging to do it, and we keep hiring kids just out of school who last three months before quitting with no notice. They'll have to be flexible—end of story." A sigh. "I just don't want to put that kind of strain on your marriage."

"Sam would love it," Yarbrough said casually. "She's a different person in the newsroom, even on that overnight shift. Be good for us. Hell of a pay cut, though. She's not getting rich at the print shop, but that'll be a drop of at least ten grand."

"Indulge me, Jim. If she produces mornings and noon, and if we find the right girl to replace Claire who can anchor both shows and will help produce in the middle of the night, we might just make it work. I'm envisioning a hungry young gal who buddies up with Samantha, and they work out the flex-time themselves. Both work forty hours a week, make around twenty-five each and all you have to do is sign off on the schedule. We'll talk about restructuring once you have someone in mind. Don't say anything to Samantha yet—let's not get her hopes up until it's done."

Yarbrough nodded. "Works for me."

"Now back to Carolyn. Samantha saw her in Gayle's desk?"

"The master control operator saw her there. Sam saw her in my office."

"Which the cleaning crew left open, right? They've done that before. So she was looking for scripts to get a head start on morning show because she wanted to sleep as late as she could? Noble, if nothing else—sure beats Claire walking in five minutes before air and mispronouncing half a dozen Arab names each morning. What was she looking for in Gayle's desk?"

"Evidence," Yarbrough said with a snort. "Sherlock Holmes on the Forrest case."

A shrug. "It isn't like Gayle is coming back, Jim. Be different if it were your desk or Faber's. I don't like snooping, either, but I don't have a problem with it in this instance. What did Samantha see Carolyn doing in your office?"

"Sam just saw her coming out. The guy in master control saw her on her hands and knees behind my desk and told Samantha."

"Was anything missing? Had she gone through your desk?"

"I couldn't tell. Nothing was missing."

"Hmmph. Now tell me again about this bizarre e-mail?"

Yarbrough removed the folded page from his jacket. Sewell read in puzzlement.

"Whose name is marked out, and why?"

"Eric. I didn't want her dragging him into this."

Sewell frowned. "He brought this to you?"

Yarbrough hesitated for an instant. "Yes."

Sewell reread the page. "This isn't appropriate, of course, but I'm not naive enough to think that our employees e-mail each other about what a great guy I am in their spare time. Frankly,

I'm curious about Redding's motivation to bring it to you. What did Carolyn say?"

"Denied sending it. Slammed her fist on my desk, which I didn't appreciate."

"Did she deny being in your office or Gayle's desk?"

"No."

"Do you believe she sent this?"

"Has her name on it." Yarbrough caught Sewell's eye. "Shawn's had her name on it."

A sigh. "You're still upset about that, aren't you? Forgive me, Jim, but she's dead—you won't ever have to fool with her again. I never tried to hide that Jack stepped in and kept her from losing her job over that e-mail. But I didn't believe for a minute she sent it. Be honest with you, I think Gayle did it."

Yarbrough's jaw tightened. He kept his eyes on the road.

"Frankly, I've always had mixed emotions about her. You did yeoman duty with her, but she was as transparent as they come—all style and no substance, dime-a-dozen talent. Yeah, Shawn screwed her. But part of taking her off the five was a talent issue, pure and simple. We wouldn't have pulled Carolyn Davis."

"Oh, because she's black?"

"Because she's good, Jim," Sewell said, an edge in his voice. "She's a better anchor than Gayle and a network quality reporter—we both know that." A pause. "This sounds personal. I know you guys have had your issues . . ."

"Rick, it's insubordination in my book when you roll all three incidents together."

"What are you recommending, exactly?"

"Station policy dictates a firing."

"You can't be serious! You're talking about going to corporate and firing her over this?"

"You scared of getting sued, Rick?"

Sewell glared. "I respect that you're upset, but it sounds like you took this e-mail personally. Take the weekend to cool off, and we'll add it to our list of things to discuss Monday."

Yarbrough was silent. He pulled into the station parking lot and cut the engine. Sewell caught his eye.

"We'll address these issues, Jim. I know you think I'm dismissing them, and I'm not. But none of it constitutes a firing—not individually or collectively. I know Carolyn's contract is up soon, and we need to make a decision about her. I'm leaning toward pushing corporate to give her forty for five years. That would probably entice her to stay."

Yarbrough looked at him in disbelief. Sewell mistook it.

"Sure, they'll argue that it's a huge increase, but we're already saving thousands by not paying Shawn's salary. As you know, our focus groups show that Jeff's appeal cuts across all racial lines and demographics, and I think Carolyn would do the same to a point—certainly as much as Shawn did. And I've seen some chemistry between her and Jeff. Downside is that she would be almost completely out of the field if she worked the evening shows, and that would cripple us. Let me think about it."

Yarbrough forced a smile. "Coming in?"

"Nah," Sewell said, starting for his Audi across the way. A bag was in each hand. "I'll be in tomorrow morning for a couple of hours. Get a lot more done in the quiet. Thanks for the lift. Have a good weekend, and let's roll up the shirt sleeves Monday."

Sewell was unlocking his car when the Taurus pulled up. The detectives popped out and strode up to Yarbrough, who was ten feet from the back door of the newsroom. Sewell broke into a trot when he heard the black detective reading Yarbrough's rights to him.

* * *

Carolyn's cell rang. It was Norris.

"Almost didn't call—didn't want to wake you up. What are you doing?"

"Cut and edged the yard, weeded the flower bed and walked three miles," she said, wiping her brow. "Now I'm washing my car. Couldn't sleep, so I thought I'd tire myself out. What's up with you?"

"You're not gonna believe this. Sitting down?"

"Hands and knees," she said, sponging hub caps. "What's up?"

"They just arrested Yarbrough. He shoved the white detective, and Washington was on him in a flash and looked like he was going to wipe the parking lot with him. Cuffed him right by the back door. I didn't have time to roll on this one, unfortunately."

She dropped the sponge and fumbled the phone.

"So another emergency staff meeting. I told Faber I'd call you, and he said not to worry about coming if you're wiped out. It's at five-thirty."

"Wow." She submerged the sponge in the pail and wobbled to her feet. "Tell Faber I'll try to be there."

* * *

Eric Redding was dressing after racquetball when his pager went off. It was the chief meteorologist at Channel Five, a middle-aged man who did the evening shows and had been at the station two decades. Eric's jaw fell at the news about Yarbrough. He said he had dinner plans but could make the meeting.

Dinner was with Claire and contingent on the husband's departure for Memphis. She would call when he was gone and wanted Eric to spend the night, but Eric was concerned he was using a would-be trip as a way to spy on her. Getting caught with Claire wasn't a good idea.

He dialed their home. He was on a first name basis with the husband and prepared for a few seconds of small talk, and Claire took on a friendly but distant persona when she answered on those occasions. He left a voice mail and said to call his cell if she wanted a ride to the staff meeting. Then he tried her cell, watching the traffic pass on Lakeland. She answered on the first ring.

"Great news, baby: My doctor called and said he could squeeze me in, so I'm barreling up there. Said he'd make sure my prescription was filled tonight."

"Very good, Claire. When is you-know-who leaving?"

"An hour ago. Made me cry, the bastard. Nearly wrecked while running errands," she said, coming close to blurting out that she was on her way to purchase alcohol, which Redding knew was a no-no. "But my doctor just called, so everything's great."

He told her about Yarbrough and the mandatory staff meeting. "Go to your appointment, sweetheart, and relax. I'll give you a recap tonight."

"We may just make a weekend of it."

* * *

Sewell was dazed when he broke the news to the staff. There was an audible gasp, since the arrest had taken place in the parking lot and many had missed it. He spoke for five minutes and introduced Faber, who would run the news department for the time being.

"Since Jim's arrest is public record, we have no choice but to go with it right away," he said. "We'll tease it at the very end of the six by saying that stunning new information has been obtained, and we won't say an arrest has been made, just like when Gayle was arrested. The teases which run during prime-time will say the same thing. Then we'll show a picture of Jim at ten, along with a statement from corporate and a bite from Rick. This is a story we need to own, folks. *The Jackson Times* will certainly have it on the front page tomorrow, but they obviously can't do anything tonight, and we don't want the competition picking it up before we do. So we'll let them wonder all night, then lead with it at ten." He paused. "I know this sounds cold, since we've all worked with Jim for several years. But this is the way the business works, and Rick's bite will emphasize that the station is cooperating fully and that Jim is innocent until proven guilty."

Carolyn stood with Norris and several other photographers during the meeting. He spoke as the meeting adjourned and the guys drifted away.

"You're here all weekend, aren't you?"

"Might as well be. Nothing else to do. Have your son this weekend?"

He nodded. "Baseball tonight, might take him camping tomorrow. May swing by and say hello after the five."

"I'll be here." She lowered her voice. "He doesn't even know I'm alive."

Norris followed her eyes and spotted Redding punching numbers on his cell phone across the way. "He might be calling you at this very moment, Davis."

A sigh. "I don't think so. He let me down very gently this morning by saying nothing at all."

"There you go again. Hell, he's standing right there. Go ask him out."

She smiled. "Get out of here. Tell your son Aunt Carolyn can't wait to hug his neck."

Norris departed. Carolyn took a deep breath and started for the weather center. A clump of salespeople walked by and blocked her view. Redding was gone when they passed. She glanced in the weather office and waved at the chief meteorologist, then spotted Redding across the studio. He was entering a room littered with broken and outdated equipment. Carolyn followed discreetly, heart pumping. She was going to ask him to dinner, right in front of the useless three-quarter-inch tape machines and analog switchers which had been made obsolete by digital technology. She stopped when she heard his voice and lingered just out of sight.

"Hey, Claire, it's me. Sewell spoke, then Faber. He'll run things for the time being. Whole thing took ten minutes. We're leading with Yarbrough's arrest at ten."

A brief pause. Carolyn kicked at a dust bunny and hoped she didn't sneeze.

"Anyway, I'm out of here. My cell is on. Call me once you've talked to Mr. Wonderful. If I don't answer the cell I'm at home. And leave the pink dress on—you don't know how good it looks on you. See you soon. I love you, honey. Bye."

Carolyn's jaw fell. Redding clicked off and started out. He walked right past her and was a step away from disappearing when she spoke.

"I have a pink dress, Eric. Look pretty hot in it, too."

Redding whirled. Remarkably poised, he offered a friendly smile. "Didn't see you. What's up?"

"I heard it all. You and Claire, huh? Sure had me fooled."

He started to reply, then his shoulders sagged. He glanced around and signaled her back into the dusty room. Resignation was on his face when he looked up.

"I'd gotten my courage up to ask you to dinner, Eric. Sure won't do that now."

He grimaced. She uttered a short laugh and kept her voice down.

"Ninety-nine percent of the people who work here would dash down the hall and blab to the first person they could find, but not me. I personally don't give a damn who you're in bed with. I just wish you'd said you had a girlfriend before asking me out. Silly me—I thought there was going to be another date."

"I'm sorry, Carolyn," he said, his eyes on the floor.

"Or did you guys have a fight and you were getting back at her?"

"There's no point in excuses. I apologize."

"I should have gotten the message this morning when you never so much as hinted that we even had a date. Beginning to wonder if I dreamed the whole thing."

He met her eyes and was silent, prepared to take whatever punishment she wanted to dish out.

"Were you going to say anything, or just let it fade away? I'm curious."

"I told her I would let it drop," he said quietly. "She threw a fit the other night."

Carolyn looked confused, then gasped. "That's why she acted like she did. I was at her house and told her we went out. You've never seen anybody go from warm to ice cold so fast."

"I can imagine. She faked the phone call from her husband to get you to leave."

She stared, then laughed to herself. "At least it's not a black thing."

Redding groaned. "No, Carolyn. Claire adores you. She just doesn't want to share me with anyone." A pause. "If you don't want to speak to me again, I understand."

"We only went out once. Don't sweat it." She kicked at another dust bunny. "How long?"

"Little over a year."

"But she's so young, Eric. What do you want from her?"

"She's been talking about leaving her husband for months. What happened the other night has her ready to do it, as in next week. She does and I'll put a ring on her finger."

Her eyes popped. "You're going to marry her?"

"I know what I'm getting into. She takes medication, and her father is an alcoholic. She doesn't make friends easily. But we're compatible. She's in no rush to get married, as long as she has a promise. And that'll give us time to make sure. Didn't do that with my first marriage."

Carolyn said nothing.

"Please forgive me. Talk is cheap, but I'd like to be friends. Dinner last weekend was supposed to be friendly—that's the honest truth." A pause. "Let me try that again: I'd very much like to be your friend, if you can live with that. If not, I understand."

Carolyn managed a nod and started away.

"One more thing," he said. A strange look crossed his face. "Sewell walked up a minute ago and asked about an e-mail you supposedly sent me this morning just before the show. You trashed Yarbrough and Claire, and bitched about having to be in so early. I told him I didn't know what he was talking about. He gave me a funny look and walked off."

Her eyes widened. She eased closer and whispered fiercely. "Jim jumped my case about that after the noon show. He showed it to me, but the recipient's name had been marked out. Never would tell me who it was sent to—said he didn't want to drag the person into it."

"It wasn't sent to me, Carolyn."

"I didn't send it, Eric, even though it came from my terminal. But I'll find out who did."

* * *

Claire's psychiatrist practiced across the street from Rankin Medical Center. He saw her once a month, strictly to determine if there was a need to continue with her medication. He needed no convincing this afternoon and swiftly wrote the refill. He promised that the pharmacy up the street would have it ready when she got there.

They did. Calmer after seeing the psychiatrist, she resisted the urge to take the pill while waiting to pay for it and figured she could even make it home before tearing open the bottle. The Rankin County medical community was thankfully located several streets from her house; the only hurdle was crossing busy Crossgates Boulevard during rush hour. Then she would take her Xanax and call Eric, who'd just left a sweet message.

Willing herself to concentrate, she peered left, then right.

Several cars passed, among them an old woman who made a left turn into the pharmacy without signaling and nearly caused a wreck. Claire took a deep breath and tried again. A full minute passed before there was an opening. She started through. Then everything went gray.

*   *   *

Carman sat on a beige leather sofa in Bennett's office. Bennett was a stocky redhead in his late forties and sat behind an oak desk which was awash in case files. Behind him were shelves of law books. He was a publicity hound, and a pair of flattering photos in *The Jackson Times* had been framed and mounted on the walls.

"I just got off the phone with Yarbrough's attorney," she said. "You're not going to believe this. Yarbrough wants a deal."

"Oh, really?"

"The attorney is local, probably supplied by the station. He sounded ready to roll his sleeves up and go to war against the overzealous police department, as he calls it, but Yarbrough doesn't want to fight." A pause. "That said, we have a good case against Darren Clarke for murder, and I don't want to have Yarbrough plead to manslaughter or attempted murder and mess it up. Can we agree on aggravated assault and limit Yarbrough to fifteen years? I think slipping a handful of pills into someone's drink shows extreme indifference to human life under the statute."

"You better believe it does. Get the lawyer on the phone and see if they'll agree to it."

*   *   *

Yarbrough agreed to plead guilty to aggravated assault and was still in his blazer and khaki's when he was escorted into the conference room. McDaniel began the questioning, pacing slowly around the room while Washington took notes. Yarbrough's lawyer was alongside; Bennett, Carman and Cowan listened on the hall speaker.

"We understand a plea agreement has been reached with the District Attorney's Office, Mr. Yarbrough," McDaniel said. "Take us through what happened Saturday night. Start with preparations which were made to coordinate the event."

Yarbrough's account was somber and in perfect lockstep with Gayle's testimony. He didn't bat an eye when asked about the money promised to Parker Ford, nor did he bob and weave when quizzed about the digital images of Ford and Shawn.

"Where are those pictures?"

"On my computer."

"We need them. Will you agree to turn the computer over to us?"

"Absolutely."

McDaniel nodded. "Now that it's out in the open that you and Gayle were involved, tell us about your work relationship with both Gayle and Shawn."

"I worked with Gayle six months before we chose to act on our feelings," he said. "Going over anchor tapes, live shots, interviewing, basic writing skills, you name it—all in an honest attempt to improve her and help the station."

"You make it sound like she wasn't qualified to be hired."

"I wouldn't say that, Detective. Even though Colonial is a large and powerful company, Channel Five operates on a shoestring budget. Gayle's starting salary was twenty-four. The difference in ten thousand dollars is a wealth of experience and talent—the polish and finesse I was trying to teach Gayle would have already been there. And Shawn was a thorn—she was watching and made comments. 'Your pet sure blew that live shot.' 'Long way to go before she's ready for network, huh, Jim?' One day I asked where it was coming from. She was coy, so I said I'd be happy to work with her—didn't want her to feel left out." A laugh. "You've never seen anyone so insulted. 'I will let you know, Jim Yarbrough.'"

"Think she was on to you and Gayle?"

"Possibly. Maybe she knew and took some perverse pleasure in torturing us. I wasn't privy to the negotiations when Shawn's contract was up in March, but Sewell called me in and said she was staying and getting a twenty thousand dollar raise and would take over the five o'clock news. I exploded, and eventually he said I could take it up with Jack Forrest."

"Did you try to do that?"

"Please, Detective. But Gayle, who's a tough kid and can take doors being slammed in her face, broke down when I told her. That's when it became personal. But I didn't have designs on eliminating Shawn so Gayle could do evening shows; I just wanted her out of there. Tie her to enough trouble that would have gotten anyone else fired, and maybe that would be enough to get her father to move her to another station in the company," he said, shaking his head. "But I digress. Bottom line is this: I put the Ambien in Shawn's drink. She told me the bartender was also spiking it, and the plan was to have the bartender alone with Shawn and take it from there."

"So you were trying to kill her and frame the bartender," McDaniel said.

"No, Detective. Again, I wanted her out of the station. We got what we wanted at the restaurant—there was a scene in front of fifty people, and some certainly realized it was Shawn Forrest who was screaming in the parking lot. We didn't know what the bartender would do with her."

Washington laughed. "You knew damn well what he would do."

"Of course he was going to sleep with her, Detective. But somebody like that wants to show off his prize, right? Gayle thought he might drag Shawn to his club and show her off, maybe let his buddies have a go at her. Again, the goal was for word to get around that our little princess, our rising star who was taking the broadcast world by storm, was really a trouble-maker. It was rumored that she had a problem with the bottle, and the competing stations and other media would have jumped for joy at a chance to tear her down. You can't imagine the resentment that the competitors had because everything was given to her."

"Were those pictures going to be part of the competition tearing her down?"

Yarbrough didn't bat an eye. "If need be."

A sardonic smile from McDaniel. "How the hell can you say you weren't trying to kill her when you put a handful of sleeping pills in her drink that already had a powerful narcotic in it?"

"We're not talking about a fistful, Detective. I put three in her drink. Counted them out."

McDaniel rolled his eyes.

"And I went to a lot of trouble to make sure exactly three were put back in Samantha's bottle. I drugged Shawn, Detective. I knew they might make her sick, but I didn't try to kill her. Gayle and I took her home and made sure she was resting comfortably. Hell, there's a lake two houses down from our house. We could have dragged her over there and let her drown if we'd wanted to."

"Gayle said you also put two pills in your wife's drink," Washington said. "Looking to get rid of her, too?"

"No, Detective," Yarbrough said patiently. "Just wanted her to sleep a bit more deeply, that's all. She was fine the next morning, other than being a little hungover."

"You've said nothing about your wife. And tell us Gayle's role again?"

"Samantha had no idea what was going on; she was jazzed about getting to hang with Shawn. Played right into our hands when she suggested we all have daiquiris at the house. Gayle's contribution was bringing the bartender, pure and simple. The money came from me."

McDaniel smirked. "I have a hard time believing Gayle had nothing to do with it. Did she tell you at any point she wanted Shawn dead? She admits she was furious when she was pulled off the five o'clock news."

"Never. Again, Detectives, the goal was to get Shawn out of the station. Neither of us stood to benefit by killing her. You guys seem to think that erasing Shawn was a way to advance my career and promote my girlfriend. Truth is, I'll never work in television again. And unless Gayle is cleared of all charges, her career is over. If you don't believe me, talk to the consultant at corporate and see how much clout I had in determining Shawn's replacement."

Cowan and the desk sergeant saw Yarbrough and his lawyer out and made arrangements to transfer him to Raymond. Carman and Bennett joined the detectives, who were still at the conference table.

"He's full of it, Counselor," McDaniel said to Bennett. "Damn straight he was trying to promote his girlfriend."

"He's protecting her, that's for sure," Bennett said, turning to Carman. "I'm sure his lawyer told him that Clarke didn't get bond and is looking at the biggest fall, so Yarbrough may have decided to cut his losses and try to spring his girl."

"Yeah, but Gomer hasn't determined a cause of death," Washington said. "What if he says the Ambien brought on the heart attack? Yarbrough's going down, and his girl may not look so sympathetic to the jury."

Bennett frowned. "Pyle better make a decision quick. I'm not suggesting anything—I trust him as much as anyone I know in the medical field—but the longer he drags, the worse it looks. But he has to be right." He stuck out his hand. "Nice work, fellas. Finish your case summary and e-mail it to me. I can check the office e-mail from home."

"We'll finish up tomorrow morning if not tonight. Just a couple of loose ends to tie up."

"Excellent. Perfect timing on the grand jury. They're meeting next week, and we'll get indictments on Clarke, Patti, Gayle, Yarbrough and Ford. Probation for Jamie, looks like."

Washington turned to McDaniel as Bennett and Carman disappeared from sight. "Listen to them, Mac, all excited about cutting deals and taking pleas after we've busted our butts to put all these folks in a sling. Sometimes I think this is more about them getting their names in the paper than it is actually putting these people away."

"I had to bite my tongue, Jerome. Let's wait and see if Mr. Smooth turns out to be the murderer after all. 'Hey, Counselor, how do you want those eggs on your face? Scrambled or fried?'"

* * *

Carolyn felt sorry for herself and picked up a large plate of Chinese food on her way home from the station. She ate in front of an NBA playoff game she had no interest in, her mind replaying the encounter with Redding. The closure was necessary, since it was difficult working with him while wondering where she stood. But the lingering hope that something might come of their magical night had been stomped out, and she felt especially alone. Her thoughts drifted to Norris, who was probably yelling encouragement to his son in a set of rickety bleachers through a mouthful of peanuts.

Her oldest sister dumped Norris after college because he wasn't exciting enough, and although she was happily married now, she'd confided in Carolyn several years ago that she cut loose a keeper. Sure, there wasn't the mind-blowing chemistry which had drawn Carolyn to her ex, nor did Norris have the education and sophistication of Eric Redding. But he was sweet and kind and would take good care of her—assuming he had the slightest bit of interest these days. He was devoted to putting his son first and said little about his love life, but he acknowledged that he went out with women from time to time. There was every possibility that like her, Norris cherished their friendship and didn't want to destroy it with an ill-fated romance. Maybe she had been smarter than she knew when she curtailed his advances at the movie that night.

The phone rang, jolting Carolyn back to the present. She answered without checking the Caller I.D. and kicked herself when she heard Eric Redding's voice.

"Claire has been in a car accident," he said, his usual poise gone. "We need to talk, and I'd rather not get into it on the phone. Is there any way in the world you can meet me at Rankin Medical Center?"

A full second passed. She almost hung up on him.

"Are you there?"

"All right, Eric," she said wearily. "Give me half an hour."

* * *

Washington and McDaniel were adding the Yarbrough statement to their case summary when Carolyn called from her car. She drove straight to Spring Center and recounted what Redding told her: Claire had blacked out in traffic and was broadsided by another car, and she was hospitalized with cuts and bruises. She was startled to learn that she was pregnant and even more surprised to discover that she was a diabetic. That, Eric said, was probably the cause of the wild spikes in her blood sugar as of late.

"Here's why this is important," Carolyn said. "Claire told Eric that she had a few drinks last night and blacked out—can't remember anything after sundown. She told me she takes medication for a chemical imbalance and isn't supposed to drink at all. Claire and Eric are involved, which I didn't know until this afternoon. See, Eric asked me out last weekend, and we had dinner. I had dinner with Claire last night and mentioned Eric, having no idea."

"And you're wondering if Claire had something to do with the knife in your door?" Washington said.

A long pause. "Yes, sir."

Washington checked with the crime lab, then turned back to her.

"Looks like they'll get to the prints on the knife and note tomorrow morning. I'll call you as soon as we hear something. Meantime, we can take prints from Claire right now. We'll know real quick if there's a match."

Carolyn grimaced. "You do that and she'll ask why, and she may go over the edge if you tell her. What if she didn't do it?"

"Then you breathe a huge sigh of relief," McDaniel said. "If you thought a jealous man had put a knife in your door, would you think twice about doing everything you could to prevent the chance of it ever happening again? Unstable women are just as dangerous, and that sounds like what she is."

"He's right, Miss Davis," Washington said. "Your friend got drunk in a jealous rage and blacked out, and it could easily happen again. You just thank your lucky stars you weren't there to open that door. You best cover yourself."

She started to respond, but he held up a hand.

"Here's what we'll do: We'll hold off on talking to her until the prints are in, if you're sure she'll be hospitalized for a day or two. But we'll have to talk to her if we get an unknown."

*   *   *

Carolyn listened to John Coltrane's *My Favorite Things* and gazed absently at the same NBA playoff game as she sipped a second glass of wine. She watched the beginning of the Channel Five late news and laughed at the coverage of Yarbrough's arrest, noting aloud that television was one cut-throat business. Then she dialed Norris's cell.

"I was about to call you. My boy hit a game-winning, walk-off home run," he said proudly. "Remembered the digital camera this time and got a great shot of him being mobbed at home plate."

"E-mail it to me."

"I will, and I've already sent a copy to his mother. I don't mind saying so, Davis—this is *Sports Illustrated* quality. Already told him I'm going to frame and mount an eight by ten for his bedroom."

Tears spilled down her cheeks. "That's so sweet, James Norris. Every boy should have a father like you."

A smile was in his voice. "Someone's been in the sauce. Didn't go well with Eric, huh?"

She wiped her eyes and recapped the evening, beginning with the encounter in the equipment room. Norris laughed.

"Two affairs right under our noses and we never picked up the scent? We're losing our touch."

"We're losing Claire, too. No way she's coming back."

"Good riddance. And I'm sorry about Eric. At least you found this out before you got involved with him. Get some rest, kid. You're dead tired, and you won't be so emotional after a good night's sleep."

"Probably not. Have fun on the camping trip—wish I could go. Where you headed?"

A long pause. Carolyn, figuring the cell connection had died, was about to hang up when he responded.

"Nowhere, with rain tomorrow. If you can get away, meet us at your place between shows. I'll bring a cooker and steaks. We'll download my pictures and let my son narrate the trot around the bases."

SATURDAY

Carolyn was aware of a thunderstorm during the overnight hours but slept soundly, coming to seconds before the phone rang. It was Washington. She gasped when she realized it was after eleven. She'd slept over twelve hours and was due at the station in less than two.

"I have some information for you. I'd like to share it in person, if you're going to be at home. Do you work today?"

"Not until after lunch. Come on."

Yarbrough's arrest was above the fold on the front page of *The Jackson Times,* and Carolyn was reading the paper and sipping coffee from a Channel Five mug when he arrived. He remained on his feet.

"The prints on the note belong to Samantha Yarbrough."

Carolyn stared, doing well not to spill her coffee.

"The knife is harder to work with because it's old. But there's a partial which matches to Samantha and another partial that doesn't match anyone in the computer."

"Oh, my God. Two people were here?"

"Possibly. I'm afraid we'll have to take Claire's prints. We can't take any chances. And off the record, our case against Gayle's date from last weekend just grew by leaps and bounds. His girlfriend passed away last night—looks like he beat her into a coma after she told him she was pregnant with his kid. Bennett just told me he'll throw the book at him."

Carolyn shook her head. "What happens to Samantha?"

"We're about to talk to her. We just confirmed she's at the print shop—said we had a couple of quick questions about the case. I'm meeting my partner there, and we'll see if we can get a confession." He paused. "She's looking at the inside, Miss Davis—this is serious business. Can you think of any reason she would have wanted to hurt you?"

"No, sir," she said quietly. "I've never had a problem with her before now. I hope to God she's not producing shows this weekend."

Washington started for the door. "We'll find that out, and I'll let you know. Chances are Samantha knows who the other print belongs to, and that will be the end of it. I've already talked to the Clinton police department, and they'll continue to send a car on regular loops through here this weekend."

* * *

"Be right with you," Samantha said, forcing a smile as the detectives entered the print shop just before noon. She wore the same apron over her blouse and jeans. There were at least a dozen customers being waited on or milling around, and Samantha was assisting an older couple with a color copier. "Go on back to my office and make yourselves comfortable."

Samantha strode in five minutes later and closed the door. She forced another smile. She smelled nice, had sprayed her hair and wore a heavy application of makeup. Not nearly as pretty as Gayle, but a reasonably attractive, outgoing woman who would apparently do anything to keep her husband out of danger. That said, she didn't appear anxious to get him out of jail. Yarbrough was being held on two hundred fifty thousand dollars bond, and his initial appearance in court would take place Monday. Both men found it curious that she was at work under these circumstances.

"Busy day. How can I help you?"

"Are you working at the station this weekend?" Washington said.

"No. Here all day."

"Do you have an axe to grind with Carolyn Davis?"

Mild surprise. "No. Why?"

"Night before last, did you call your husband and tell him that Carolyn was in his office?"

Samantha spoke over the intercom and said to hold the interruptions unless there was an emergency. She sat behind her desk.

"I did. The master control operator saw her in there."

"Doing what?"

"On her hands and knees behind the desk, like she was looking for something. I thought Jim needed to know. I would have let him know regardless of who it was."

"Your husband accused Carolyn of sending an e-mail just before the morning news yesterday," Washington said, easing closer and slowing his cadence. "He showed her a copy, but he had marked out who got it. Carolyn heatedly denied writing and sending it. That ring a bell?"

Samantha shook her head slowly, her eyes on Washington. Her guard was up now.

"It sounds like your husband was trying to use it as leverage against her—possibly to get her fired. He talked to Rick Sewell, because Sewell spoke to the person who allegedly received it. That person had no idea what Sewell was talking about. Other words, it didn't go to him."

Samantha was silent.

"That e-mail was sent at five-twenty-two," McDaniel said, consulting his notes. Samantha jerked at his voice, having been lulled by Washington's quiet intensity. "Carolyn said the only people in the building at the time were you and her, Eric Redding, the master control operator, the two studio camera operators and the three people in the control room. That's six technical staff, and all would have been in place when it was sent."

"Not necessarily . . ."

"Well, none of them would have had access to her computer," Washington said. Samantha's eyes jerked back to him. "Carolyn said she and Redding were on the set, so that leaves you." He paused, letting the moment linger. "Did your husband ask you to get into Carolyn's e-mail program and coach you on writing and sending that e-mail? And after it was sent, did he instruct you to go into 'Sent Messages' and wipe it off the hard drive, so there would be no record of it?"

Samantha was silent.

"Did your husband ask you to send it to him? Is that how he had it when no one else did?"

Samantha started to respond, then bit her tongue.

"Let me remind you, Mrs. Yarbrough, that we have the capability to trace the origin of all e-mails," McDaniel said. "Other words, simply going into 'Sent Messages' or 'Deleted Messages' doesn't necessarily make them vanish without a trace."

A sharp exhalation. Samantha looked at the ceiling, then her desk. "I was trying to protect my husband. Carolyn knew about them."

Washington feigned ignorance. "Knew about who, Mrs. Yarbrough?"

"Jim and Gayle!" Tears filled her eyes. She gritted her teeth and willed them back. "That conniving slut talked her way into bed with him the first week she was here. We were separated for six months, then he moved back in when he swore it was over."

Washington turned to McDaniel, then back to her. He was unable hide his shock. "You're telling me you knew about them but sat across from her at dinner last weekend and had her over to your house?"

"I don't expect you to understand, Detective. Jim told me it was over, and I believed him. I liked Shawn and felt sorry for her. And like I told you the other day, Shawn talked about killing herself."

Both men frowned. "When?"

"When it was just Shawn and me. I told you that, Detective. 'This is killing me, Samantha. I don't know how much more I can take.'"

McDaniel was flipping pages. "That's not what I have, Mrs. Yarbrough. You said . . ."

"That's exactly what I said. Maybe you guys were in such a hurry to pursue your own angle that you didn't stop to consider suicide," she said, getting to her feet. Her face was dark, her voice hoarse. "A father who forced her into broadcasting and wouldn't even let her work where she wanted. An alcoholic mother. A cheating husband, whom she'd just found out about that day. She told me they hadn't slept together in two years!"

Washington zeroed in on her. "Mrs. Yarbrough, did Shawn Forrest specifically tell you she wanted to kill herself, yes or no?"

"Not in so many words. But it was pretty clear what she was getting at."

Washington gave her a long, cool look. "When did you find out your husband and Gayle were involved again?"

"Last Friday. The day before we all went out," she said quietly. "I caught them in our bed."

The words hung in the air. "So how could you go through with . . ."

Samantha's smile was brittle. "I chose not to confront them, Detective. They didn't see me. I drove back here, locked myself in this room and cried. Then I got mad. Decided I'd teach that little tramp a lesson the next night."

"Explain."

"I was ready to kill her. I have a big bottle of Drano under the sink," Samantha said, looking away. Then she lifted her head. Her teeth were bared now, her face ashen. "It was my idea to make daiquiris. It was my idea to have them all out to our freakin' house! That's why I went running out to Shawn in the parking lot—a light bulb went on and I was imagining Gayle

Kennedy choking to death on our kitchen floor. The whole time Shawn was spewing on me about her horrible life, I was waiting to make my move. And in the end I chickened out. But there will be a next time, believe me."

Washington let the moment linger. "A knife and a post-it note were found. The knife was wedged into the door of a carport. The message on the note said, 'Watch your back.' The prints on both are yours, Mrs. Yarbrough. Were you trying to send a message to Gayle?"

A long moment passed. Then Samantha nodded, her eyes on the desk. McDaniel stepped forward and spoke, his voice startling her again.

"There's a reason we asked if you had an axe to grind with Carolyn Davis. She lives in a small house off College Street, here in Clinton. The house has a carport. Gayle Kennedy lives in an apartment on Old Canton Road in north Jackson. No carport."

All remaining color drained from Samantha's face. She lowered her head.

"Where'd the knife come from?"

"Claire Bailey's desk," she said, her voice a whisper. "Our morning anchor. I'd seen her use it to open envelopes."

"We're going to have to take you downtown, Mrs. Yarbrough," Washington said. "If you'll come quietly, we won't take you in cuffs in front of your staff."

Samantha wiped her eyes and got to her feet. "I need to call my lawyer."

"You can do that downtown."

She paged an assistant. A young woman knocked a moment later. Forcing a smile, Samantha said she had an errand to run and told her to handle things until she was back. The young woman complied without a word. Samantha gathered herself and walked out with the detectives, offering no resistance.

* * *

Norris and Barry met Carolyn after the five o'clock newscast. Faber was helping produce and told her to take a long dinner break, citing the slow news day. Light rain was still falling, but Norris set up his grill in the carport and cooked mouth-watering steaks and vegetables. Carolyn added potato chips and Pepsi and set up a card table and chairs. She grinned as father and son burned through the food, keeping time to Earth, Wind and Fire on the boom box Norris brought from his van. The humidity and occasional mosquito wasn't enough to send them inside.

After the meal Barry insisted that his father transfer the baseball pictures to Carolyn's computer, and he beamed when she hugged him after seeing the home run. Norris presented him with a wrapped DVD. It was the Kevin Costner baseball film, *Field of Dreams.*

"Take a load off, Davis," Norris said. He cleared the dishes and situated his son in front of the movie. He returned with a pair of ice cold bottles of Michelob and two huggers. "Get me caught up."

A tired smile. "Washington came by the station a couple of hours ago. Samantha put the knife in the door. It was meant for Gayle. Samantha apparently copied the wrong address."

Norris's eyes popped.

"There's an unidentified print on the knife which might belong to Claire. That makes sense because it's Claire's knife— Samantha grabbed it out of her desk." She sipped her beer and caught a wisp of charcoal smoke as the breeze picked up. "Eric called right after that."

Norris grinned. "Ask you out again?"

A snort. "Said everything is going to work out just peachy. Claire is exhausted but in good spirits, and Eric wants the three of us to have lunch when things settle down, as he put it. Must think we're all going to be best friends."

"Sounds like they're perfect for each other."

"They belong in a rubber room. Then Faber and Sewell cornered me. You're looking at the new morning and noon anchor, at least for the time being."

Norris's grin disappeared. "Great."

"Faber and I talked a long time. He thinks Sewell is in serious trouble. Corporate folks are coming—two of them will help run the newsroom until the place is stable again. And even though my contract isn't up until August, he thinks they'll open the checkbook."

"And I've got swampland to sell you in the bowels of Madison County."

"True, but he's management. Can't believe he'd float that if there wasn't at least some truth to it." A sigh. "Of course, opening the checkbook to those folks is a thousand dollar raise, and they're liable to make that early shift permanent."

"At least that way you'd be kept up to date on the happy couple's progress."

She giggled, then became wistful. "Maybe I'm screwing up, but I don't have the desire to send tapes all over the country like I used to. I went on line and looked at the help wanted in the trades, and there's an opening for a weekend anchor and reporter in Montgomery. Pays thirty-six. Same thing in Monterrey, California, for a little more. And a station in upstate New York has a full-time reporting position with fill-in anchoring and will go forty-eight. I'd love to make that much money. But the cost of living would eat up the gain in salary." A long sigh. "Maybe I got my big-city oats out of me when we were in Atlanta. Beginning to think I ain't going anywhere, Norris. Mississippi born and bred and here to stay."

"That's not such a bad thing."

She sipped her beer and shrugged. "Sisters are here, couple of girlfriends from college." A smile. "And if I left, there wouldn't be anybody to drag you to Waffle House in the middle of the night."

Norris laughed and got to his feet. "Let me check on my boy. Get you anything?"

"I'm great, thanks."

He returned a minute later with a synthetic Wal-Mart sack and remained on his feet. "Wanted to reward the kid for the big game last night. One of my all-time favorite flicks."

"Everybody says it's great, but I've never seen it."

"You will. Picked you up a happy, too. It's in there."

She fished out a small, white paper bag with the familiar logo of a Jackson jeweler. A gift-wrapped package was inside. Her hands began shaking when she opened the small box, and her heart pounded when she saw the ring. She looked up, eyes filling with tears. A broad grin was on his face.

"Too wet to get on my knees." He paused. "Will you marry me—Carolyn?"

A sob escaped her. "Oh, James. Are you sure about this? I was thinking last night about how wonderful a friend you are. I couldn't bear . . ."

He slipped the ring onto her fourth finger. It fit perfectly. Carolyn stared at the diamond cluster, tears sliding down her cheeks.

"I talked to your sister this morning. Warned her not to tell."

A disbelieving grin spread across her face.

"The last time I talked to her was the day I heard you were joining us after you and your ex split. Promised I'd take good care of you. I meant it in a professional sense, but she told me today that she knew right then I would propose—I'd know when the time was right." He exhaled, a hint of nervousness finally escaping. "I told you all along that I was going to take stock of things when my son started college—my ex and I are trying to get him through his teen years without the complication of step-parents. But I couldn't wait. The ex likes you, by the way. She gave it her blessing for what it's worth." He kissed her lips for the first time. "I love you. Will you marry me?"

Barry appeared in the doorway. "Well, Dad? What'd she say?"

Carolyn laughed and sobbed some more. "Yes. Yes, yes, yes."

Barry hugged them and returned to the house. Norris touched her cheek. "Eric asking you out was a wake-up call. But that thing in your door was a message from God: 'Norris, get that girl under your roof right now.'"

She smiled through her tears. "I love you, James. I would be honored to be your wife. I want to get married soon, somewhere around here so my kin folk can come, and nothing fancy. You know me—I'm easy to please. And I'll be a good step-mother for Barry."

"I know you will. And you're still Davis. You always will be."

"You'll always be Norris." She got to her feet and fanned herself. "Let me hug your boy goodbye, then back to work. Watch the late news tonight."

He laughed. "Uh-oh."

"Won't say a word. But there will be a gleam in my eye nobody saw at five."

MONDAY

Two middle-aged men from the Colonial office in Atlanta sat in on the morning news meeting. Faber was in charge, but he was smart enough to let the corporate types shape the coverage of the day's events. Carolyn was on her third cup of coffee, having anchored the late news last night before the quick turnaround to begin her new shift. Faber had taken her aside and told her to be patient for a few days. Once a news director was hired and stock was taken of the current staff, he promised to go to bat for her. In the meantime, he would do his best to make sure she was done each day after the noon show.

Both men from corporate were in jeans. One was dour, the other far too upbeat for a Monday. This man gushed over the station's involvement with Fifth Street Elementary and animatedly explained the on-air possibilities—the goal was impressing upon the viewers that Channel Five was the station in the market on their side. Carolyn, to whom much of the hot air was directed, sat patiently and offered the occasional encouraging comment. She excused herself when her cell rang and stepped out the back door. The rain was gone after lingering all weekend, leaving the city with a brief, springlike respite before the heat and humidity returned. She savored the hint of cool in the breeze, watching cigarette butts, gum wrappers and a crushed soda can get carried along in the parking lot.

"It's Washington. I'll be brief. The medical examiner just

announced his decision." A long pause. "The heart attack killed Shawn, not the suffocation. He's convinced it happened first. Said there just isn't enough evidence of a struggle to indicate that she fought back."

Carolyn gasped. "Oh, my God! This means she wasn't murdered?"

"Possibly. Your buddy Yarbrough may have known what he was doing after all. Even if he serves his whole sentence, he's out in fifteen. His little honey is the big loser."

"But I thought she cut a deal!"

"No. Off the record, she talked before trying to get a deal and gave us the store. We found out that her lawyer does loan closings. No criminal experience at all. Never ceases to amaze me that the folks with the biggest attitudes seem to make the biggest mistakes."

Carolyn moaned. "How long do you see her on the inside?"

"Depends on what she's indicted for. Hopefully she'll get more than probation," he said, not trying to hide his sarcasm. "Anyway, press conference at eleven at Rankin Medical Center. A fax will be sent out, but I thought I'd give you a heads-up."

"Thank you, Detective. We'll go break that story right now."

"Last thing: My partner lost his mother-in-law this morning. She'd been sick for months and had moved in with them. I thought you would want to know, since you said you've been there."

"I have. Give him my best. And if you don't mind, get back to me when arrangements are made. I'll stop in at visitation and speak to him and his wife."

"Thank you, Miss Davis. That would be very kind."

"You bet. Call me Carolyn, by the way. And it won't be Miss Davis much longer—I got engaged over the weekend to our photographer James Norris. You've met him."

"I sure have. Congratulations, Mrs. Norris! I'm happy for you."

"It'll still be Carolyn Davis on the air, but I'm thrilled. Thanks for letting me know, Detective."

The upbeat corporate news honcho was ecstatic that Carolyn had the medical examiner's decision before anyone else. He helped Faber set up the studio and hovered as Carolyn wrote the copy. She was on the air five minutes later. Faber lingered at the set as she finished and the station rejoined a syndicated talk show. He led her to a quiet corner of the studio, not far from where Eric Redding revealed the truth about his relationship with Claire. Hard to believe so much had happened in such a short period of time.

"Both those corporate guys really like you, and their blessings will score points with the consultant and Big Jack. Make everything count right now, and your ship may just come in."

EPILOGUE

Blair Bennett thanked his lucky stars that the Hinds County Grand Jury was still in session.

The eighteen-member panel was in its final week on the job, and the next grand jury wouldn't meet until July. Bennett felt that sterling police work, a few breaks and his own willingness to make reasonable deals with the smaller players in the case had him in the enviable position of striking while the iron was hot. He called Washington and McDaniel to the stand, and both painted clear and intelligent pictures of each player and location. Late that afternoon Bennett and Carman were relaxing in Bennett's office when a young assistant district attorney stuck his head into the room. Bennett hadn't admitted it to Carman, but he was envisioning a glowing write-up in *The Jackson Times* and perhaps some national press.

"You got true-bills on all seven, Blair."

Bennett picked up the phone and dialed Washington.

"We ran the table, Detective—got indictments on all seven. I want them all served today."

* * *

A few days later Samantha Yarbrough began serving her six-month sentence at the Hinds County Penal Farm. Originally charged with stalking, Bennett agreed to let her plead to a misdemeanor charge of threat by notice. Jamie Fontenot was charged with obstruction of justice for lying to a police officer and was given a suspended sentence and a year of probation.

Gayle Kennedy, still in jail because she couldn't post bond, was in the position of possibly taking the biggest fall in light of Yarbough's plea. She fired her lawyer and convinced the judge she was indigent, citing no job, no savings and no representation from the station. A lawyer from the public defender's office was assigned, and he persuaded her to plead to the same aggravated assault charge as Yarbrough. Her sentence was also fifteen years.

By then Parker Ford had a stack of charges pending against him, including manslaughter in the death of Tracey Walton, sexual intercourse with Shawn by use of stupefying substance, and a variety of felony narcotics violations. Bennett wanted the death penalty, but the combination of crimes didn't meet the criteria. Ford was insisting on representing himself after going through a series of lawyers, and a trial loomed in April. Bennett was pushing for life without parole as a habitual offender, anxious to get Ford off the streets for good.

Patti St. John pled guilty to accessory after the fact to murder in exchange for her testimony against Darren Clarke. Although her sentencing would be withheld until after Clarke's trial, she faced a maximum of five years and began serving it immediately in order to get credit for time served. Once she was behind bars, five people were serving sentences in connection with Shawn's death.

Clarke's trial began on a cold, misty day in February, exactly nine months after Shawn's body was discovered. The Channel Five live truck was a fixture near the Hinds County courthouse, and Carolyn was the cornerstone of the station's coverage. Rod Faber was now the news director, and she quipped to him that this wasn't a California trial and probably wouldn't last more than a week. She was set to do live shots at noon, five and six each day with a recap package at ten. It was the first full week of the February rating period, so there was the usual pressure to beef up the newscasts in a never-ending quest to increase viewership. The trial was a big deal; crews from CNN, MSNBC and the FOX News Channel were all on hand.

Jury selection and opening arguments consumed the first day. The following day Washington and McDaniel took the stand and described the crime scene and their meetings with Clarke. Carolyn watched as both detectives were grilled by Clarke's attorney for what he considered a rush to judgment. The detectives were cool under fire, but Jessica Hunter, the director of the Mississippi Crime Lab, blew her stack as the lawyer hammered at the credibility of her work. The judge had just banged his gavel and warned Hunter about her behavior when someone approached Blair Bennett's table with a note. Bennett conferred with Linda Carman, then asked to approach the bench. Carolyn watched as the judge called for a recess and asked both sides to his chambers.

"A rough start for the prosecution," Carolyn said during a live shot from the front steps of the courthouse during the Channel Five noon news. "As we've told you, Defendant Darren Clarke's attorney, Robert Grubb of Hattiesburg, made a number of pre-trial motions to have all charges dismissed based on what he says is a complete lack of evidence, and this morning he took Jackson police and Mississippi Crime Lab personnel to task for what he called sloppy evidence gathering. At issue is a suitcase which disappeared from Shawn Forrest's car the morning her body was discovered. Homicide detective Tim McDaniel testified that the suitcase was found the following day by a maintenance worker at Boardwalk Apartments, some fifty yards from Shawn's car. Grubb cited this as perhaps the most glaring example of sloppy police work he's seen in years."

Footage of Grubb cross-examining Jessica Hunter ran as

Carolyn continued. It had been shot by Norris from the back of the courtroom.

"Meanwhile, Grubb promises an expert witness who will testify that the contents of Shawn Forrest's bloodstream would have caused her death instead of suffocation, which is what the prosecution is contending, and he promises a vigorous cross-examination of Dr. Ben Pyle, the state medical examiner. Pyle sent shock waves through the medical and legal communities last spring when he stated that a heart attack killed Shawn Forrest, although he couldn't determine beyond reasonable medical certainty if the suffocation or the drugs caused the heart attack. In fact, one of Grubb's pre-trial motions centered around that very point; he asked why Clarke was even on trial for murder when two people had already confessed to drugging her, and the medical examiner himself couldn't definitely determine that her death was a murder. Grubb also promises testimony from a witness who will claim that Shawn Forrest talked about killing herself.

"The prosecution hopes to rebound this afternoon with testimony from Patti St. John and Jamie Fontenot, two young ladies who were in the company of Clarke the night Shawn died. That's where we stand, and we're in the midst of an unexplained delay of almost an hour," Carolyn said, now back on camera. "There has been no official word for the recess, but it was obviously enough of a concern for presiding judge Thurman King to halt the proceedings. We'll have an update at the end of the newscast or earlier if we find anything out. Carolyn Davis live at the Hinds County Courthouse for Channel Five News—back to you in the studio."

Carolyn and Norris hustled back to the courtroom and waited out the delay, which lasted an additional ten minutes. Judge King waited until the jury was seated, then announced in a somber voice that a mistrial had been declared. There was a second of shocked silence, then gasps and bursts of conversation. Grubb was on his feet immediately and asked Judge King to allow bond for Clarke. Norris trotted out to the courthouse steps and set up his camera as the motion was being heard. Carolyn dialed Faber and told him what had happened. Five minutes later she was on the air, just in time to introduce Blair Bennett. He was twenty feet away, having been cornered by members of the media near the courthouse doors. Norris followed her lead and aimed his lens at Bennett. Carolyn hustled that way to ask questions.

"There are allegations of jury tampering," Bennett said, addressing the group in response to the barrage of questions. His face and tone were impossible to read. "We received that information about ninety minutes ago. I'm disappointed that Judge King granted bond to the defendant."

A reporter from *The Jackson Times* wedged forward. "The tampering is widespread enough to warrant an entire new jury, rather than employ the two alternates?"

"All I can say is that there will be a new trial. Thank you."

Bennett broke away, and Norris panned the group until he reached Carolyn. She grabbed Grubb, who was anxious to comment on the mistrial and stressed that the murder charges had been nothing more than political grandstanding on the part of Bennett. He added that he would be filing a motion tomorrow to dismiss the case. Carolyn was summarizing the events after Grubb left when there was a trio of loud pops on the far side of the building. Still live, Norris and Carolyn ran in that direction, as did others in the media. Carolyn gasped when she rounded the corner, then did her best to describe the scene. Norris, whose camera had picked up the audio of the gunfire, adjusted his focus and aimed his lens at the body on the sidewalk.

It was Darren Clarke.

* * *

Carolyn's final live shot of the day was during the six o'clock news. She was on the front steps of the courthouse and addressed

Norris's camera when Jeff Walker threw to her.

"A bizarre and tragic end to the long-awaited trial of Darren Clarke, the man charged with murder in the death of his wife, former Channel Five anchor Shawn Forrest."

Carolyn paused, watching the monitor several feet away. Footage of Clarke being loaded into an ambulance aired, and Norris had picked up several seconds of dramatic ambient sound as the ambulance sped away. She resumed as the video cut to a door leading to the courthouse basement, then an awning across the street.

"It was from this side door of the courthouse that Darren Clarke was ushered out of the building minutes after the mistrial was declared and he was granted bond. Three shots rang out from across the street, the third hitting Clarke in the chest and killing him. As we told you earlier, Channel Five News confirmed that the shooter was Leigh Forrest, the mother of the victim. Mrs. Forrest, of Alpharetta, Georgia, was arrested on the spot and offered no resistance. She was booked by Jackson police this afternoon and will make her initial appearance in court tomorrow morning."

"Carolyn, do we know anything more about the jury tampering allegations?" Jeff said from the studio.

"Jeff, I spoke with Hinds County District Attorney Blair Bennett a short time ago and asked that very question. I also asked if there was a possibility of a link between the shooting of Clarke and the possible jury tampering. He said he could not comment at this time. As to a possible trial of Leigh Forrest, he said he would immediately seek an indictment on murder charges."

* * *

Carolyn spent several hours on additional pieces which would run on the late newscast and didn't arrive home until after nine. Norris pushed aside a paperback novel and pulled her into his arms in front of a roaring fire. She rested her head on his shoulder, savoring the moment. Being married to her best friend agreed with her, as did the new contract offered by Colonial Broadcasting. She'd accepted a five-year deal at forty thousand a year, reporting from nine until six Monday through Friday and handling fill-in anchor duties when necessary. There was a young brunette from Baton Rouge who now co-anchored with Jeff at five, six and ten each night, but Carolyn much preferred her field assignments and was thankful for the even-handed, all-business approach employed by Faber.

"Forgot to tell you this, Norris: Claire called twenty minutes after the shooting and invited me out to their house for supper. They didn't have the TV on and didn't know what had happened. I called back on the way home. Claire was asleep, so I chatted with Eric awhile."

"How's the happy couple plus one?"

"Plus two. Claire's mother has moved in."

"Moved in or visiting?"

"Moved in. Eric said Claire realized after their daughter was born that she wasn't ready for motherhood after all. Her mother is basically a nanny—cooks, cleans, takes care of the baby and will be there indefinitely."

"What the hell does Claire do all day?"

"She writes poetry and short stories on a laptop and says the creative juices flow best when she's curled up in bed, so that's where she stays. Eric said the mother brings meals to her on a tray. This sounds beyond dysfunctional."

"And Eric's cool with all that?"

"Seemed fine with it. Know what else he told me? He's thinking about quitting television and trying out for the independent league baseball team. Said he pitched in high school and still has a deadly knuckleball, whatever that is."

Norris burst into laughter. "Is he on drugs?"

"He's such a nice guy, but I've decided they're both a few

251

bricks shy of a load. If I cut off contact with them, though, Claire will start crying and beg me to be her friend."

"She's not your friend, Davis, never has been. We're husband and wife for God's sake, and I'm not even supposed to know she married Eric and had his baby? You're her friend because you listen to her problems and don't tell her to her face that she's crazy."

She blushed. "You listened to my problems for years and didn't tell me to my face I was crazy."

"You've never been that crazy. By the way, Faber just called. Said you kicked butt today. We're invited to join him and his wife for dinner this weekend as a thank-you for all the hard work. He and his wife don't drink, so spiked daiquiris won't be a problem."

Carolyn grinned, then paused. "I got a good look at Leigh Forrest as they were cuffing her. She's older and heavier, but I would have sworn it was Shawn. Eerie looking into that face. By the way, you can't convince me Jack Forrest wasn't trying to influence that jury. And Bennett lucked out—he was looking at a certain acquittal. I talked to a couple of jurors off the record who weren't impressed at all with the case."

"I talked to a photog from the newspaper while you were talking to Washington. He said, 'More dead air—first Shawn, now Clarke.' Also said his wife knows a woman who played in a tennis league with Shawn. Said Shawn was the most insufferable human being she'd ever met—hated everyone and everything. Hundred percent convinced she killed herself and did it partly because she knew how much attention her death would get."

"If that's what she wanted, she got her wish. And it won't end any time soon—Bennett is itching to try Leigh Forrest and save face with the voters after this debacle. So we'll saturate the airwaves with Shawn again in a few months. And that Parker Ford trial will be a circus with him representing himself."

A pause. "I was thinking about how both of us heard those gun-shots and went charging over there. We're living right, Norris—that could have easily been a drive-by that hadn't played all the way out."

"I thought about that, too. You with a story to tell and me with pictures to get—it's in our blood, isn't it?" He pulled back. "Speaking of hazardous duty pay, I got a raise."

Her eyes lit up.

"Old friend at Jackson State called as I was walking out the door today, offered me a chance to run their campus radio station and teach some courses. Stuck my head in Faber's office and fudged—said an offer was on the table and thirty was mentioned. That's one reason he called just now." A proud smile. "I move to thirty effective immediately."

Carolyn grinned. "Look at you, bluffing your way into a raise when I had to practically beat one out of them. And what are you going to do when you make that courtesy call to your friend and he offers thirty-five?"

"Turn him down." He covered her feet with an afghan. "I never had any doubt about marrying you, Davis. But I must admit I wondered if working with you might be a little much."

Her lips curled into a smile. "And?"

"Wouldn't trade it for the world."

* * *

Washington and McDaniel were almost finished with their latest addendum to the Shawn Forrest case summary when Washington's cell rang. It was Parker Ford, calling from his jail cell in Raymond. He was days away from being sent to Parchman, where he would spend the rest of his life. He floated several theories about the shooting of Clarke, news of which had spread quickly through the jail, then badgered Washington about intervening on his behalf. Washington patiently explained the situation again, then hung up when Ford resorted to idle threats. McDaniel was grinning, aware who was at the other end of the line.

"How's our boy?"

"'I know things, Big Man. You said you'd help me, and you lied,'" Washington said. "He just doesn't get it, Mac. We didn't need his testimony—Patti and Jamie gave us more than enough to put Clarke away, and Leigh Forrest just put him away for good. How many more times do we have to go over this, Parker?"

McDaniel grinned. "He probably thinks if he works on you long enough, he'll talk you into breaking him out of the big house. That's after you get his Probe out of impound, and you guys can make a run for the border and buy up more of that Mexican Valium he was selling from that amp of his."

Washington laughed as he got to his feet and slipped on his jacket. "Those Allman Brothers records will never be the same, will they?"

"Not so fast, fellas," the desk sergeant said, stepping into view. "Some kids found a body in a parking lot a couple of blocks off State Street. Crime lab is on the way."